SILENCERS
AND SERMONS
THE EXTRACTORS

JD HARRIS

authorHOUSE

AuthorHouse™
1663 Liberty Drive
Bloomington, IN 47403
www.authorhouse.com
Phone: 1 (800) 839-8640

Published by AuthorHouse 06/24/2016

ISBN: 978-1-5246-1592-5 (sc)
ISBN: 978-1-5246-1591-8 (e)

Library of Congress Control Number: 2016910372

I want to thank the following:

My wife Cheryl for her undying support and input.

Barbara Lipe for her advice and insight as a writer.

CHAPTER 1

JT Logan sat in a small airport, two hundred kilometers outside Madrid, reading a John Grisham novel. The sound of heavy boots caught his attention, and he raised his eyes to see two militiamen in crisp, black uniforms towering over him. He was the only other person in this part of the terminal. "Excuse us, señor. Are you Mr. JT Logan?"

"Yes, I am. What can I do for you?" The officer had spoken to him in Castilian Spanish, and JT responded in kind.

"I understand that you are carrying a gun. Is this true?"

JT hesitated; he figured someone had set him up. "No, sir. I thought it was illegal for a foreigner to carry a gun in Spain."

He saw the guards observing him to see if they could detect any nervousness that would indicate he was armed. The guard finally said, "That's true. Would you mind if we checked?" The other militiaman put his hand on his gun; JT could hear the leather holster creak.

JT figured it was an effort to intimidate him. He could see that the guard's gun was in a holster, covered by a flap, and buttoned down. He knew he could knock both men out before either one could come close to reaching his sidearm. He laid his book on the chair next to him and stood up. Dwarfed by his six-foot-four-inch frame, the two militiamen—who were barely five and a half feet tall—met his piercing blue eyes. "No, sir," JT said coolly, "I don't mind."

"Turn around, please, and lock your fingers behind your head."

JT complied. The guard was rough, and JT figured he was trying to make a point. When he patted down each leg, the man hit him in the balls, but JT simply winced and said nothing.

The guard scowled menacingly. "Okay, sir, you may sit down. Who do you work for, and what is your business here?"

"I work for the Trans Global Insurance Company, based in Paris. I'm here trying to get to the States."

The guard switched to English. "The international airport is in Madrid, and there are many flights to the States from there. Why are you at this particular airport?"

JT switched to English also. "I'm hoping to catch a ride on a private plane to Paris and then to the States. I'm just trying to save a little money."

"We have word that you are an assassin, Mr. Logan, and that you were involved with the kidnapping of a young woman in Madrid."

JT smiled at them, which seemed to irritate them. "Officer, I'm not carrying a gun, so you can see that your information is false. I did not participate in a kidnapping. Whoever told you that is obviously trying to throw you off their trail. You're being duped."

The guard narrowed his eyes. "What does this word 'duped' mean?"

"It means to be made a fool of, but I'm sure you're smart enough to see that now. Check your source of the erroneous information, and you will find whoever you're looking for."

The guards faced each other. They then took him over to a section that held ten rows of empty folding chairs and had him sit on the far end of the fifth row. He saw he was as far away from the doors as he could get. "Please sit here and wait until we can check something out." As they began walking away, he could hear a plane pull up on the tarmac outside the building. JT wondered if it was his plane. He couldn't tell because the curtains that covered the airport's glass wall went all the way to the floor.

As the guards walked away, he noticed the curtain move a little, and he felt fresh air from somewhere. The curtain pulled back slightly, revealing a man standing by an open door. The man peered through the curtains at the militiamen at the desk and motioned to JT.

The guards still had their backs to him. One was on the phone, and the other was listening to his partner. JT stood up quickly, walked over, and stepped through the curtain and followed the man through the door. The man shut the door, locked it with a key, and started running toward the plane. JT followed down the grass to the tarmac and around the back of the Gulfstream. JT could feel the heat from the engine exhaust.

They went up the steps, and as soon as they got in, the door closed. The plane surged forward before JT could sit down. As it turned onto the runway, JT looked out the window at the building. The front part of the glass building had no curtains, so he could clearly see the militiamen, their guns drawn, searching for him.

The plane lined up on the runway. He could feel the vibration as the pilot revved up the engines to full throttle and released the brake. The plane surged forward so much that it pressed his head back against the headrest. After they were airborne, the man, who was in working-class shirt and pants, came back to JT's seat. "You are Mr. JT Logan?"

"Yes, I am, and I appreciate you extracting me from what could have been a bad situation. How did you know it was me?"

"I was going on a description of you. They said you were tall and built like a muscleman. Also you were the only one in that part of the airport." JT did have a slim waist and a bigger-than-average chest and biceps, but that was from his days in the army. He lifted enough weights on a regular basis to maintain his physique.

The man turned his gaze toward the front of the plane. "It's all in a day's work. Settle back, and we'll get you something refreshing to drink."

JT reclined his super-comfort seat and closed his eyes. He heard a voice in French. "Excuse me, sir, can I get you a glass of wine or a cocktail?"

He met the eyes of a beautiful, retro-style, Marilyn Monroe–looking blonde. She had bright red lipstick and wore a tight, white blouse that amplified what were larger-than-average breasts and a tight black skirt. She was also wearing heels.

JT quickly came to his senses. "A glass of red wine would be nice."

She stood up to her full height in the plane, something he could not do. "I'll be right back."

A few minutes later, she returned. As he reached for the glass, their eyes met and lingered as she sat down across from him. "Is there anything else I can get you? Anything at all?" She gave him a seductive look. She sat with her shoulders back, which emphasized the size of her breasts.

He and his liberator were the only passenger on the plane. "No, thank you, this will be fine."

He closed his eyes and sipped the wine. He heard her get up and walk to the back of the plane. He hadn't had sex in eight months, but he didn't know anything about her—and in this day of STDs, he wasn't interested in exploring that possibility. The wine and the physical exertion he had gone through the past week made him sleepy. He sat the glass in the armrest and drifted off to sleep.

When he felt someone shake his shoulder, he opened his eyes to find her staring at him with that seductive smile she had. "We'll be landing soon. Raise your seat, please." He complied, leaned over, and then lifted the window shade. He could see the Eiffel Tower silhouetted against the rising sun in the distance. A few minutes later, he felt the plane touch down.

After the plane came to a stop, he moved toward the door that had just opened. He walked down the steps to see a man leaning against a black Peugeot, appearing rather intimidating in his black suit. When he saw JT, he stood up and approached him. "Mr. Logan?"

"Yes."

The man opened the door, and JT slid in on the black leather seat. The man shut the door, went around the back of the car, got in the driver's seat, and drove off without saying anything. The traffic was bumper to bumper with cars, motorcycles, and even bicycles. The motorcycles and bicycles drove between the cars. Even though the windows were up, JT had no problem hearing all the honking, beeping, and shouts of frustration from outside.

The driver stopped in front of the ancient, six-story building in District 16 that housed JT's apartment.

JT got out amidst the commotion of Paris. He glanced around; if any of the fifty or sixty people who were hurrying by within a hundred feet were looking for him, he couldn't detect who it was.

He went inside, got in the elevator barely big enough to hold him, and went to the sixth floor. The building was hundreds of years old but had been retrofitted with an elevator that took the place of a closet on all six floors. By Paris standards, JT's apartment was a huge place. The unit he owned covered the whole end of the building; the floor below held ten six-hundred-square-foot apartments in the same space. He got out, walked to his apartment, and went in. As expected, a man he did not know was sitting on the couch under the far window, a briefcase by his feet. The man rose and smiled. "Mr. JT Logan, I presume?"

"Yes, sir, and call me JT, please."

"Of course, of course. I am Maria's uncle, Franklin. I so appreciate you getting my niece away from those ... those ... terrorists. I hope you killed them all."

JT looked at him without comment. The man hesitated. "Oh, that's right, you can't discuss it." The man was every bit as tall as JT and about a hundred pounds heavier, which was very unusual for a Frenchman. He was wearing a very expensive suit and had diamonds on his watch and the three rings he was wearing. He reached into a briefcase on the table and pulled out a laptop. He opened it and turned it on. After a few minutes, he started typing and then finally looked up. "Do you have an account number?"

JT bent over and typed it in. Franklin sat there a minute and then looked up with a smile. "Five million into your offshore bank account, correct?" JT just nodded. If he was being taped, he didn't want anything being recorded that could incriminate him.

Franklin stood up as JT started for the spacious bedroom of his apartment. Franklin followed him to the door. "There will be a man outside your bedroom door while you sleep. Have a good night's rest, and you will be leaving at seven in the morning for your flight to the States."

"How will I be going, by commercial or private plane?"

"Oh, private—well, it's an Airbus, but it's a chartered Air France, loaded with tourists. You will have first-class accommodations to make a man as big as you are as comfortable as possible. You will land in New York, and there will be another plane to take you to your next destination." He smiled, walked out the door, and closed it.

JT opened a drawer, took out clean underwear, and went into the shower. He stood in the steam from the shower for ten minutes before washing and getting out. He got in bed and fell asleep almost immediately. His biological clock still off from his recent travels, he awoke fifteen hours later. He got up, shaved, and got dressed.

He walked out to find a man, who introduced himself as Simon, in the kitchen. He spoke in French. "I was just going to come and wake you. I'll have some croissants ready in a minute." JT sat down and poured himself a cup of coffee. Simon set a plate of warm croissants down, and JT picked one up and put it on a small plate. He spread butter over it and then some jam on top of that. It was wonderful because the croissants were still warm and the aroma filled the kitchen. He ate four of them even though he was on a no-bread regimen.

Afterward, he went back and packed a suitcase. It was small enough to be a carry-on. They went out to where the black Peugeot was blocking the inside lane of traffic; cars were parked bumper to bumper along the curb as far as he could see. They got in, and he was driven out to another small airport, though this one was big enough to handle commercial jets. Simon pulled up to the steps, and JT got out and climbed the stairs. The flight attendant, in her crisp company uniform with a nametag declaring her to be Cherise, stuck out her hand. "May I see your ticket, sir?"

He showed her his phone.

Her eyes got big, and she motioned him to follow her. She went to a first-class seat and stood in front of the woman sitting there. "I'm sorry, Miss, but you will have to go back to your original seat."

The woman, who was about five feet tall, stood up. "I was told I could sit here if the man didn't show up." She put her hands on her hips in defiance.

Cherise smiled the smile of a professional flight attendant. "He's here. I'm sorry, but you will have to return to your original seat.

The woman looked at JT and then back to Cherise. "Since he's late, let him sit back there."

The pilot stepped in and very sternly addressed her with a heavy French accent. "Madam, you must return to your seat or leave the plane." She stood there not moving. The pilot was just as firm. "Madam, you are interfering with the operation of an international flight. If I have to call the *policier*, you will be detained indefinitely."

The woman picked up her belongings and went back to the back, giving all three of them a dirty look. The pilot smiled and motioned JT to the seat. "You may be seated, monsieur."

He sat down and wondered why it was always Americans who made fools of themselves in foreign countries. For that matter, he didn't understand why she was mad—at five feet tall, she could have fit in the overhead bin quite easily. The door was closed, and the announcements were made. The air the compression unit was blowing put pressure on his ears, and they hadn't even taken off yet. It was another thirty minutes before the plane rolled to the runway and then another fifteen before he felt the plane throttle up and catapult forward.

On the eight-hour flight JT watched four movies and played solitaire until they finally announced their approach to LaGuardia. After landing and clearing customs, he left the secured area and saw a woman with a sign that read simply, "JT." He walked over and introduced himself. She asked for his last name, and when he told her it was Logan, she motioned for him to follow her. He walked behind her and got in a car that took him out of the city to a rural airport where he saw several jets.

He got on a Lear jet, and they took off immediately. This time, he was the only passenger on the plane.

He landed in Memphis a few hours later. When he left the terminal, there was another woman with a sign with his name on it. She picked up her cell phone and called a car from the cell phone lot, and about ten minutes later a black Range Rover SUV pulled up. He put his bag in the back, walked around to the driver's side, and got in. He drove downtown to the Peabody Hotel and let the valet take the car. After he registered, a bellman took him to his suite, told him his clothes were already there, and handed him an envelope. JT tipped him, and he left. JT opened the envelope; in it was a key that he put in his pocket. He then went to the bedroom.

There was a knock at the door, and JT peered out the peephole to see a courier with a package.

He opened the door, and the man smiled at him. "I have a special delivery for Mr. James Thomas Logan." JT nodded and reached for the package. The man pulled it back. "May I see some ID, please?" JT took out his driver's license and showed him. The man smiled again. "Sign here, please."

JT signed the sheet, took the package, shut the door, and put the box on the table. He opened it; inside was a locked metal box. He pulled the key out of his pocket, unlocked it, and raised the lid to reveal a .40-caliber Ruger semi-automatic. He picked up the loaded clip and stuck it in the handle until it clicked. He pulled the bolt back and saw the bullet slide into the chamber as he let go of it. He picked up the clip-on holster and put the weapon in it.

Also inside the box was a cell phone. He picked it up and dialed a number.

A voice on the other end answered, "Hello."

"Robert, JT here."

"Man, it's good to hear from you. I didn't think you were going to make it in time. You are in Memphis, aren't you?"

"Yeah, I'm at the Peabody. What time do I need to be at the church?"

"In two hours—five thirty, sharp."

JT smiled. "I'll be there before then."

"Hey, wait a minute, JT. I thought you would come out and stay with us. We have plenty of room."

"No, that's okay. The company is picking up the tab here, and besides, you probably have your four road dogs with you, and it's bound to be crowded."

Robert laughed. "With all the women they have up here, you're right about that. I'll see you at the church."

Forty-five minutes later, he went down and asked for his car. They brought it up, and he maneuvered through downtown and got on I-240. He followed it around, got on I-40, and took the exit for the church. It was one of the largest churches he had ever seen. He parked where he saw several other cars and walked in the front door. Standing in the vestibule was Robert, surrounded by the four men JT knew were never far from his side.

Robert was a mid-level mercenary who made a decent living fighting other people's battles. He had been in pretty good shape at one time, but drinking and carousing had taken its toll on him.

Robert spotted him, walked over, and hugged him. "Damn, man, how are you?"

"I'm fine, but you might want to keep your profanity down while you're in church."

"Oh, hell, that's right." He looked around to see if anybody else had heard him. "Come on, man, I want you to meet the woman I'm going to marry. In fact, you may be related to her—her last name is Logan, also."

JT smiled at him. "What's wrong with her?'

Robert frowned as he adjusted his 101st Airborne cap. "What do you mean?"

"Well, if she's marrying you, there has to be something wrong with her. Is she blind or mentally challenged or what?"

Robert grabbed his shoulder and laughed as they walked. "No, man. She's beautiful and smart. She's a neurosurgeon and a lawyer to boot."

"A doctor and a lawyer ... are you sure about this? One slip, and you're screwed."

Robert leaned back and laughed again. "No, I'm sure. She can support me, but I still have to have my team. You know, you get on the jazz every once on awhile and have to see some action. Hey, when are you going to get me hooked up with that company you work for?"

"I put your name on the list. I'll have to check and see where you are." JT knew his company would never accept Robert or anybody like him, because he liked to brag about who and how many people he killed. "Does she know what you do for a living?"

Robert shook his head. "I'm a troubleshooter that has to take a few trips out of the country occasionally, as far as she knows. Government contracts mostly." He smiled as they walked toward the sanctuary.

JT stopped him as they walked in. "I'm curious. I know that foursome that hangs around with you are your closest friends. Why did you pick me for best man?"

Appearing a bit embarrassed, Robert looked down and back up. "You're right—they are. I couldn't pick one of them for hurting the other three. You were next on my list, so I picked you so I wouldn't hurt my friends. I hope you're not mad."

"Nah, that makes sense. I just wondered. Are they going to be groomsmen?"

"Oh, yeah. She has three friends and two sisters on her side, so they'll be up there with us."

They continued their walk to the front of the sanctuary, where JT saw a pretty, redheaded woman about his age talking to the minister. She wore matching jacket and slacks with a white blouse, and she had a great figure. Robert walked up. "Excuse me, honey. I want you to meet someone. Jessie, this is my best man, JT Logan. JT, this is my bride to be, Dr. Jessie Logan. I told him ya'll might be related, having the same last name."

JT looked into the prettiest face he had seen in a long time, and he envied Robert.

She shook JT's hand, and he found it to be firm but soft. "Where is your family from, JT?"

"South of LA. And you?"

"Dallas-Ft. Worth area, so we're probably not related."

JT shook his head. "Probably not."

Robert introduced him to the preacher, Pastor Willis, and laughed as he turned to Jessie. "JT asked me what was wrong with you. He thought you had to be blind or mentally disabled to marry someone like me." They all had a good laugh.

The preacher clasped his hands. "Okay, let's get this rehearsal done." Jessie introduced JT to Angela, who was going to be the matron of honor. They went through the rehearsal three times before everybody knew what they had to do.

They left for the Peabody for the rehearsal dinner. JT got there first and waited in a plush chair in the lobby. The others finally showed up thirty minutes later. They went in to a banquet room in the restaurant and sat down, and as the salad was being served JT engaged in small talk with Angela. She told him where she was from and what she did. Suddenly they heard, "Angela, I need to talk to you—*now.*"

They all turned to see a man standing there waiting for Angela. She got up and walked out to him in the hall. They couldn't hear them, but it was obvious they were arguing. JT ate but kept his eyes on the couple. Robert leaned over to Jessie and asked, "Who is that?"

Jessie glanced at the couple still arguing. "That's her jackass husband, Billy. He's super jealous of her and needs to stop messing with her. Her daddy is one of the most powerful lawyers in Shelby County, and he'll ream him a new one. If I ever see another bruise on her, I may take him to court myself."

Angela finally came back in and looked over at Jessie as she sat down. "I'm sorry, Jessie."

Jessie shook her head. "Don't worry about it."

They went on eating, and halfway through the main course someone tapped Angela on the shoulder. It was her husband again. "Come out here right now and talk to me, or I'll drag you out." He turned and walked out.

Robert stood up, but JT stood up also. "I'll handle this, Robert. Stay seated."

Robert looked at JT. "No, I'm going to kick his ass."

JT shook his head. "You'll make things worse. Let me try and cool this thing down. Stay here."

Angela started to get up, but JT pushed her back down. "You too."

JT walked went out the door that had been closed by now. Her husband turned, obviously expecting to see Angela, and JT held up his hands. "Hey, I need to talk to you. Hey, man, I don't know what the problem is, but look at it from our standpoint. You're messing up something that's very important to these people. I understand you and your lady are having problems, but can't this wait until after this dinner is over?"

Billy put his hands on his hips. "Are you the best man?" JT nodded. "Well, you are the problem."

JT frowned at him. "Me? Why me? I just got into town a couple of hours ago."

"I don't allow no man to get near my wife. Where are you going after this, to some party probably?"

JT shook his head. "I don't know what the rest of them are going to do, but I'm going up to my room and go to bed. I'm suffering from jet lag. Look, I'm just going to walk your wife down the aisle when this is over. I do not intend to butt into your marriage; in fact, I'm not looking to get involved with anyone right now. Trust her, man—she's not going to do anything but do her part in the wedding."

As he waited for Billy to respond, JT assessed the other man. He suspected Billy had a good build at one time but had let himself go. He was stocky and wore a tight T-shirt that showed off his pecs and biceps, but it also showed off the roll around his middle.

Billy looked at JT. "You're lucky I have a cage match tomorrow night, or I'd kick your ass."

JT worked to keep his expression neutral. "I'm sure you could, and I appreciate your not doing it. Like I said, I'm not the least bit interested in your wife, and she's doesn't show any interest in me or any other man at this dinner. Honest, she's cool. I'm just asking you to chill out a little and have your talk with her later, okay?"

Billy stared for a second. "Okay, but if I see anything between you, I'm coming after you. Do you understand me?"

JT nodded. "Yes, sir, and that will make me behave on that threat alone."

Billy turned and walked off, and JT went back in and sat down knowing Billy was all mouth. He doubted he really had a cage match—he was too out of shape.

Robert asked, "How did it go?"

JT shrugged a little. "I asked him to be cool and settle his problems at home. I told him I wasn't interested in his wife and she wasn't interested in me. He agreed and left."

Angela turned to him. "If that's how it really went down, you were talking to someone besides my husband." JT smiled, but she didn't.

After the dinner, they walked out into the lobby of the historic hotel. They watched the duck master bring the ducks out of the elevator and walk them out on the red carpet that had been unrolled for them. He herded them to the fountain in the middle of the lobby and let them swim around for a while before he took them back up on the roof.

Jessie looked around. "How about a drink before we leave?"

JT shook his head. "Count me out; I'm suffering from jet lag. I'm going to go up and pass out, but thanks for the invite."

Jessie scanned the lobby. "I was trying to see if Billy was hanging out waiting. Angela, I can't let you go home—I'm afraid he'll kill you in a jealous rage. Come home with me."

Angela had tears in her eyes. "I'm afraid of him, but I have to go home sometime. If I stay out tonight, it will be worse tomorrow, and I'm afraid he'll disrupt the wedding."

Robert walked up. "You're right—Billy's waiting outside in the valet lot. Let me and my boys handle him."

JT stopped Robert. "I don't think that would be a good idea. If you got arrested, we don't know if we could get you out in time for the wedding."

Jessie cut her eyes at him. "I agree—don't do anything that will make you miss this wedding. JT, will you keep him occupied and let me have my car brought around to the other door so we can get out of here and worry about tomorrow later?"

JT nodded and walked out. He spotted Billy and approached him. "Hey, man, I just want to talk."

"What have you done with my wife?" Billy asked belligerently.

"I haven't done anything with her. I haven't seen her since the dinner, and I told you I'm not interested in her." He walked past so Billy would have to turn away from the hotel to talk to him. "I'm not going to tell you how to run your marriage, but you need to do something about this jealous rage you have. It's going to get you in trouble someday. Everything you think is happening is not happening—you just think it is."

Billy sneered at him. "I think you should stay out of my business. That's what I think."

Glancing over Billy's shoulder, JT saw one of Robert's boys get into a Lincoln Town Car and drive off. He nodded at Billy. "You're right, man; I was just trying to help what appears to be a great couple."

Billy sneered. "I don't care shit about the bride and groom."

JT smiled. "I was talking about you and your wife. Sorry I bothered you." He turned and started to walk away.

Billy walked up behind JT, grabbed his shoulder, and yanked so hard it tore his coat at the shoulder.

JT responded by spinning around and slugging Billy in the nose. Billy's head hit the pavement, and he was out cold, so JT walked back over to the valet. "You ought to call the police and an ambulance for that man lying over there."

The Memphis police had an ever-present force downtown, and they were there in a few minutes. JT told them about Billy's jealousy and how he'd disrupted the rehearsal dinner. He looked at the officer. "Oh, yes, I almost forgot—I have a gun permit, and I do have a weapon on me." He held up his hands.

"Where is your weapon?"

"It's on my belt under my right arm."

The officer felt for it. "Do you mind if I hold onto it until we're finished?"

"Not at all. Whatever makes you feel more comfortable."

"Let me see your driver's license and your permit."

JT took them both out and handed them to him. The officer looked at them. "Damn ... a permit issued by the CIA. Are you an agent?"

JT smiled as he shook his head. "No, sir. I'm not an agent, nor have I ever been one. Saying I was would be lying and a disgrace to all the real agents. I used to be a contract agent, and I made a lot of enemies in my younger days, so they let me carry this as protection."

"What are you doing in Memphis?"

"I'm best man at a friend's wedding."

"When are you leaving?"

"I don't know, Officer. I'll have to wait until my company gives me another assignment."

The police officer nodded and went over to talk to some high-ranking police officials with a lot of brass on the uniforms. JT stood there listening to the traffic and the crowd heading for Beale Street. After Billy was put in the ambulance, the officer returned and handed him his license and permit. He then took the magazine out of JT's gun, ejected the shell out of the chamber, and handed it all to JT. "I appreciate your telling me about the gun. Please don't load that until you are out of the area."

JT nodded. "Yes, sir. You can count on it." He dropped the magazine and extra round into his pocket and stuck his gun back in the holster.

He walked back into the hotel, took the elevator to his floor, and went to bed. Before he could drift off to sleep, his phone rang. It was Robert, and he could hear the party in the background. "Hey, man, come on out to the house. We're having a blast, and there are some fine-looking women up in here." He could tell Robert had been drinking.

"No, thank you. Don't get shit-faced and show up with a hangover tomorrow."

"I won't. I'll see you tomorrow." The phone went dead.

JT shook his head. *That dumb bastard.*

CHAPTER 2

The next morning JT woke up feeling a lot better. He showered and got dressed with a vest to conceal his holster with his jeans. He went down to the restaurant and had a breakfast of scrambled eggs, bacon, grits, and sausage gravy over his eggs. *There's nothing like Southern cooking.* He ordered cantaloupe, coffee, and a glass of whole milk to top off a breakfast he had missed for the last eight months.

He went back to his room, changed, and walked to the health club. He worked out for an hour and a half and then went back to his room and showered again.

It was a quarter past eleven, so he went to the closet and pulled out the leather garment bag that contained his dress blues. He was allowed to wear the uniform because he was an inactive member attached to the First Air Cavalry, a unit that had long ago traded in its horses for helicopters. Robert and his crew had been out of the army for more than nine years, but Robert still wanted a military wedding.

Because JT was attached to the Air Cav unit, his uniform included brass decorative spurs on his shoes and a black cowboy hat. He put on the pants and shoes and decided to make a few phone calls before he got ready for the wedding that was three and a half hours away.

Before he could pick up his phone, it rang. Seeing it was Robert, he answered it, hoping the groom to be, wasn't drunk or in jail. "Hello?" There was a long silence. "Hello, Robert? What's up, man ...? Robert, are you there?"

"Yeah, man, I'm sorry; I don't know what to say. I'm really sorry about this. I mean, I hate putting you in this situation."

"What are you talking about, Robert? Are you drunk, in jail—what? Talk to me, man. Where are you?"

There was another long pause. "I'm in Hattiesburg, Mississippi. We're getting on a flight to South America. I got a job to do that pays well and—"

"Bullshit, man! Are you telling me you're not going to show up at the wedding?"

"Yeah, man. I'm sorry, I just can't do it. After thinking about it last night and seeing Angela having trouble with her husband and Jessie talking about her father being a lawyer ... I just decided I couldn't do it."

"You sorry bastard, this is low, even by your standards. What did Jessie say when you told her?"

Another silent pause. "I haven't told her. Man, I'm sorry to do this to you. Tell her I'm really sorry about this."

"Me tell her? You call her and tell her. You owe her that much, but you need to get on that plane and fly your ass back to Memphis, do you hear me?"

"Sorry, man, I'm really sorry." JT heard the phone go dead.

JT stood there. "I'm not believing this shit. Now I've got to go break the news to the bride," he muttered. He went into the bedroom and finished putting on his uniform, which consisted of white shirt, bow tie, and a waist jacket with his rank and ribbons. He grabbed his cowboy hat, walked downstairs, and asked them to bring his car around. He got in, drove toward the interstate, and talked out loud to himself. "I have to tell the bride she's being stood up at the altar. I have to tell the bride the groom is an asshole. I have to tell the bride ... what in the hell am I going to tell the bride?"

He drove while formulating a plan to hunt Robert down and literally kill him. He knew he would have to kill Robert's posse to get to Robert, but that was fine with him. He finally arrived at the church and didn't want to go in, but he knew the sooner he told the bride, the better.

He walked into the church and asked a woman carrying flowers, "Where is the bride's room?" She led him to a door with a gold plaque on it that read, "Bride's Room." He knocked on the door.

The door opened about an inch, and an eye peeked out from behind the door. "Can I help you?"

"Yes. I'm the best man. Tell Jessie I need to see her. It's important."

The eye looked away and then back. "Come back in a couple of hours—we're not dressed." The door shut.

JT stood at the door and contemplated walking in but figured they probably really weren't dressed. He knocked again; no answer. He knocked again, this time with enough force that the door opened quickly. The same eye was looking at him. "You can't come in, sir. We're trying to get ready for the wedding." The door started to close, but JT stuck his foot in the way.

"Tell everybody to cover up because I'm coming in, in thirty seconds." He kept his foot holding the door open and after twenty seconds pushed the door open and walked in. There were four women wearing an assortment of slips, bathrobes, and bras and panties. He shut the door behind him as they scrambled to cover up. "Excuse me, ladies, but we have a situation on hand. Where's the bride?"

They pointed to another closed door, and he walked over and knocked rather forcefully. The door opened, and an older woman put up her hand, but before she could say anything, he pushed his way past her. Jessie spun around and grabbed a robe to cover her white bra and panties. He noticed she had a garter belt and hose on. "We have a situation that needs your immediate attention. Ask her to leave for a minute."

The woman looked at Jessie and back at JT. "Who is this man, dear?"

Jessie tied the belt around her robe and told the woman, "He's the best man, Aunt Cecelia. Give me a moment, please." Aunt Cecelia's eyes opened wide, and Jessie looked at her. "Please?" The woman walked out and shut the door.

Jessie stepped up with fire in her eyes. "Okay, what's the problem? If he's drunk or in jail, I'll kill him. Where is he?"

In spite of having rehearsed on the drive over, JT found himself at a loss for words. He finally took a deep breath and exhaled. "He's not coming ... to the wedding ... I mean—"

She practically screamed, "*What?* Are you telling me he's standing me up? Where is he? Give me a phone!"

"You can use mine," JT said, pulling the phone from his pocket, "but he's not answering. He has his turned off."

She took JT's phone from his hand and dialed Robert's number. She hung up and called him again. The third time she started dialing, JT took the phone away from her. "You can call him all you want, but he's not answering. Do you understand that?"

Tears started down her face. She made a face at JT as if she wanted to kill him. "Let me tell you something about your best friend—"

"Hold it right there. First, of all, he's not my best friend. Those four dogs that hang out with him are his best friends. I'm fifth on the list, and there is no sixth, so I'm the best man. If I catch up to him, what you have planned will pale in comparison to what I'll do to him. Now, if it will make you feel better by hitting, cussing, or spitting on me, then go ahead. I'll take it, but I had no prior knowledge of this."

Jessie appeared unsteady, as if she was going to lose consciousness. JT grabbed her, and she fell in his arms. He sat her in a chair, and her shoulders heaved as she cried. She finally sat up. "The only reason I convinced myself that I loved him was because my dad's last wish is to see me married. He's got cancer, and I really don't expect him to live another month or two. If he dies brokenhearted, I'll ..."

"Let me call a man who works for me. He's what I call my pathfinder. In tight situations, he can always find me a way out. Hold on for a minute."

She shook her head. "The only way out of this is that he shows up here in the next few minutes, and I wouldn't have him if he did. I can't believe I convinced myself that I was in love with him. I just can't believe it; I'm really not that stupid."

JT took a few steps back and used speed dial. "Hello, Pathfinder, I have a situation I need out of." JT told him the whole story.

There was a long pause on the phone, and then the voice came back. "It seems to be a pretty simple solution. The main point here is to make Dad happy, correct?"

"Correct."

"Then you marry her."

JT paused. "That's not a solution, Pete. I need a solution."

"Think about it, dude. You can divorce her after dad passes on. See ya." The phone went dead.

JT looked at the phone and then at Jessie. She narrowed her eyes, obviously hoping to find a glimmer of something she hadn't considered. "What?"

JT took in a deep breath. "Here's the plan. I'll marry you, and after your dad passes away, we can divorce or annul the wedding or do anything you want to get out of it."

She turned around and then back. "That's not a solution."

"That's what I said. But it's that or someone has to go out there and make the announcement that there's not going to be a wedding, and you'll have to tell your father." Her head snapped around at him when he said that.

She paced the room silently. Finally, she stopped. "Would you do that? What story are we going to tell the people, and who's going to tell it?"

JT scratched his chin. "First, we have to tell the preacher and see if he will go along with it." He went to the door and opened it. "Somebody go get the preacher, quickly."

He started to shut the door, but Aunt Cecelia glared at him and said, "Just who do you think you are, ordering us around like we're in your army?"

"I'm the man who's helping your niece out of a bad situation."

She stood up, walked quickly away, and went out the other door. A few minutes later, the preacher came in. Together Jessie and JT told Pastor Willis the story. He shook his head and sat down. "I can't participate in a sham wedding, not in the church. The only way to make this happen is to do it legally."

"That's what we're talking about."

He looked at them. "But you don't have a marriage license and you haven't gone through the church's mandatory counseling before marriage."

JT looked at him. "So you won't do this then? We know three days have passed before today, and you can give us a Cliff's Notes counseling session. All we have to do is get a marriage license."

The preacher rose and began pacing up and down like Jessie had been. He turned to them. "I'll see if Mrs. Hendricks, who works in the permit office and issues marriage licenses, will cooperate. She's a member here. If she will, I won't break the rules ... but I might be willing to bend them a little. I'll be right back." He walked to the door and turned back. "You realize that, if I can pull this off, you two will be legally married." They both nodded, and he left.

JT turned to Jessie. "I'll send your guard dog back in here, and I'll go out and push the preacher. If we get this done, I'll go out before the congregation and make up a story that will be so absurd some of them will have to believe it. Get ready to get married, and I'll be back."

He walked out and saw Aunt Cecelia sitting with her arms at her side. "Go back in there and help her get ready to get married." Aunt Cecelia remained sitting and crossed her arms. JT stepped up. "Go on, we don't have a lot of time." She jumped up and went through the door, and he turned to the rest of them. "I suggest you get dressed. There's liable to be a lot of male traffic through here between now and the wedding. Get up and get to it." It seemed everybody responded to his command voice, for they all jumped up as he went out the door.

He went to the pastor's office; since he was an associate pastor, his office was in the basement. When he walked in, a woman in her sixties was filling out papers and stamping them with her notary public seal. She handed them to the pastor, saying, "You sign here, here, and here; and the bride signs here and here; and the groom signs here and here."

JT signed, and as the pastor signed he mumbled, "May God forgive me for this." He handed them to JT, who left to return to the bride's room. As he arrived, Angela was going in.

He stepped up quickly. "I need you to do something for me. Take this envelope in, give it to Jessie, and then bring them back to me when she's finished, okay? Please?" She smiled and walked in the door. In less than five minutes she came back out and handed them to JT. He smiled at her. "How's your husband?"

"He's in the hospital with a concussion. Everything is going to work out. He didn't know I didn't come home last night, because he wasn't at home. Thanks."

JT smiled again. "You bet." He went back to the pastor's office and gave the papers to him.

Pastor Willis motioned to a chair. "Thanks, and have a seat. I imagine you could do with a bit of rest. You know, this is a good thing you're doing. Not many men would go out on a limb like this. Would you like some water?"

JT asked, "You don't happen to have any leftover communion wine, do you?"

The pastor let out a boisterous laugh. "No, we use grape juice in the Baptist Church. I have some, but I don't think that's what you want." He reached into a small refrigerator and handed JT a bottle of water. "Where do you attend church, JT?"

JT took a drink of the water before answering. "Well, I'll tell you, Pastor. I was raised a Baptist, by a Baptist preacher-father, along with a couple of brothers, but I have been traveling the earth so much the last twelve years I forget when it's Sunday, much less where the nearest church is. The last time I was in church was Notre Dame in Paris, and that was about eighteen months ago."

Pastor Willis looked up at the ceiling. "I would love to see some of the old churches of Europe someday."

JT glanced at the diplomas on the wall. "The prettiest ones are in Rome. I was visiting a church in Rome, I forget which one, but the guide was telling us that the cobblestones we were standing on out front were part of the Great Appian Way. He said the ancient Romans laid them six hundred years before the birth of Christ. My friend looked up at him and said, 'Who in the hell did you think laid them, the ancient Mexicans?'"

The pastor threw his head back in laughter. "Your friend zeroed in on the who and not the why, didn't he?"

JT smiled. "Yeah. We visited the Vatican, and he bought a rosary for a friend of his back home. I asked if he was going to get a priest to bless it, and he said, 'For all the good it'll do, I bless it myself,' and he made the sign of the cross over it." The pastor laughed hard again.

Willis looked at JT. "While you're in Memphis, maybe you will take time to visit our church. So you were active in the church growing up?"

"Only to the point of singing a little with the family. We had to do it that way because I can't sing."

Willis laughed with his head back. "This is making me feel better. Do you remember any one particular time about that?"

JT stared off into the distance and smiled. "Yes, we were asked to sing as a family at a revival. Mom had been feeling bad, and we didn't know if she would be able to sing. When they announced us, we walked up on the stage, and Momma walked up with us. When she got to the top, Daddy said, 'Bless your heart, dear.' She turned and said, 'Bless your heart, dear.' The spirit must have moved the rest of us, because for the next minute all that was heard was, 'Bless your heart, Daddy,' 'Bless your heart, son,' 'Bless your heart, CD,' 'bless your heart, JW,' 'Bless your heart, JT,' and 'Bless your heart, Momma.' Finally, Daddy stepped up and said louder than he meant to, 'Okay! That's enough heart blessing—let's sing.'"

Willis doubled over laughing. He finally composed himself, wiping tears from his eyes. "Thanks. I needed that at this particular moment."

JT looked Willis in the eye. "Back to your original question, I might come with my wife in the near future."

Willis stood up with a more serious expression on his face. "I hope so. She's a dedicated member here who saved my wife's life when she had a brain tumor. No doctor could find what was wrong with her, but an hour with Jessie and she knew the problem, and one operation fixed it." He paused, and then said, "It's about twenty minutes before the wedding. I understand you want to make a small speech."

"No, sir, I'm going out there to tell one of the biggest whopping lies that has ever been told in this church. You might want to wait in hiding until I'm finished so you won't be considered complicit in our crime."

Willis leaned over on his desk, laughing again. JT walked to the sanctuary and went in. He walked up to the podium and picked the wireless mic up off its stand. He put it to his mouth. "Is this thing on?" People in the back waved and nodded.

He stepped up to the front of the platform. "My name is JT Logan. The fact that Jessie's last name is Logan also is purely a coincidence—we're not related. Now I'm going to tell you a story that I don't think any of you are going to believe, but here it is. I'm going to marry Jessie Logan today." There was a hushed gasp over the whole church. "This is why that's going to happen. As you see by my uniform, I am in the military. Sometimes the military will loan out their people to certain government agencies. I can't discuss to who or how that works, but please take my word for it. If certain people had learned my identity and that I was getting married, my future bride and other people I worked with would have had their lives put in danger. I expected my duty to be over about five weeks ago, but we ran into some unexpected problems. I wasn't cleared to come here until late yesterday.

"I asked my friend Robert to stand in for me until I could get here. I asked him to be seen taking her places and being seen with her generally, and he agreed. We couldn't even have napkins and invitations printed with my name on them because of the secrecy. I got here, and Robert and I were supposed to switch places. Now here's the really unbelievable part. Robert works for an agency that does some overseas work, and he was called up in the middle of the night last night. He's on another continent as we speak.

"Believe it or not, Jessie and I are finally going to be married, and we hope you will continue to bless us with your presence on this occasion, but I do have a problem. Robert took his team with him, and I am short a best man and four groomsmen." He saw a man in a dark suit sitting about six rows back. "Sir, you in the dark suit, could I ask you to come up and stand with me?" The man nodded and stood up to make his way to the end of the pew. "Can I ask you to do one more thing for me? Would you see if you could find four other men in dark suits? I prefer dark for the pictures being taken, but I will take any color of suit."

JT had his cowboy hat under his arm, and he spotted a kid about ten years old sitting on the end of a pew, about ten rows back. He walked down the steps and up to the kid. "Could I ask you to do something for me, young man?" The boy looked up at this man towering over him with all his ribbons and decorations on his uniform. "Would you hold my hat and give it to me as I walk down the aisle with my bride?" The kid's eyes got big as saucers, and he nodded as he took the hat and held it as if it were made of gold.

When JT returned to the platform, the four men and the newly appointed best man were standing there with Willis. He felt his pocket to make sure the wedding ring Robert had given him was still there. The wedding march started to play, and they turned to look back down the aisle. The bridesmaids walked in at intervals, and finally behind them was Jessie. She wore a beautiful wedding dress with a train dragging the floor about ten feet behind her. Her father was holding her hand as he was pushed down the aisle in a wheelchair. He had oxygen on to help him breathe. When they got to the steps, the preacher made his announcement that marriage was a union ordained by God and asked, "Who gives this woman to be wed to this man?"

Her father said in a weak voice, "I do." Jessie leaned down, kissed him on the mouth, and then walked up the steps as the man pushing the wheelchair maneuvered it to the end of the first-row pew.

JT stepped up beside her. The preacher cleared his throat and started. He left out certain sections that had been in the rehearsal, and JT figured it was so he could have deniable plausibility. He asked if Jessica Theresa Logan took James Thomas Logan as her lawful wedded husband. JT realized they had the same initials as well as the same last name. The service went on, and JT found himself thinking, *I've been shot and was never this scared. I've jumped out of airplanes and never been this scared, and I was a prisoner of war and was never this scared.*

Finally, Willis smiled at both of them. "I pronounce you husband and wife. You may kiss the bride." The kiss was soft, sweet, and brief. He could see Jessie's red eyes under her veil. They turned, and Willis said to the guests, "I present to you Colonel and Dr. Logan."

When they walked out, JT took his hat from the kid and handed him a hundred-dollar bill. He heard the kid over the music. "Mom, it's a hundred dollars!" Everybody laughed as his mother tried to shush him.

When they got downstairs to the reception hall, the first woman to join them hugged Jessie. Jessie turned to him. "JT, this is my sister Lenore."

Lenore looked at JT and then back at Jessie. "I want to talk to you, soon." She gave JT a look as she got in line next to them. JT thought, *Well, that's one that didn't believe my story.*

Another woman walked up, and Jessie turned to him again. "JT, this is my other sister, Hazel." Hazel gave him the same look Lenore had.

The guests began going down the receiving line. As they shook hands with him, many people said how romantic the wedding was. JT wondered if anyone believed him.

The kid came by, and his mother asked JT, "Do you realize you gave him a hundred-dollar bill?"

He smiled. "I do realize that. That hat is mighty important to me, and it was well worth it."

After they got out of the receiving line they walked around the hall chatting with people, and some of them were still remarking about JT's story. After an hour, Jessie finally said to him, "I have to sit down. These shoes are killing me." He walked her over to a row of chairs. She pulled her shoes off and rubbed her feet.

The kid walked up. "Colonel, you want me to hold your hat during the reception? It won't cost you anything."

JT laughed. "Sure. What's your name?"

"Bobby, Bobby Briggs. Colonel, can I ask you a question?"

"Sure, Bobby. What is it?"

"Did you earn the Silver Star and the CMH?"

JT was a little surprised at Bobby's knowledge of his military ribbons. "Yes, sir, I did. I'll tell you about it sometime."

Bobby looked down and back up. "My dad's in the military, but he's a Marine. He's in Germany."

JT sat down next to Jessie so he was at eye level with the boy. "Tell him I appreciate his service to our country. The Marines are a mighty fine outfit. I've owed them my life on more than one occasion, and I hope to meet him someday."

Bobby grinned and then took on a serious face. "Why don't you wear your CMH? If I had one, I would wear it with my pajamas."

JT laughed, and Bobby sat down beside him.

Jessie looked over at him. "What is a CMH and a Silver Star?"

"Just awards for not being late to chow for five years in a row. Do you want something to drink?"

"Please, I would love it. We have to cut the cake in a few minutes."

JT went to get her a cup of green punch. When he brought it back, Bobby was on the other side of the room showing some other boys JT's hat, and he was pointing back at him. Jessie was staring at him.

"What?"

She studied him for a few seconds more. "The Silver Star is the third-highest medal awarded for bravery, and the Congressional Medal of Honor is the highest award for bravery, and the president presented it to you? You impress me."

"Good. I was beginning to think you generally disapproved of me. How'd you find that out in the few minutes I was gone?"

"Bobby told me." She smiled and looked down. "I do appreciate what you're doing, and I'm ashamed I haven't expressed my gratitude before now."

He smiled at her. "It's a pleasure."

They cut the cake and danced the first dance. Then JT walked over, shook her father's hand, and introduced himself. The old man seemed grateful, and JT didn't know if he believed their charade or not. He was clearly too sick to question it. JT leaned down. "How about I push while you dance with your daughter?" A smile beamed across his aged face as he nodded.

JT pushed the wheelchair over to Jessie. "Dear, your father would like a father-and-daughter dance." With tears in her eyes, Jessie reached down and took his feeble hands. She stepped sideways and around to the music, holding her father's hands as JT maneuvered the wheelchair. Afterward, there was much applause.

She had her sisters take their father home, and they celebrated into the night. As people started to leave, JT walked up to his new bride. "What now? I haven't given any thought past this point. What were you and Robert going to do ... uh, I mean go?"

She laughed. "To be honest with you, we were playing it by ear. I have my clothes in the car, but I'm afraid to leave town. My father is too frail."

JT frowned. "Of course you shouldn't leave the city. Why don't we get your clothes and go to my hotel room?" When he saw her expression, he added, "I have a suite with two bedrooms. You have no obligation to me in any way." He smiled at her as she asked Angela to get her suitcase.

They drove back to the Peabody, walked up to the room, and went in. JT looked at the extra bedroom. "I've already taken the master, but give me a few minutes, and I can move out. I'll stay in the other room."

She stepped in front of him. "You'll do no such thing. I'll sleep in here, but what about tomorrow?"

JT shrugged. "It depends on how Dad feels I suppose." She smiled.

JT went in, took his uniform off, and took a shower. He came back out in a pair of long gym pants and a long-sleeved T-shirt. His phone rang, and he answered it and started speaking French. He had a short conversation, telling the person on the other end that it was past midnight in the States and he would call them back tomorrow. He put the phone down and turned to see Jessie standing in the door with her gown and housecoat on.

She looked at him. "You speak French very well. Where did you learn it?"

He poured a glass of water. "In France."

She laughed. "That makes it sound like a stupid question."

"Sorry, my company is based there, so I had to learn French to survive."

She walked in and sat down on the end of a very plush sofa. "What do you do exactly?"

He got another glass of water for her and then sat down on the other end of the sofa. "I work for the Trans Global Insurance Company. We insure high-value items like, jewels, gold, art ... people."

"Are you in sales? How do you put a value on them?"

He shook his head. "No, I'm not in sales. Gold is worth so much an ounce. The people who make the jewelry put the price on them as well as the art galleries with paintings. We get a percentage of the value when we recover it."

She nodded in understanding. "So, if you are not in sales, what do you do?"

"I'm in recovery. If someone steals your jewelry, I find out who did it and ask them to give it back."

"Do you get dental with that?"

He laughed. "No benefits. It's strictly commission-based transactions, but let me ask you a question. Why be a doctor and a lawyer?"

She stared out the window into the black of night and then back at him. "I was in a lawsuit years ago, and the lawyers wouldn't listen to me. I switched lawyers, and she listened to me and defended me based on medical facts. I decided I could do better, so I went back and got a law degree."

Confused, he asked, "So, do you practice medicine or law?"

"Both, but I make most of my money these days by testifying in court and consulting. I still have a limited number of patients to keep my surgical skills honed ... You know, you should probably be a lawyer."

He shook his head and laughed. "I don't like lawyers. Why do you say I should be one?"

"Because you very successfully changed the subject from you to me. I didn't realize it at first. What is it that you don't want me to know?"

He cut his eyes at her. "What makes you think I'm hiding something?"

"Because I was asking about your business, and you changed the subject so I wouldn't ask the question you didn't want me to ask. What is it?"

He smiled and shook his head. "No, I was just interested in you. I don't know what you're talking about."

She looked at him very slyly. "How do you insure people? That was the last item of the things you said you insured, and you said it softly and quickly as if you were hoping I wouldn't notice. So how do you insure people?"

He turned away for a minute. "I told you I was into recovery. I don't insure anybody."

"So, how do you recover people?"

He thought a minute. "Let's say you went to some third world country, and the government or outlaws or whoever decided to grab you and hold you for ransom. It would be the job of the man in that department to go in and get you."

She nodded. "How do you figure how much I'm worth?"

"It depends on how bad they want you back. The people who sent you there, I mean. They should take out a policy on you before you go because it would be cheaper that way. If you don't take out a policy, then the cost can go up, sometimes double in price—supply and demand."

"You said the man in that department of recovering people. Are you that man?"

He smiled again. "I am sometimes. I do it all, except sales."

Her phone rang, and she got up, walked into the bedroom, and answered it. The white silk housecoat accented her figure. He could hear her talking. "Uncle Benjamin ... It couldn't be helped, and it was a last minute thing ... I didn't think about that at the time. I don't know, but I will think of something. I can't help it—are you listening to me? I'm in the honeymoon suite at the Peabody doing nasty and vile things with my new husband. I'll talk to you in the morning, and we will come up with a plan. Good-bye."

He looked at her as she came back in. "Is everything okay?"

She nodded. "I apologize for that. I'm in several business dealings with two of my uncles, and they ... are a little upset with me right now. I screwed up."

He turned and stretched his legs out on the couch facing her. "Let's talk about a couple of things. This thing about doing nasty and vile things to me, do we need proof, a few photos maybe?"

She laughed big and hit him on the foot that was near her leg. "I was just trying to get him off my back. We don't need proof."

"Okay, the next thing we should talk about. Why was he mad at you? What did you do wrong?"

She didn't answer for a minute and then said, "You know, I think we should have an agreement to not delve into each other's private life too much, agreed?"

He wrinkled his brow. "Oh, after you give me the third degree about my business, you want to limit the prying and delving now. That's not fair."

She nodded. "You're right. I shouldn't be so nosy if I'm not going to let you be. We'll say no more, okay?"

He nodded. "Okay. I just thought you might need to have a prenuptial agreement. Oh, we can't do that—we've already said, 'I do,' haven't we? Is that what your uncle was complaining about?"

She sighed. "Yeah. I had Robert sign one so their interests would be protected. I forgot about it in the three seconds you and I discussed marriage. He's pretty upset, as Uncle Brad will be."

JT sat deep in thought for a minute. "I bet a good lawyer could come up with a postnuptial agreement, couldn't they?"

"Wouldn't be any good if both parties don't agree to it."

"I'd sign it—I'm not after your money. Have them draw it up and give me your lawyer's information, and I'll forward it to my lawyer. No conditions—whatever you had before we married is still yours, and reverse of course—not that my money would be any concern to you. My lawyer's in town on another matter anyway."

She gave him a really big smile. "You know, the longer I know you, the more I like you. You should still be a lawyer."

"Thanks. Well, since it's almost dawn, I think we should get some sleep."

She looked at her watch. "It sure is; I didn't realize it was so late. Good night."

CHAPTER 3

JT blinked through the muted rays of the sun, filtering in through the drawn curtains over the bedroom window. He picked up his watch; it read 11:45. He reached for the house phone. "Room service? Would it be possible to get breakfast this late? Great. Coffee, scrambled eggs, bacon, biscuits if you have them, toast if you don't, and a pitcher of orange juice and fruit for two. Thank you."

He got up, shaved, and put on his gym clothes. Thirty minutes later he heard a knock on the door. He opened it, and a man pushed in a tray with stainless steel food covers gleaming in the light from the window. JT tipped him, and he left. He poured himself coffee and added cream and sugar.

As he took his first sip, there was another knock on the door. He looked out and saw two older gentlemen standing there. He opened the door. "I'm Jessie's Uncle Benjamin, and this is my brother, Brad. May we see Jessie, please?" The two men were like slightly younger versions of her father.

"She's not up yet. Can you call her later and make an appointment?" They raised their eyebrows in disbelief. "Really, we had a late ... night last night." They frowned, giving him sober faces. The two older men with wire-rimmed glasses and three-piece suits looked at each other.

He heard Jessie from her room say, "It's okay, JT. Let them in." He stood back and opened the door so they could come in. He walked over, poured another cup of coffee, and doctored it as he had seen Jessie do at the rehearsal dinner. He took it to the door and knocked. She opened it but didn't come out. He offered her the coffee. "Oh, thank God. I appreciate this." She took the coffee and shut the door.

He went back to his coffee and warmed it up. "Sorry, gentlemen, that I can't offer you anything. Had I known you were coming ...?"

They shook their heads. He sat down, spooned up some eggs, and took a couple of pieces of bacon. There were biscuits under one cover and gravy that he hadn't ordered, and he put some sliced cantaloupe on the plate.

Jessie came out, and he handed her the plate. "Oh, thank you, kind sir. I woke up famished."

JT fixed himself a plate and walked to the door of his room. "If you gentlemen will excuse me?" He went in and shut the door.

* * *

Uncle Benjamin asked, "Where's he going?"

Jessie looked at her uncle as she took a sip of coffee. "His room. Why?"

Benjamin lowered his voice. "What are we going to do? Do you realize he'll own half of everything we have when you divorce?"

Jessie slowly ate her breakfast. "I told you I would come up with a suitable solution, did I not?"

Brad glanced at his brother and back at her. "There is no suitable solution."

Uncle Benjamin started to say something, but Jessie cut him off. "Listen to me, you two. Have Ed draw up a binding agreement that has the same language in it as a pre-nup, and he'll sign it."

They both blinked in apparent shock. "Are you sure?" Brad asked. "Have you discussed this with him?"

She looked at them disapprovingly. "Get it done. I'll send you his attorney's information, and we'll have an agreement as soon as the two lawyers can get it done. I understand his lawyer is in town anyway. Now, if you'll excuse me, I need to get dressed." They continued to blink at her in amazement, and she scowled at them. "He's not after my money."

Brad stood up. "If he learns how much we're worth, he will be."

"Then that should motivate you to get this done as quickly as possible." They got up and walked out, and she closed the door behind them. She finished eating, went to her room, and got in the shower for a long time.

* * *

JT came out, walked to the kitchenette, wiped the counter down, put the dishes on the service cart, and pushed it into the hall. "Did you get enough to eat?" he said as she walked out after her shower.

"Too much. It was good, and I thank you very much."

He smiled. "Are your two uncles surprised at my appearing as dumb as they assume I am?"

She chuckled. "They'll be all right, but expect a quick turnaround on this. What's your lawyer's name?" He opened his address book on his phone and gave it to her. She downloaded it to her phone and handed him his phone back. "What kind of phone is that? I've never seen one before."

"A satellite phone—it switches to satellite from a cell tower when there is no reception. I very rarely have no reception."

She looked at him, amazed, and then her phone rang. She answered it with a voice of concern. "I'll be right there." She looked at JT as she put her phone back in the pocket of her robe. "Dad's back in the hospital. I have to go."

They both went to their rooms, and she came out wearing tan slacks, a white blouse, a white sweater, and boots. He came out in blue jeans, white running shoes, and a buttoned-up gray shirt that perfectly fitted him. Not tight, but cut so he had ample room for movement while still showing off his physique. His weapon was in a leather case he carried. He looked at her and said, "Let's go."

She frowned. "You're certainly welcome, but you don't have to go. I know this will be boring to you."

"We have to keep up appearances for Dad, don't we? What kind of husband would he think me to be if I didn't accompany my wife in her time of need?"

She smiled, and they walked out the door. As they made their way down the long hallway, she took his hand, held it, and smiled at him again. "Don't take this wrong—this is just for appearance's sake."

They had his car brought around, and as they waited in the Memphis humidity, she said, "I have no idea where my car is. It may still be at the church if someone didn't take it to my house."

"We'll find it. Where are we going?"

"To Baptist Hospital in Collierville." JT texted his lawyer to meet them there, and then they got in his Range Rover and drove off. Her phone rang. "No, Uncle Benjamin, I'm on the way to the hospital. Dad was taken in this morning. Well, tell him to bring it to the hospital then. Good-bye."

She hung up, and his phone rang. He answered it on the steering wheel, and the call came over the car speakers. "JT? Arian here. I heard from your wife's lawyer, and they're being difficult. I figured you're doing this for her, so I put simple language in that said everything she had before the marriage was hers, you forfeited any claims to it, and the same for you."

He narrowed his eyes. "So, what are they being difficult about?"

"It's a one-way street the way they have it worded. What's hers is hers, and what's yours is hers. I told them that was never going to happen, so you might want to have your wife talk to them. I can't believe you got married, and I can't wait to hear the details."

"Nothing to tell—she got me drunk, and I woke up married." He smiled as Jessie hit him. "Arian, say hello to Dr. Logan."

"Doctor? Wow, maybe you should rethink this. Hi, Dr. Logan."

"Hello, Arian. Call me Jessie. Don't believe him about being drunk, but it is an interesting story. I'll jerk a knot in my lawyer. Thanks."

"Thank you, and I've never known JT to be under the influence of anything in the last fourteen years. By the way, what was your name before you married?"

Jessie smiled. "Believe it or not, it was Logan."

"Seriously, JT?"

"She's not lying. It's Logan. In fact, we're both JT Logan. We've already done some preliminary research, and we're not related."

"Good to know. I'm on the way to Collierville Baptist now. Good to talk to you, Jessie. Bye."

Jessie picked up her phone and pushed a button. "Rhonda, let me talk to Ed ... I don't care if he's talking to the president of the United States, put him on the phone." She raised her voice a few decibels. "My dad is back in the hospital, and I don't have time for this crap, so put him on the fucking phone." A few minutes of silence followed. "Ed, my husband just heard from his lawyer. Make it swing both ways, and get it right this time. I'm not going to tell you again. If I have to do my own legal work, I don't need your firm, do I?" She hung up.

They drove in silence a few more minutes before he glanced at her. "Get him on the fucking phone? Remind me to never make you mad."

That brought a smile to her face. "Did I really say that? Now you know why I have never married in the last thirty-eight years." She glanced at him with a slight frown. "How old are you?"

He grinned without looking at her. "Believe it or not, I turned thirty-eight my last birthday. Do you want a copy of the birth certificate?"

"Seriously? When is your birthday?"

"February the second."

Her eyes got big. "No kidding? You're actually three days older than I am? I thought I was going to have to go through the humiliation of having a younger husband."

He looked at her. "February the fifth?"

She nodded.

"Why haven't you gotten married in the last thirty-eight years? You're a beautiful woman with a kick-ass figure—not that I've noticed. You're a doctor and a lawyer and got to be loaded. It seems there would be a line from here to Atlanta to get hooked up with you."

She didn't smile. "My sister Lenore has a mentally challenged child, and Hazel has a physically disabled child, both from birth defects. It's in the genes, and while I love my two nephews, I'm not going to produce more of the same. Men want a family I won't give them."

They got to the hospital, and she pointed. "Pull up to that gate with the guard." The guard came out, JT lowered the window, and Jessie leaned over. "Billy, it's me. This is my husband's car. Can you get me a sticker for it and let us in?"

"Sure, Dr. Logan." He raised the gate. They parked and got out, and the guard came up. "If you'll leave me your keys, I'll have your sticker put on, and I'll bring them to you."

JT dropped the keys into his hand and followed Jessie into the hospital. When Jessie opened the door to her father's room, JT saw the doctor bending over her father, so he backed out into the hall and waited. Five minutes later, Jessie walked out with the doctor. They talked a minute, and he left.

She came over to JT. "His white cell count got too high, so they brought him in. Come on in and say hi to him."

JT walked around the bed because Mr. Logan was lying on his left side facing the wall. Jessie sat down on the other side of the bed in a chair near her sisters.

"How are you, sir?"

The old man opened his eyes and smiled. "After three daughters, two of which married losers, I finally got a son I can look up to. Promise me one thing, JT."

Lenore and Hazel raised their eyes.

"Anything, sir."

"Promise me you will watch out for my daughter for the rest of her life."

JT smiled. "Sir, every married couple hopes they will grow old and die in each other's arms. Of course, it doesn't always work out like that, but I will give you my oath on this. No matter what happens between us in the future, I will look out for her the rest of her life. That's a promise I don't give lightly."

Mr. Logan smiled and closed his eyes. Jessie came around and hugged JT. "Thank you. You made him very happy." Seeing that her dad had fallen asleep, she lowered her voice. "The more and more I come back to reality, the more and more I am in awe of what you have done for me. My best friends haven't come to my aid. Of course, they are all women, but you know what I mean. I hope I'm not being a burden on you or keeping you from doing something you need to do."

He smiled and shook his head. "No. I didn't know what I was going to do with the three months of downtime I'm required to take after ... after working for eight straight months. I left a relationship ... some time ago, and I'm not looking for another right now. Now that I think about it, I guess getting married would be called a relationship." She laughed, leaning on his shoulder. Their eyes met. "What I'm trying to say is, I could use a good friend right now, one who can be objective, even if she is preoccupied most of the time."

She laughed again. "I think I would like that, JT. I think I could be good at that. Thank you." Aware that someone had walking up to them, they turned to see a man in an expensive, three-piece suit. "Ed, did you get it straightened out?"

"Yes, Jessie, I did. I was looking after your best interest. I didn't mean to make you mad or go against your wishes. Is there somewhere we can sit down?"

Jessie's sisters glanced at her as they started to leave. "I guess we need to get back to the losers we're married to," one of them said sarcastically.

Jessie motioned Ed and JT to follow her. She led them out of the patient area and down the hall to a meeting room. She unlocked the door, and inside was a small conference table and chairs. Jessie propped the door open, and Ed asked, "Are we expecting someone else?"

Jessie looked at JT. "Your lawyer is coming, right?" He nodded, picked up his cell phone, and started texting. He finished, and they heard his phone ding.

He smiled. "She's coming up the elevator."

They waited for about five minutes, and Jessie looked up as a beautiful brunette with a Barbie doll–figure walked in. JT said, "Hey, Arian, have a seat over here by me. We have to be a 'we and they' for this."

Arian sat down, looked at Jessie, and then back at JT. "My God, JT, she's beautiful." She stuck out her hand and shook hands with Jessie. "My name is Arian Moss.

Jessie smiled. "Thank you, but you are the one who's beautiful."

JT raised his arms. "Well, you're both beautiful, and I'm beautiful, so, Ed, by comparison, you're ugly as a bowling shoe."

Jessie and Arian laughed long and hard. Ed barely broke a smile as he shook Arian's hand.

Arian raised her eyes to Ed. "Is this the final draft that you sent?" He nodded.

She took the time to read over it. "It appears to be in order, so all we need are signatures." She pushed a hard copy to JT. "Sign where the green sticky markers are." He did, and she gave the sheet to Ed. He had Jessie sign where the orange sticky markers were, and they did the same with a second copy.

"Well, that about covers it." Arian looked at her watch. "It's five o'clock. Does anybody have time for dinner?"

Jessie stood up. "Sure, we do, but Ed has to go." He smiled sheepishly and left the room.

She checked on her father, and then they drove into Memphis and went to the Folks Folly Steak house. When they were seated, the waiter came and recited the menu. After they ordered, Arian looked at them. "Okay, how long have you been seeing each other, and how did you keep this a secret? When word came out that you were married, nobody knew anything about it ... So?"

Jessie glanced at JT with a smile. "Be my guest."

JT smiled as he leaned back in his chair. "Well, let's see. Where to begin? About a month ago Robert called me and asked if I would be his best man at his wedding."

Arian narrowed her eyes. "Robert with the four ...?"

JT nodded. "That's the one. He—"

Arian interrupted. "He's a creep. Haven't I always told you there was something wrong with him?"

"He is, and you did."

Arian sat silently as JT told the story. Before long, Arian's jaw dropped, but she remained silent, and she was still sitting there with her mouth open when he finished his tale. She looked at him. "You mean you ..." She pointed at Jessie. "And you ... seriously?" JT and Jessie both nodded their heads. "I can't believe this. You're not just pulling my leg, are you?"

"No, but if you want, stick it up here, and I'll give it a yank."

She stared at JT and then Jessie as though to see if she could detect an untruth. He returned her gaze and raised his hand. "That's the way it happened. Honest Injun, I mean, honest Native American. I need to be politically correct here, I suppose."

Jessie was laughing at JT, but Arian still had her mouth open in disbelief.

Keeping a straight face with some difficulty, JT said, "We have progressed in our relationship. Friday we were casual acquaintances, and today we've become friends. That's progress, isn't it?"

Arian nodded. "That sounds reasonable if you leave out that little tidbit about getting married in between."

Jessie stopped laughing and put her hand on Arian's arm. "He left out a very important part, because it shows what a great guy he is." She proceeded to tell Arian about her father.

As she finished the story, Jessie's phone rang, and she retrieved it from her pocket. "I'm sorry, I have to take this. It's about a legal case I'm working on. I'll be right back."

Arian asked JT as Jessie walked off, "What kind of legal work does she do?"

JT smiled. "She's a lawyer too." Arian's mouth dropped again.

* * *

Jessie stood outside the entrance of the ladies room. As she listened, she watched JT and Arian. Arian was smiling and talking, and he nodded or shook his head occasionally. Jessie saw her reach up, pull his face toward her, and kiss him on the side of the mouth. They continued to talk and laugh.

Jessie finished her phone call, went back, and sat down. "I'm sorry to disrupt our dinner."

Arian scooted her chair back and stood up. "Excuse me for continuing the disruption, but I have to go to the ladies room."

She left, and Jessie turned to JT. "I need to know something ... No, I want to know something, and if this is getting too personal, tell me. Do you and Arian have a history? I saw her kiss you, and that seems to be an unusual lawyer-client privilege."

He smiled. "No, she and I have been good friends since I hired her firm to represent me fourteen years ago. We don't get to see one another more than once a year—everything is done by phone. Besides, she's married and has been for fourteen years."

"Marriage doesn't stop some people. What does her husband do?"

He laughed. "Her husband is a beautiful blond named Jeanie. She's a lawyer and the other half of the law firm."

"You mean she's a lesbian?"

He nodded. "You know how it is with most lesbians—one takes on the male role, and one takes the female? I used to think that one requirement of being a lesbian was that one or both of the women had to be ugly as hell. Well, Jeanie is as beautiful as Arian is, and they've been together all this time."

Jessie looked at him for a second. "How old is she?"

JT wrinkled his brow. "She's forty-four or forty-five. I can't ever keep that straight."

This time Jessie dropped her jaw. "I figured her to be in her early thirties. I hope I look that good when I'm her age."

* * *

They finished dinner, and Arian headed back to the airport to catch her Atlanta flight. Jessie looked at JT as they got in the car. "I like getting to know about you. Are there any other secrets I would want to know about?"

"Oh, hell, yeah, but I'm not telling."

She laughed. "Drop me by the church so I can pick up my car. No, let's go back, check out of the hotel, and move you to my house. I have an extra room with a lock on the door for your protection." She gave him a really big grin.

Once JT had checked out, he took her back to the church, where she got in her Lincoln Town Car. He then followed her to a beautiful five-bedroom, four-bath house in Germantown.

Jessie showed him to a room, and he looked at the bedspread with its floral design, the curtains with their pastel colors, and the chest of drawers with bowls of potpourri sitting on doilies. It was a little too frilly for his taste, but he figured it wouldn't be permanent. He opened the closet, and it was full of clothes, so he stepped back. "Houston, we have a problem." She laughed as she walked into the room. Pointing to the closet, he said, "It looks like someone already lives in here."

She put her hands over her mouth as she laughed. "Oh, I forgot I had this stuff in here. If you'll help me grab these clothes, I'll clear it out."

He stopped her. "Wait. Let me see your room, please."

"Sure, why?"

They walked into the master bedroom, and JT went straight through to the master bathroom and started opening doors. He came out and put his hands on his hips. "I knew it— two walk-in closets, and both are beyond full. Where are you going to put the clothes in the other closet? I'm betting any other closets in the house are full also."

She laughed as she walked up and hit him on the arm. "I'll find a place—don't worry."

He hesitated before he spoke. "What were you going to do with Robert's shi—stuff?"

"I'm telling you I'll make room. That reminds me, I have some stuff of his in the back. I don't know what it is, but I'm going to burn it."

JT made a face as if he were horrified.

"What?"

"I've married a hoarder. What other perversions are hibernating in your soul?"

She stepped over quickly and playfully hit him on the shoulder. Then she rubbed her fist. "Why does it seem like that hurts me more than it does you?"

"Because it does—you hit like a girl." She smiled and pulled back as if she were going to hit him again, but she didn't.

They removed the clothes from the closet, took them to a third bedroom, and laid them on the bed.

He arranged his clothes like he was in the barracks. Shirts were hung one inch apart with the right sleeve facing out. Next were pants, and they were also one inch apart. After that were jackets, coats, and his garment bag with his dress uniform.

She walked in and exclaimed, "Oh my God, I've married a neat freak!"

He slowly looked around at her. "Let's let the marriage counselor decide if a neat freak is worse than a hoarder or not." She bent over laughing, which put the six pair of high heels in the bottom of the closet in her line of sight.

"Let me get these high heels out of your way." She started gathering shoes.

"Nah, leave them. I might want to wear them later."

She laughed. "I don't know how long this marriage will last, but we may have to build onto the house." She dropped her smile, and it was obvious she'd remembered the marriage was supposed to last only as long as her father lived. She looked up at him with tears in her eyes.

He gave a reassuring smile. "I don't know either, but I hope it lasts a long, long time."

She smiled with tears in her eyes and started to walk out with the armload of shoes. When she got to the door, she stopped and turned back to him. "Thank you for making me feel better."

He realized what she was thinking. "That's what friends do."

A few minutes later she returned and asked, "Where do you live when you are not marrying damsels in distress?"

He half smiled. "All over. I have an apartment in Paris, a place here and there, plus I have friends I stay with around the world."

* * *

Two nights later, JT's phone woke him. He recognized the ring he assigned to European calls, so he answered it. A voice on the other end said with a German accent. "Mr. Logan?"

He replied in German, "Yes, what can I do for you?"

"My name is Freidrick Schell. Someone has taken my wife, and I was told you could help me. I can pay whatever you are asking."

"Okay, Mr. Schell. I am in the States, but I will have one of my colleagues contact you and discuss this personally with you. Don't say any more over the phone. Can he reach you at this number?"

There was a pause. "Yes, of course, but I was told you were the one who had the best chance of doing it."

"I am part of a team. We all participate. I want my colleague to contact you so we can get working on this right away—time is of the essence. He will use my name, so you will know he is legitimate. He will contact you shortly. Good-bye."

"Good-bye."

JT got up and walked to the kitchen as he auto-dialed a number. He got himself a glass of water and leaned back against the counter. Still in German, he addressed the person on the other end. "Scottie, we got a hit. Contact Mr. Freidrick Schell in Hamburg, I'll text you the number. It's his wife, so do a thorough background on him. He says he can pay whatever we ask, and that's a red flag to me. It doesn't always mean somebody is trying to set us up, but everybody that has tried to set us up has said that. Get back to me as soon as you can. Bye."

As he ended the call, the kitchen light came on. Jessie stood in the doorway. He looked over at her. "I'm sorry; I didn't realize I woke you."

She smiled and shook her head. "You didn't. I've had a restless night, and I was awake." She paused briefly and then asked, "You were speaking German, is that right?"

He nodded. "But that's only because I was talking to a German."

She laughed. "You're trying to avoid the subject. How many languages do you speak?"

He gave her a little smile. "None correctly. I can speak conversationally in a couple of languages."

"You realize you just evaded my question, don't you? Remember, I'm a lawyer."

He walked over to her. "You remember the talk we had about not delving into each other's past? Well, this is one of those things, okay?"

She nodded and folded her arms as if she were cold.

He touched her shoulder. "Go back to bed and try to get some sleep."

She shook her head. "I can't sleep. Daddy is too much on my mind. Maybe I ought to get dressed and go up there."

"Just to watch him sleep? They'd call you if they needed you, wouldn't they?" She nodded. "Wait here a minute." He went back into his room and came back out with a blanket and a pillow. He sat her down on the couch. "Lie down, please. Sometimes a change will help you sleep."

She smiled, sat down, and then stretched out on the couch. She laid her head on the pillow, and he pulled the warm blanket up over her. It was about sixty seconds before he heard her soft purr. She slept until nine thirty the next morning.

* * *

She awoke when she smelled coffee. "I'm sorry, I was dead asleep. What time is it?" She looked at the clock before he could answer. "Oh my God, I didn't realize it was that late." She took the coffee he handed her. "Thanks ... for everything."

He winked at her. "I just hope you can break the habit of having me put you to sleep."

She smiled as she went into her room to shower and dress. When she came out, she was dressed in a black business pantsuit with gray pinstripes. JT wore blue jeans and a long-sleeved dress shirt. He had put scrambled eggs, bacon, and toast on the table. He poured her a second cup and put cream and sweetener in it. "Thanks, but I wish you hadn't gone to the trouble. I'm not really hungry."

"Sit down and eat. You know breakfast is the most important meal of the day." He brought his plate in and sat down.

She looked at his plate. "Tell me if I'm delving into something I shouldn't, but I never see you eat bread. Why?"

He pursed his lips. "I used to have trouble with arthritis in my left knee, high blood pressure, trouble keeping the weight off, and a few other problems. A doctor in China put me onto not eating anything made from wheat. The wheat we grow today is different from the wheat that used to be grown—they've altered it genetically to get better production. I admit to falling off the wagon every once in a while. I had some croissants before I left Paris, and when I got back to the States I had biscuits and gravy one morning in a few moments of weakness. At any rate, it cured a myriad of other minor problems I had." He smiled at her.

"Really? I may need to try that. I have a little arthritis and ... a few other problems that that diet might help."

He smiled a mischievous smile. "I also used to hoard clothes. I had them in every closet in the house, but now I'm cured."

She wadded up her napkin and threw it across the table at him as she laughed. She continued to smile. "Let me make another observation. You put ketchup on eggs? I've never seen that before, and it's really disgusting."

"I've done that ever since I was a kid. My mother couldn't break me of it and would, in fact, hide the ketchup in the mornings. She quit when she realized I had my own stash from McDonald's."

Jessie put her fork down so she wouldn't drop it laughing.

He waited until she composed herself. "One other thing you should quit using is sweetener. It causes problems like weight gain, and I read research where it is worse on your teeth than meth. Use sugar—it doesn't have that many calories per spoonful, and unrefined sugar from sugar cane would even be better. Just a thought."

She examined the package of sweetener. "Hmm, you might be onto something there." She eyed him. "From the looks of your body, you are."

"If you saw my body when we do those vile and dirty things you told your uncle about, you'd be impressed."

She held his gaze as she smiled and slowly nodded. "I bet I would."

After she finished eating, she said, "Can I ask about that conversation in German?"

He got up, picked up the dirty plates, and looked her in the eye. "No." He walked into the kitchen.

* * *

JT and Jessie enjoyed each other's company, and the next six weeks consisted of daily hospital visits, walks in the park, sitting, and talking about life. Jessie had taken time off to get married and to watch her dad.

A few weeks later, the light in his bedroom coming on awakened JT. Jessie said, "JT, the hospital called. They want me to come right away."

He looked at her, and she was trembling. He got out of bed and grabbed her by the shoulders. "Slow down, get your clothes on, and we'll go as fast as possible. Go get dressed."

She went back to her room. JT got dressed, and Jessie came out of her room in blue jeans and running shoes and was pulling a blouse on over her bra.

They went out and got in his car. He drove only a few miles over the speed limit because he couldn't afford to get a ticket and have his name show up in public records. After a few minutes she asked, "Can't we hurry?"

He glanced at her briefly. "If a cop stops us, we'll be thirty minutes or more getting a ticket. We're going as fast as I dare. We'll get there in time."

They pulled into the doctor's lot, and she had the door open before he came to a complete stop. He jumped out, auto-locked the car, and had to run to catch up to her. She ran in, though when she was in the hospital she slowed to a fast walk. She had her phone up to her ear. "Lenore, pick up, dammit ... Let me see if I can get Hazel." She dialed the phone again. "Hazel, you need to come to the hospital right away." She paused. "I've tried to reach her, but she doesn't answer. You try it on your way, and I'll keep trying." She looked at JT. "I've told her time and time again, 'Keep your cell phone by your bed.' She doesn't have it charged half the time."

When they got to the room, the doctor was there, listening to the old man's chest. JT started to back out, but Jessie grabbed his hand, and he stayed with her as the doctor stood up. "I'm afraid he's got pneumonia, and this looks like it could be it. He's not coherent, because we've got him pumped full of morphine."

Jessie went over to her father, and JT pushed a chair up until it hit her in the back of the legs. She sat there, cried, and held her father's hand, though there wasn't much hand to hold because of all the tubes coming out of it. They had depleted the veins in his arms, and even the catheter port had failed.

Forty-five minutes later, Hazel walked in. Jessie asked, "Where's Junior?"

"Someone had to stay with the Mikey, Jessie. This whole hospital thing scares him." Jessie nodded in understanding. "I called Lenore's neighbor to see if he could knock on the door and raise them." Jessie nodded again.

An hour later, as the old man's breathing started to get shallow, Lenore came in the door with her husband. "Why didn't you call me, Jessie?"

Jessie looked up with rage on her face, and JT put his hands on her shoulders. "We did—both of us tried."

Lenore appeared to be spoiling for a fight, and she held up her phone. "I haven't had any calls to my phone." Jessie grabbed it before Lenore could pull it back.

"It's dead, Lenore," Jessie said after checking the phone. "The battery's dead. I've told you about that a hundred times." She threw the phone back at her sister; Lenore didn't react quickly enough to catch it, and it landed in the floor and broke into several pieces.

The old man started talking, and Jessie explained to Lenore, "He's not coherent; he's talking out of his head from the morphine drip."

Then they heard the old man distinctly say, "JT?"

With everyone else looking at him. JT walked to the edge of the bed. "Yes, sir, Mr. Logan, I'm here."

The old man slurred his words. "Take care ... Jessie. All ... life."

"Yes, sir, you have my promise, I'll take care of her all of her life." The old man nodded, and his eyes half closed. JT heard him exhale and then nothing. He turned to Jessie. "He's gone."

The three sisters broke down crying. JT closed the old man's eyes and observed the time. He held Jessie and, feeling her legs fold, knew she was fainting. He picked her up, carried her to the doctor's lounge, and put her on a sofa.

She came to and continued her crying. He pulled out his handkerchief and gave it to her. Lenore and Hazel came into the lounge, sat, and cried. A nurse came in. "Dr. Simmons is on his way back down here from his office upstairs. I'm going to put the time of death at approximately ..."

JT said, "It was 1:28 a.m., exactly." She nodded and walked out.

The doctor came in and sat down across from them. "I'm sorry, but he declined so fast. I wish we had had more time to notify you."

Lenore said bitterly, "That's no excuse. If you had been watching him like you're supposed to, we would have known sooner."

Jessie got up and walked over to the doctor. "Dr. Simmons, I appreciate all you did for my father. Don't pay any attention to my sister—she's just distraught, and on top of that, she's stupid."

JT had to bite his lip to keep from laughing.

Jessie walked back to JT, took his hand, and walked out.

"Where to?" he asked.

"Home."

When they got home, she headed straight for her room. "I want to be alone, please."

He didn't see her again until the next day. She walked out in a business suit again. "I have to finalize the arrangements. You going or staying?" She didn't look at him. JT didn't like the coldness in her voice but decided this wasn't the time to pursue it.

"I'm going."

She walked past him. "Let's go, then."

He stood there until she stopped at the door and looked back. He just stared at her to let her know he didn't appreciate the way she was treating him. He grabbed his key and walked out behind her. They got in the car, and nothing was said as they drove to Memorial Park Funeral Home and Cemetery. He followed her in. Her sisters and their husbands were already there.

Lenore looked at Jessie. "It's nice of you to finally show up. We've been here for twenty minutes."

Jessie sat down, opened her briefcase, and took out a folder. JT went to the back of the room and sat down as Jessie returned Lenore's contemptuous look. "I told you we'd meet at 2:00, and it's 1:56, so I'm early, for your information."

At two o'clock on the dot, the funeral director came in, introduced himself as Mr. Grayson, and gave his condolences to everyone.

"Now, Dr. Logan, I think we have everything set. There will be one recorded hymn at the beginning and one at the end. The service is to be no longer than twenty minutes—the preacher is aware of that—and in lieu of flowers, the family wishes donations to be made to the American Cancer Society. Anything else we need to discuss?"

Lenore stood up with fire in her eyes. "Jessie, you're the youngest. Do you think because you're a doctor and a lawyer, you're going to hijack Dad's funeral? I want Charlie's niece to sing 'How Great Thou Are' and—"

Jessie interrupted her. "Charlie's niece couldn't sing on the best day of her life— anything. I'm not going to have her warbling at my dad's funeral. Why don't you book her for yours before the prices go up?"

Lenore's expression was determined as she sat back down. "You still don't have the right to decide everything. I want four of dad's favorite hymns sung by someone and not a recording." She crossed her arms. "Don't you have anything to say, Hazel?"

Hazel cleared her throat. "Yes, I agree with Lenore—we should have a say in what happens here. Not just you."

JT thought, *Damn, I should've sat near the door in case a fight breaks out.*

Charlie looked at Jessie. "We'll decide on a hymn and when it will be played. You two have the same right. That seems only fair."

Jessie leaned back in her chair as she put the folder back in her briefcase and looked at Charlie and then the funeral director. "Mr. Grayson, I have paid the $15,000 for my dad's funeral. If they come up with $5,000 each, then let them do what they want. But until you see cash in hand, it will go as planned." She stood up and walked out.

JT stood up and nodded to the others. "Brothers and sisters, good day." He caught up to Jessie as she got to the car. They got in, and he backed out, asking, "Where to?"

"Home." Another one-word answer.

They drove home without saying anything to each other. When they got home, she went to her room and slammed the door. His phone buzzed, and he looked at the text, which read "Grounded, 2 in 5. ???" Scottie was telling him the background work on Mr. Schell's wife had been completed and that the second phase was starting in five days. The three question marks meant "Where are you?"

He texted back, "death in the family problems, will advise 1," meaning he would let them know in twenty-four hours.

He went to his room and turned on the TV to see if there was any publicity on the world news about Mrs. Schell. As he watched, he picked up the phone and pushed a number on his speed dial. "Hello, Margaret? I need transportation to Scottie's house for Thursday, please." He was telling her in code he needed a ride to Manheim, Germany.

"Sure, but you should stop by for a visit on your way," she replied, which told him he was needed in the home office.

Twenty minutes later, he got a text that read, "Tuesday, 3:00pm, M-A Ready."

That meant he had to leave from the Memphis-Arlington airport, which meant the first leg was going to be a prop and a small one. He preferred jets. He didn't know how to tell Jessie he was leaving; she was in a fragile state of mind, and he didn't want to push her. She stayed in her room all day Saturday and Sunday.

JT didn't bother her but always left food in the fridge for her.

Monday they got in the car and drove to Memorial Park for the funeral service. JT stayed in the back; he had seen his share of bodies, and he didn't want to see the old man's.

When the service was ready to start, he saw the sisters and their husband sit down in the family room off to the side. There was an empty seat beside Jessie, and he started walking toward it, but Jessie stood up, grabbed Aunt Cecelia's hand, and sat her down beside her while casting a quick look at JT. He returned to the back of the chapel and sat down.

When it was over, the family was led to the limo. The door was shut after they got in, making it clear there was no room for him. He didn't put his car in the procession—he wasn't about to run and try to catch a funeral procession. Instead he went to a bench under a big tree and sat down to wait. It was about an hour before the limo pulled back in and Jessie came to where he was sitting on the bench. He got up and walked behind her to his car, and when they got in, the atmosphere was ice cold.

On the way back, JT finally had to say something. "Jessie, I don't deserve to be treated this way."

"I'm sorry you had to miss the graveside service," she said while looking straight ahead.

"I know what happens there. I didn't need to see it. I've already made my peace with your father."

She glanced over at him. "I want you to know that I release you from the promise you made to my father about watching out for me."

He stared at the road ahead. "It wasn't a promise, it was an oath, and it was between me and him. You have nothing to do with it, nor do you have the right to cancel it."

They pulled up into the drive of the house. After she got out, she said to him across the top of the car, "I need to be by myself for a few days."

He narrowed his eyes at her over the car as he shut the door. "Not a problem. I have to leave on business tomorrow anyway."

As he walked in ahead of her, she asked, "Where are you going?"

He didn't answer; he just walked into his room and shut the door behind him.

He thought, *Well, this will work out. She's needs to be alone, and I need to go to Europe.*

* * *

Jessie stayed in her room the rest of that day and into Tuesday evening. She came out to get something to eat and heard a car pull up; it was JT's Range Rover. She was heading back to her room when the back doorbell rang. A man she didn't recognize was at the door. She walked over and opened it. "Yes, may I help you?"

The man smiled and said, "I was told to drop this car off here. Is it okay right there? I can move it if you need me to."

She glanced out the window at JT's car and then back at the young man. "Yes, that's fine, but where is he?"

The man shook his head as he handed her the key. "I don't know, ma'am. I was just told to drop the car here."

She took the key as another car pulled up. The man ran and got in it, and they backed out. She didn't know what to do. She had brushed JT off, and she felt she would appear weak if she called. She didn't sleep well the next few nights.

* * *

JT's plane touched down in Manheim. He went to a waiting car and was driven around for an hour, passing the same landmarks from different directions. Once he and the driver were sure no one was following them, they pulled into a warehouse. The door was quickly shut behind them.

He got out, and Scottie walked over to him and shook his hand. He was a muscular guy with black hair and good looks, the only flaw being a small scar on his right cheek. "I'm glad you're here, JT. I've been planning, but change anything you want."

They walked into a room that had a topographical map of a farm and surrounding woods on one wall. Sixteen men in black military fatigues sat facing the map. Scottie told JT, "She's being held in the basement of this farmhouse. We'll go in, in two teams. One will approach from the high ground in back of the house, and one will approach from ground level. I haven't come up with code names yet but—"

JT looked over at Scottie. "Upstairs and downstairs."

Scottie nodded. "I like it. Bad Billy here will be upstairs team leader, and I will be the downstairs team leader. You move in with whichever team you want, but I suggest the downstairs team. We're going to run into some bad boys with heavy artillery. You guys each have the weaponry to take them out, and I know damn well you have the skills." Scottie stepped up to the map and pointed. "There are guards posted here, here, here, and here ... and here. Each man takes out the men he's assigned to. Stay out of other's people's business unless someone calls out for help. If you get hit, sing out. We have two medicos, one with each team." He turned to JT. "How'd I do?"

JT studied the map. "Have you rehearsed this yet?"

Scottie looked down and back up. "Yes, sir, three times."

"Who was playing my part in the rehearsals?"

Scottie raised his finger. "I was."

JT nodded. "Then you'll be the extraction leader on this. You've been wanting this opportunity, so here it is."

Scottie frowned. "You mean I'm heading this whole extraction? Where will you be?"

JT looked at the map again and back at Scottie. "I'll be under your command as upstairs team leader. Put Bad Billy downstairs."

Scottie had a huge grin on his face. "Thanks, boss. I won't let you down."

JT smiled back. "I know you won't. If I thought you would, I wouldn't let you do it. When's lift off?"

"Tomorrow afternoon at fourteen hundred. It's supposed to rain Saturday and Sunday all day, and I'd like to do it under cover of the rain, but I want to be on the ground before it starts raining. We'll go in by paraglider chutes and be extracted by slickers." He turned to the other men. "Check your gear, especially your radios. Make sure we're all on the same channel—I don't want anybody walking around out there deaf. Downstairs team probably be the first to see the lady in question, so, Mikey, bring the lady to JT's team. They will take her out. Remember, we are dropping in on Farmer McNasty's place. Any questions?"

"What about dead or wounded?"

Scottie paused. "I didn't plan on that, so let's don't have any dead or wounded. If anybody feels faint ..." He pointed at the map. "We have safe spots in the dense woods here for the downstairs team and here for the upstairs team, and we don't leave anybody behind. Extraction by three Hueys right here at one hundred hours Saturday, so don't be late. There will be green phosphorus markers to land by and a drone with Hellfire missiles covering our retreat if needed. One other thing—we can pick up a bonus if we see this man and eliminate him." Scottie passed a picture around. "The CIA wants him dead or alive, and he might be there, so memorize this face."

JT looked at them all. "Scottie will be supreme leader when we leave the plane. I'll be under his authority. Now get some sleep."

After the other men left, Scottie said, "Thanks, JT. I really appreciate the confidence you have in me, but now I have butterflies in my stomach."

JT smiled. "That's natural. If you didn't have butterflies I wouldn't trust you with our lives. Do a good job, and you may get the job permanently."

Scottie frowned. "You're not planning on leaving us, are you?"

"Nah, I was considering an executive position. We'll see." JT started to walk off.

Scottie said, "Can I ask one more question, JT?"

JT stopped and turned around. "Sure. What is it?"

"How do you convince yourself to go in, knowing you or your men may die?"

JT stood deep in thought for a minute. "Everybody has a different mindset. I convince myself I'm going to die on this extraction, and I do my best to not worry about dying so everybody else will get back okay. You have to believe you're going to die, or it won't work. If you start worrying about dying, get out of the business." He turned and walked off, leaving Scottie to figure it out for himself.

* * *

Jessie had gone to the office on Wednesday and busied herself with a court case she was working on, and Pastor Willis's wife had an appointment Thursday morning for a checkup. By noon Thursday, JT was really on her mind. She resigned herself to the fact that they needed to talk about what was next for them.

She dialed his number, and it rang twice before he answered. It was good to hear his voice, but she didn't let him know.

"Hello, Jessie. What's the problem?"

She paused a minute. "Does there have to be a problem for me to call?"

"The way you've been treating me, yes. What do you want?"

She cleared her throat. "We need to sit down and talk about ... about us. Can you come over tonight?"

"I thought you wanted to be alone for a couple of days."

She steeled herself against his logic and didn't want to appear weak. "Well, I did, but this is more important. Can you come over tonight?"

He was silent for a few long seconds. "I'm at the home office, and I have business here, and it will take a few days. If I knew you were going to do this, I would have stayed there."

She frowned. "You're in Paris?"

"Yeah. I'll be here for a few days, maybe longer."

"Are you going to do any of that—"

"Please don't discuss that on the phone. I'll see you when I get back. I'll call you when I'm through, because I'll be out of range of a tower for a few days, so you will not be able to reach me."

"You said you never lost signal with that phone. Why are you going to lose it now?"

"I said I hardly ever lost signal. I'm not taking my phone where I'm going. I'll call you when I get back. Take care. Bye." The phone went dead. She wanted to call him right back because hearing his voice made her feel better, but she didn't. She didn't like this needy feeling she had for him, especially since she knew he wanted out of the marriage.

* * *

Friday, the extraction teams suited up in full camouflage combat gear and were driven in a covered truck to an airfield. They got on an old C-130 and strapped themselves in. JT realized it had been almost two years since he had jumped by parachute.

They rode, listening to the roar of the engines, and after hours of flying, they stood up and did their "check of threes" that all sky divers use. The back ramp of the plane lowered, and they moved to the climb-out. JT was in front of the upstairs team, and Scottie was beside him in front of Bad Billy, who was heading the downstairs team. When the green light came on, he and Scottie ran for the door and jumped spread-eagle into the ink-black night. Their teams were right behind them. The air was freezing, and the drop at over one hundred miles an hour was breathtaking.

JT waited two minutes and then yanked the ripcord. The rectangular chute opened with a *pop*, and JT started floating to earth. He strained to see the phosphorus markers; he knew they would land in the right vicinity, but he wouldn't know how fast the ground was coming up without the markers. He finally spotted the markers to his left and pulled hard on the steering toggle that controlled his direction; the others followed. He glided to the left and landed right in the middle of the circle of markers. He knew Dutch had risked jumping in daylight to put these out for the teams.

When he hit the ground, he rolled and started gathering up his chute, immediately running for the outside of the circle so no one would land on him. When he got to the outside, he dropped his chute and keyed his mic. "Upstairs north of the circle." He heard several replies of "Roger that." He waited while men started running up, and he counted until he had all eight of his team. He motioned them to follow, and they spread out with twenty yards between them in a staggered formation.

They took up their positions as diagrammed on the map board. JT heard on his radio, "Report," and clicked the mic that was clipped to his shirt. "Upstairs in position."

Bad Billy's voice came over the radio next, saying, "Downstairs in position," and then Scottie ordered, "Move out."

JT took his team across the ridge and down the hill until they came to an outbuilding that hadn't been on the map. After hand-signaling for one man to go around one side of the building, he went to the other side. Dutch met him in front, and together they quietly looked in the window. Inside the building were four heavily armed men playing cards and laughing. JT motioned to Dutch, pointed at him, and held up two fingers. Then he pointed at himself and held up two fingers. Dutch nodded. They opened the door, and each of them fired their silencer-equipped Sigs. The four men dropped. JT went to the side of the building to signal an all-clear to the rest of the men and indicated that one of them needed to come up and clean up the bodies. The man nodded and went in, and JT heard the *zip, zip, zip, zip* of the man's silencer as he put a round in the head of each man to ensure he was dead.

They moved on down the hill as it started to rain and came to the caretaker's house. A woman who looked to be at least eighty years old was sitting on the covered porch, asleep in a big chair with a blanket over her. A dim light bulb over her head cast eerie shadows as it swung in the breeze. JT decided not to kill her although he knew he should. Rule number one was never let the enemy behind you, and every person encountered was a friendly or an enemy. He knew she wasn't a friendly, so that technically made her an enemy, but he motioned them to give her a wide berth; they went around her. He had someone slip up and check the caretaker's house to make sure it was empty.

As they approached the main house, JT heard another *zip* from a silencer, followed by the sound of a body falling. He was about to step out from behind a tree when a guard walked right in front of him. JT put his gun to the man's head and pulled the trigger. Warm blood spattered JT's face.

He caught the man and lowered him to the ground so he wouldn't make a noise when he fell. He then moved to the root cellar doors. He started to open them when he heard a voice whisper in German, "What are you doing? Get back to your post." He heard somebody's silencer silence him, and somebody grabbed the man before he hit the ground. JT had worried about the night being so dark, but it turned out to be an advantage for them. The teams all had night vision equipment, but the lights from the windows of the farmhouse interfered so they couldn't use them.

He knocked on the root cellar door and stepped to the side. The door rose, and a man peered out into the dark. JT put the muzzle up to the man's temple and pulled the trigger. He grabbed the man by the hair so he wouldn't fall back into the cellar, but the hollow-point round had taken the top of the man's head off, so the body dropped with a big thump.

He signaled his team to rush the cellar; once inside, they found the room dark and empty. They eased open the interior door, which according to their intel led to the kitchen, and saw a man facing the stove and another turning the knob on an old-fashioned radio. JT held up two fingers, there were two *zips*, and both men crumpled to the floor. JT walked past the fallen men to another door. Instinct told him to pull his knife. He cracked the door open and saw a man sitting in a hallway in a chair. He was asleep, so when JT got to him, he pulled the man's head forward and buried the knife in the back of his brain. The man slumped forward without a sound.

Charles grabbed the dead man and laid him on the floor. When he then pulled out his cell phone and took a photo of the man, JT realized it was the man the CIA wanted dead. Then Charles took up a defensive position, watching another closed door further down the hallway.

After signaling the men behind him to clean up the two bodies in the kitchen, JT stooped down in the dim light to take keys off the dead guard. He then went to the closed door, found the correct key, and unlocked the door. He pushed it open and saw two women instead of the one they expected.

JT held up two fingers. Two of his men whispered to the hostages in German and French that they were being rescued. The two men had the women climb on their backs. They exited the building as they had come in, and when they were ten yards away from the house, they could barely hear silencers going off out front. JT keyed his mic. "Upstairs cleaned. Extraction complete. Over."

He heard a crackle in his earpiece, and then Scottie came on and said, "You have the pigeon already?"

"Yes, one pigeon we're after and one pigeon of opportunity. A piece of cake. Ready to move to the departure point."

Scottie came back on the radio. "Upstairs, downstairs, no pigeons your location; clean up and move out." They started back in the direction they had come. As they got to the caretaker's shack with the old woman on the porch, JT saw she was still asleep. In fact, he could hear her snoring, so he waved everybody by him as he watched the old woman. When the last man had passed, he waited two minutes and started out behind them.

JT caught movement out of the corner of his eye and turned to see a grenade coming his way. He jumped behind a stand of trees as the grenade went off. He didn't remember falling to the ground, but he felt like he had a red-hot iron stuck to his body on his left shoulder, the left side of his back, and the left side of his ass. He turned over and saw the old woman walking rapidly with a cane down the hill. JT aimed and put four rounds in her back, and she fell to her knees and then face down. If any guards were still alive, he knew the grenade explosion would have alerted them. He tried to get up but couldn't. All of a sudden, the medic was cutting his shirt open with a knife, and JT heard him say, "He's hit in several places. Pick him up and carry him." He felt his body being lifted, and then everything went black.

When he woke up he was on his stomach on a stretcher in a chopper. It landed, and he was pulled out and carried to a covered truck. He passed out again, and the next time he woke up he was back in the warehouse, still lying on his stomach. He didn't feel any pain, no doubt thanks to one of the several IVs running to his arms. He lay there without opening his eyes and heard a man say, "How did he get those scars across his back? He looks like he was whipped with a bullwhip."

Scottie replied, "He was a prisoner of war when he was in the army. The fortunate ones were killed. That's all you need to know."

JT opened his eyes. Scottie saw him and stooped down. "Anybody else hurt?" JT asked, his voice weak.

Scottie smiled and shook his head. "You're the only one. Didn't you hear me in the briefing talk about no wounded?"

JT smiled and closed his eyes. "That was a rookie mistake I made. I should have killed that old woman in her sleep the first time I saw her. I put other men in danger by pulling that dumb stunt."

Scottie put his hand on JT's arm. "Maybe, but no one else was hurt, so you get to pay for your mistake by getting hit in the ass. It's going to be tough sitting for a while."

JT looked back over his shoulder. "How bad am I hit?"

"You took shrapnel from the grenade in the left shoulder, the left side of your back, and the left side of your ass. Some of it went fairly deep. No broken bones or punctured vitals, but you're going to need physical therapy to get over this."

"How long before I can get home?"

Scottie closed one eye like he was thinking. "You've been sewn up and given some blood and antibiotics, but I need you out of the country and, better yet, off this continent. They'll be looking for us. We already have the money deposited in the bank, and the target we did for the CIA means the ride to and from is free. I should have you home with your wife inside twenty-four hours."

JT nodded. "I'll divide the money up so you get the extraction leader's share."

Scottie patted his arm again. "Thanks, boss. Oh, by the way. We identified the girl as some big German industrialist's daughter. Margaret negotiated the rate, and tomorrow we'll let him know she was rescued. It's going to be a good payday."

JT woke up when they moved him from plane to plane. Hours later, Scottie shook him and woke him up. "We could get you to the US, but I just learned we don't have a doctor we can trust anymore, so you're going to recuperate in Mexico."

JT shook his head. "No, take me home. My wife's a surgeon."

He heard Scottie say to the others, "Damn, he's married to a doctor."

JT opened his eyes again groggily and laughed. "She's a lawyer too."

Scottie bent over. "Why are you risking your life doing this if you're rolling in the dough?"

"Same reason you are. You get on the jazz, and you have to scratch where it itches."

JT came to when he heard the back doorbell of Jessie's house ring somewhere off in the distance. He heard the back door open and realized he was on the outside.

Jessie screamed, "What happened to him?"

Bad Billy lied, saying, "He was hurt in a boiler explosion in an old factory is the word I got. I wasn't there."

"He needs to be in the hospital."

Billy walked in beside the stretcher. "We need to put him down—where do you want him?" She led them to her bedroom. Six men picked up the sheet he was lying on, lifted him up, and put him on the bed. He was still on his stomach covered by another sheet.

Billy turned to Jessie. "The authorities might look at his wounds and ask why we didn't hospitalize him over there. Being in a third-world country would explain that, but they may want to know how he got into the US."

Jessie said, sounding scared, "He needs to be in the hospital."

"Ma'am, we wanted to stop him when we got to Mexico, but JT insisted he be brought here. If this is not something you want, let me know, and I'll take him back out. If he goes to the hospital, he'll probably go to jail."

She looked at him as though she were trying to process all this. "No, leave him. I'll care for him." Billy gave her a few packets of morphine and antibiotics, and he and his men left. JT felt her pull the sheet down. The fresh bandages didn't seem to bother her, but when she saw the whip scars on his back, she stood up and covered her mouth as she gasped. The tears really started to flow.

When he woke up the next morning, something smelled familiar. It smelled like Jessie, and he realized he was at her house. Jessie was sitting beside him with eyes red from crying. He looked up at her until she came into focus. "Hey, sweet thing. Miss me?"

She kneeled down. "This is not funny. If you weren't hurt so bad, I'd hurt you myself. Now, where have you been, and what have you done?"

He shook his head the best he could while lying on his stomach. "We agreed—no delving into each other's past."

"I know that, but this is the present. Now how did you get these wounds?"

He raised his eyes at her as the room started to spin. "A boiler blew up in a factory in a third-world country."

"I heard that, and I don't believe it. Why did they have to sneak you in under cover of dark then?"

"I'm sensitive to light."

She raised her voice. "Don't make jokes. Where did you get these whip scars across your back? I know they're old, but still ..."

He smiled. "From a whip. I'll tell you about it sometime." He passed out again.

He awoke again, and Jessie was still by his side. When she saw he was awake, she leaned over. "JT, we have to talk about this. What did you do? How did you get hurt? How did you get the whip marks across your back, and don't tell me from a whip. Now, are you going to tell me or not?"

He stared straight ahead for a minute. "We had an agreement, at your insistence I might add, that we wouldn't delve into each other's business. You don't get to change the rules because they don't suit you anymore. I'm sorry they brought me here. I must have been loaded with morphine when I asked them to bring me. Hand me my phone, please."

"Who are you going to call?"

"Scottie. He can get me to Mexico, and I'll come back and we'll talk when I'm not under the influence of narcotics."

She picked it up and moved it further out of his reach. "I'm glad you came here, and I'll take care of you, even though I may wind up in jail. I owe you that."

He eyed her again. "Speaking of that, if it ever comes down to the authorities or your sisters or whoever, you were told, by me, that I was injured by a boiler explosion. That's all you know."

"Will you ever tell me what happened to you, about your wounds and your scars on your back?"

He hesitated. "Not under our current rules of engagement. I don't need to know certain things and you don't need to know certain things if we're going to get a divorce."

Tears started down her cheeks. "I guess we can't avoid talking about that forever." The doorbell rang; both were secretly relieved. She got up and closed the bedroom door as she walked out. He heard the back door open, and the voices of her sisters seem to pierce the air.

He heard Hazel say, "Why did you close your bedroom door, and why are you crying?"

Jessie voice came back. "JT was injured in an industrial accident, and he's asleep. I'm just worried about him."

Lenore said, "Why is he still here? We know this marriage was fake, so why don't you get rid of him and get on with your life? He's after your money if you're not too blind to see. What's going on in your mind, Jessie?"

She was silent for a minute. "I'm married at the present moment, and the marriage was not a fake—I'm legally married to him. What goes on between my husband and me is none of your business. If you keep pushing, I'm going to have to ask you to leave."

Hazel replied, "Jessie, we know he married you at the last minute so Dad wouldn't be disappointed. Dad was the only one who believed that cockamamie story anyway. What are you doing with your life? We're just trying to help."

It got quiet, and then Jessie said, "Listen, sisters, I appreciate your concern, but I have to handle this by myself. Thank you for coming, though."

"Well, Lenore," Hazel said, "I think we've just been thrown out. Let's go."

JT heard the door open and then shut. It was quiet until the bedroom door opened and Jessie came back in. She leaned down and lightly ran her fingers over the scars on his back.

"JT, can I get you anything?"

"I'm powerful hungry. I can't remember the last time I ate."

She stood up. "Let me make you some beef broth."

"Just beef broth? How about a beef steak?"

"No, you've been taking pain killers. Something that heavy might make you sick, and if you throw up, you're going to pull your stitches loose. I'm cutting back on your pain medication, and I'll increase your solid food intake as I do." She sat there. "Are we ever going to discuss the divorce?"

He closed his eyes. "I'm no lawyer, but discussing that while one of us is under the influence would negate anything said during that time, wouldn't it?"

"You should have been a lawyer," she said, and he could hear the smile in her voice. "I'll be back in a minute."

He didn't open his eyes as she walked away. "I'd never be a lawyer, I don't even like lawyers." She chuckled as she went to the kitchen.

She came back with a cup of hot broth. "Do you feel you could roll over on your right side some? If not, I'm going to have to pour this in your ear."

He laughed and then winced at the pain caused by the laugh. "Don't make me laugh—it hurts." He pushed with his arm and turned onto his right side. "If you put some pillows behind me to keep me from rolling over on my stitches, I might lay on my back a little."

She got three pillows and laid them behind him, and then she helped push him over to where he was lying on the right side of his back. She picked up a remote and raised the head of the bed up so he was halfway sitting up. Then she spoon-fed him the broth.

He looked around the room. "I'm in your bed. Where are you sleeping?"

She answered as she gave him another spoonful of broth, "Well, I slept in this chair last night, but I'll be sleeping beside you until you're better."

He took another sip of broth. "You know you're safe for the time being," he said with a grin.

"I'm probably safe anytime; you're not the kind of guy to take advantage of me."

He smiled sleepily. "Don't you bet on it."

She smiled at that. "You know you talk in your sleep when you're under the influence of drugs, don't you?"

He frowned. "What did I say?"

She hesitated a second. "Maybe I better not say anything. That's one of those areas that we don't want to delve into."

"No, I need to know what I said, please."

"Will you tell me what it's about if I do?"

A feeling of concern swept over him. "If I can, I will."

She was quiet for a minute and then said, "You mumbled something about upstairs and downstairs, being in place, and something about you should have neutralized the threat ... Well?"

He stared at the wall and then finally looked over at her. "Upstairs and downstairs were just code words to identify two groups of people, and I can't tell you the rest. Knowing might put you in danger, especially if you ever had to testify in court. I can't see that happening, but worse things have occurred."

She appeared to choose her next words carefully. "If ... when the divorce goes through, will you tell me all about this?"

"Never. If the divorce didn't go through, I might." He saw her eyes widen. "In the meantime, can you help me up? I have to pee something fierce."

She stood up and put the broth cup down. "No, you can't get up yet or you'll pull your stitches loose. I'm going to have to put in a catheter."

He gave her a horrified look. "Seriously? How about a urinal or a section of water hose and a bucket?"

She laughed. "You big baby, you're a typical man. You go get yourself beaten and shot up, but nobody messes with your dick. We'll try a urinal." She walked back with a plastic urinal and handed it to him.

He tried to move his left arm, but he couldn't because of the wounds and the bandages. He shook his head. "I can't hold it and me with one arm."

She pulled the covers back, exposing his naked body. He held the urinal close, she took his penis and put it in, and he filled it up. She took it and emptied it, and he looked at her as she walked back in. "I'm not through yet." They went through the ritual again, and he filled it halfway up. He said, "That felt so good, my eyes watered." She laughed.

She crossed her arms. "That's another reason why you're not getting solid food. If you do, you'll have to get used to a bedpan."

His eyes widened. "I'm good with broth." She laughed again.

He looked at her for a long time. "It's good to see you laugh again and talk to me. I didn't deserve the treatment you gave me."

Tears formed in her eyes. "You're right. You didn't, and I'm sorry." She stood there for a minute and then turned and walked out.

* * *

JT was awakened by the back doorbell ringing. A few minutes later, there was a knock on the bedroom door, and Jessie said, "Are you decent? You have visitors."

"Sure, come on in."

Jessie came in, followed by Angela and a woman he had noticed at the wedding.

He looked at Angela. "How's things going for you?"

She smiled weakly. "Okay. I have a restraining order against Billy, but I'm afraid that won't stop him from getting to me. We'll see what happens now that I'm staying with my parents."

Jessie brought the other woman forward. "JT, I don't know if you remember Candice or not. Things were happening at the wedding pretty fast."

"Hi, Candice. I remember you."

Candice turned to Jessie. "Well, we just wanted to say hello and sorry about your accident." They waved and left. Angela looked back as she left, and JT felt like she was pleading with him with her eyes.

"Jessie, before you go, can I have my phone?"

She narrowed her eyes and frowned.

"I'm staying."

She walked back, picked up his phone, handed it to him, and walked away. He sent a text to Margaret: "Need side of house repaired, may need a total paint job." She would know he wanted someone to do a side job for him and that a person needed to be dealt with and possibly killed. Within an hour he got a text back. "Repairman ordered, expect him soon."

Jessie didn't bring up the divorce anymore, apparently waiting for him to be perfectly clearheaded when they talked. She slept beside him and checked on him every couple of hours.

It was two days later when Jessie came in to say, "There's a man named Dutch here. He said you were expecting him."

"Oh, yeah. Show him in. He's an old friend." She went out and brought the man back in. "Dutch, it's good to see you, man. How's the wife and kid?"

"Fine, fine, JT. You seem to be recovering okay."

"Yeah, with the nurse I got, I'll be up and about in half the time." Dutch smiled, and they both looked at Jessie. She turned, walked out of the room, and shut the door. Dutch sat down in the chair.

Dutch looked at him and said in German, "Okay, man, what have you got?"

"A friend of mine has a husband who is always in a jealous rage over her if she gets within twenty yards of another man. I'm afraid he may kill her or mess her up. I need her protected, and more than that I need him neutralized or eliminated if need be. I'll trust your judgment on that."

Dutch nodded. "I like this type of job because I can't abide a man that hits a woman."

JT scrolled through his phone and came up with Angela's information that he had downloaded from Jessie's phone while she was in the shower. Dutch downloaded it to his phone. JT looked up at Dutch. "After this is over, make sure you delete that."

Dutch smiled and stood up. "Of course. Take care, man. I'll let you know."

JT nodded his head.

* * *

Dutch walked out, and Jessie walked back in. "Okay, is that some more of this business we can't discuss?"

"Why can't he be an old friend that came by to see me?"

She folded her arms. "At least you didn't lie to me. He didn't ask how you got hurt, so he must have already known. What was he doing here, JT?"

"It has nothing to do with what happened to me. It's business I'm farming out to him so I won't have to do it myself. There's no danger to me or you."

As far as she was concerned, that wasn't a good answer. "JT, I want to know what he was doing here."

JT narrowed his eyes. "I'm not going to tell you, so quit asking. You sound like we're married."

Her tears brimmed over. "When do you want to talk about divorcing?"

He looked back at her and leveled his gaze. "Saturday morning without fail." It was Sunday, so she knew it would be a long week.

During the next week, JT started getting up and walking a little bit with crutches. It was clear that he could feel each wound with each step he took. One day he walked into the kitchen and told Jessie, "I've been shot nine times, bayoneted once, and beaten with a bullwhip, but I never hurt like this."

She thought she was going to cry when she heard that, but she refrained.

When Jessie woke up the next Saturday morning, JT was not in bed. She could smell coffee and bacon so she got up, put her robe on, and went to the kitchen. JT stood at the stove cooking while holding onto one crutch. "Have a seat," he said. "It'll be ready in a sec."

She sat down and poured a cup of coffee. He brought her a plate of eggs, bacon, and fruit. "No more bread for you," he said with a smile.

She had a hard time smiling back. She didn't know if she could eat or not; she felt sick to her stomach.

After he finished eating, he picked up his plate, put it in the dishwasher, came back, and leaned on the chair he had been sitting in. "Are we ready for the divorce talk?"

She nodded and stared at the table, fighting back the tears. He leaned on the table. "Talk to your lawyer and have a divorce drawn up. You divorce me, I'll divorce you, or whatever works out in your best interest. Tell him to make it quick. I'll move out today, because I can't stand to look at you anymore."

The tears rolled down her cheeks.

He dropped his head and then raised it back up. "I can't stand to look at you anymore because I have fallen in love with you. If I can't be more than what I am to you, then it's best we separate and not see each other again."

Her mouth dropped open, and she narrowed her eyes in surprise and shock. After a few minutes, she finally stood up, walked around the table, and put her arms around his neck. "I have fallen in love with you too. Please don't leave me." She kissed him. It was the first time they had kissed since the wedding, and it was warm and sweet. He held her, and when they pulled apart enough to look into each other's eyes, he had tears running out of the sides of his eyes.

JT could hardly talk. "I thought you wanted a divorce. I thought you wanted me out of your life. I know you don't like what I do."

She shook her head. "I don't know when I fell in l love with you. I guess it was when my dad died. Your reason for being married to me was no longer there, but I needed you. I thought you wanted out. I thought *you* wanted a divorce. That's why I was so mean to you—I didn't want it to be over. What you do has nothing to do with loving you."

He looked into her eyes. "Will you marry me?"

She laughed. "We're already married." They kissed again, and he seemed a little unsteady on his feet, so she walked him to the bed. "You've been up long enough. I need you to get well, because I am going to do unspeakable things to you when you're able."

He lay down. "Do them now. I'm ready to die if need be."

CHAPTER 4

Jessie's sisters came back over the following week. JT lay in bed, listening to them talk. "Jessie, we just want to help. You need to get this divorce over with and get on with your life. This is not good for you."

There was a long silence. "We're not getting a divorce. We're staying married."

"What?" Hazel sounded shocked. "Jessie, he's after your money—you got to know that."

"Then I'll give it to him," Jessie said, and he could picture the smile on her face. "I don't know what happened, but somewhere along the way, we fell in love."

"Bullshit," Lenore said. "He's snowed you. Watch—he won't have a job, and he'll live off you, like he's doing now. You really need to think about this. Maybe you should talk to Pastor Willis—he'll help you get through what you're feeling."

After a brief pause, Jessie said, "Perhaps you're right. I'll call him this afternoon."

"That-a-girl. Let us know what happens." With that, the sisters left.

* * *

The next afternoon, JT was sitting at the dining room table when the back doorbell rang. Jessie went to the door.

"Pastor Willis, thank you for coming. JT, look who's here." JT stood up with the help of a cane and shook the pastor's hand.

They offered him a seat and asked if he wanted anything to drink. He replied, "I was up this morning early, and I have a late night ahead. Do you have anything with caffeine?"

Jessie got up and started toward the kitchen. "How about a cup of fresh-ground coffee?"

"That'd be great."

She came back with the coffee just as JT finished telling the pastor about the boiler exploding and wounding him. She sat down.

After taking a sip, Willis asked them. "What did you want to see me about that's so important?"

Jessie glanced at JT briefly and then said, "Well, something has happened we didn't expect to happen with this marriage."

Willis looked up from his coffee. "We're not going to jail, are we?"

They both laughed. "No," Jessie replied, "somewhere along the line we fell in love. We're not getting a divorce."

There was a long silence as Willis processed the information. "That's ... that's wonderful!"

Jessie asked the pastor, "What I want to know is, is there anything we need to do to make sure we're married?"

Willis appeared deep in thought. "You already have a marriage license. We can't redo that without getting people in trouble. I asked the senior pastor if I was legal in doing what I did, and he told me I didn't break any rules but that I bent them too much for them to ever straighten back up. You're legally married, but I wouldn't mind if we had the ceremony again in my office so you can say the words with conviction, and that would be pleasing to God."

She smiled. "That sounds good. Check your schedule, and let us know."

Willis stood up, shook JT's hand, and hugged Jessie. He looked from one to the other. "I think this is wonderful, simply wonderful. The Lord sure moves in mysterious ways."

After he left, Jessie turned to JT. "Do you mind? I thought it would be nice."

"I don't mind. I think it'll be nice too." He took her hand and walked her to the bedroom. "I think it's time we consummated this marriage."

She smiled as he shut the bedroom door. "Do you feel up to it? I'm not sure you're healed up enough."

He kissed her. "I'll let you do most of the work." They made passionate love for an hour. She had about decided to get up when the back doorbell rang. She jumped up, grabbed her robe, eased the door open, and looked out back.

JT protested, "Hey, don't cover that beautiful body up yet. I'm not through with it."

She pulled her robe on, tied the belt, and opened the door. "It's Lenore and Hazel. I'll be right back, but get showered. You've had enough physical exertion today."

He laid his head back down and was lightly snoring before she'd closed the door.

Jessie opened the back door, and Lenore stared at her with a slight frown. "You weren't asleep, were you? It's two in the afternoon!"

Jessie shook her head. "I was in bed, but I wasn't asleep."

Lenore seemed puzzled, but Hazel opened her mouth and put her hand over it. "Oh, we're sorry. We're going." She grabbed Lenore and pulled her away as she explained in a whisper that they had interrupted a private moment.

Jessie went back, saw JT was asleep, and took a shower. When she got out, she shook him.

"You're doing okay, and I need to get back to work. I have a court case in two weeks and surgery the next week. Then I have to fly to Dallas to give a speech. Maybe you can go with me if you're up to it."

He nodded. "Maybe. I just had a Jessie pill—I'm exhausted." He went back to sleep as she smiled.

* * *

When Jessie testified in court two weeks later, JT was walking with a cane, but he went along and watched. He was impressed. She was obviously very intelligent, and she conducted herself well on the stand. When she did her surgery, he asked about it. He was interested in her work as a doctor. The time finally came for him to accompany her to Dallas. She was to give a speech on medicine and the law at a medical convention.

Jessie said to JT one morning. "I'll have my assistant get our tickets to Dallas."

JT shook his head. "Let me get a company plane. I need to log some hours anyway." The day came, and they drove out to the Memphis-Arlington Airport. Three twin-engine Cessnas sat on the tarmac outside a hanger. They pulled up to one, and he took their luggage and put it on board. He drove his car into the hanger and locked it up.

He helped her in the right-side door, and she gave him a confused look. "I'm going to sit up front with the pilot? Where are you sitting?"

He smiled. "I'm the pilot." He closed the door with her staring at him. He went around, still with a noticeable limp, and did his final check on the plane, examining the props and the tires and checking the fuel level visually. He finished his pre-flight checkup and got in the plane on the left side. He put his headphones on, gave her a pair, and showed her how to put them on.

"Can you hear me okay?" She nodded, and he laughed. "It's okay to talk to me."

She looked at him. "I didn't know you were a pilot. There's a lot I have to know about you yet, and that agreement we had to not delve into each other's business is no longer in effect."

He nodded. "A lawyer once told me hearing the answers are not as important as asking the right questions."

She smiled. "I have a question for you—are you a lawyer? You sound like one."

He shook his head as he started up the left engine. "No, I'm not a lawyer." He then started the right engine. "I don't like lawyers." He grinned at her.

She began to ask a question but stopped when she heard a new voice over her headphones. "Five-niner-niner-three, you are cleared for takeoff. Wind is out of the west-northwest at 3.6. Have a safe flight."

"Thank you, Arlington. Have a good day." He taxied out on the only runway there, rolled down to the end, and turned around. He throttled the engines to the rpm's he wanted and began to roll down the runway until he lifted off. He banked the plane, headed southwest, set his instruments, and turned to her. "Okay, we can talk now." They chitchatted until they got to Dallas and landed at a small field to the south of the city.

A green Range Rover was waiting. She got in and asked him. "Why do you like Range Rovers so much?"

"I fit in them better than most cars. My height is in my body, not my legs. I know guys four inches shorter than I am, and we wear the same size inseam. This vehicle has the headroom I need."

He set the GPS to take him to the downtown Hilton. As they drove through an intersection she saw a bunch of people milling about the street.

"What are these people doing, waiting on a parade to start?"

He smiled. "No, this is Dealey Plaza, where President Kennedy was shot."

She looked behind them as they drove through. "I grew up outside of Dallas, and I've never been here."

They got to the hotel, valet parked, and had their luggage taken to the room. It was as nice a room as you could find at a Hilton. She sat down on the bed. "I'm going over my speech, okay?"

He nodded. "Sure. I'm going to sit outside on the balcony and make some phone calls."

She watched him as he slid the balcony door open. "Don't make any that require you to go to Europe, okay?" He smiled as he closed the door.

He had gotten a call from Dutch when he was in the car with her but hadn't answered. Dutch didn't call right back, so he knew it wasn't urgent. He pushed the direct dial button, and Dutch answered in German.

JT said in German, "Dutch, what's up?"

"I got that repair on the house done. You had some broken boards and a few cracked windows. I don't think you'll have a problem with it, but if you even suspect that you do, call me. Can you check with your wife and see how she likes it?"

JT smiled. "Yeah, man. I'll see if she's noticed. Thanks." He knew Dutch had met up with Angela's husband and cracked his ribs and broken a few bones. He'd probably told Billy to stay away from her or he would be back to do it again.

JT saw Jessie standing at the window. He looked at her, and she slid the door open.

"I get worried when you talk to people in a language I don't understand. Why do you do that?"

He smiled. "I don't speak so you can't understand when you're eavesdropping. I speak so the person I am talking to can understand. Maybe he doesn't speak English."

She frowned slightly as she slid the door closed and got back on the bed.

He turned away, gazing out over the city. He pushed another speed dial button and said in Arabic, "Margaret, anything come up since our last dance?"

She replied, "Somebody must be listening to you since you're talking in Arabic. We had a hit on a society lady from London. She was shopping in Marrakesh and hasn't been seen since. The ransom demand came through this morning. Scottie is doing the background check. Do you want me to send you the particulars on it?"

"No, I'll be on a need to know basis. If it's a go, Scottie will score for us. I'm still too broken up to play football."

"Get well soon, boss. We need you for moral support if nothing else."

"Thanks, Margaret. Bye."

He got up, went back in, and decided to take a nap. He lay down beside Jessie, and she rolled over with her speech in her hand. "You're beginning to scare me."

He turned to her. "By taking a nap? I thought I was supposed to—"

"That's not it. Were you speaking Arabic? I've not heard a lot of it, but that sounded like what I've heard from TV."

He sighed. "I can converse in French, German, and—"

"No, you speak perfect French and probably perfect German. I feel like you're hiding something from me. I feel like I know you less than I did a month ago."

He thought a minute before answering. "Look, I've spent most of my life where everything I did or said was kept a secret. You don't tell anyone—you know, 'loose lips sink ships.' I won't lie to you, and I'll never do anything to put myself in danger without telling you. I need to get used to sharing thoughts and secrets with another person. Give me time, okay?"

She leaned over and kissed him. "Okay. I won't push anymore ... Yes, I will, but I won't push so hard." He smiled.

The next day, her speech was at two in the afternoon. JT went into the room and sat in the back. He walked without a cane now but still had a limp. He wanted to see how she presented herself. She talked about medical stuff that he knew absolutely nothing about, and it was almost like she was speaking another language; he knew how she felt now. After forty minutes, she summed up and looked at her audience, which was about 80 percent women. "Are there any questions? We have about twenty minutes."

There were various questions and then silence. Finally, one woman stood up. "Dr. Logan, I've known you for over ten years, and I've followed your work. Nobody here knows about your recent marriage. I've heard it is one of the most romantic and unusual stories anyone has ever heard. Will you share it with us?"

Jessie looked surprised. She glanced back at JT, and he smiled and nodded. She smiled at the audience. "I don't know how romantic it is, but I do know it is unusual. I will give you a brief outline. A few months ago, I was supposed to marry a man I had been dating for eight months. I convinced myself that I loved him because my dying father's last wish was to see his thirty-eight-year-old daughter married. I'm the last of three sisters. The day before the wedding, at the rehearsal, I was introduced to his best man, who had just come in from ... from out of town. The next day, three and a half hours before the wedding, the best man came barging into my dressing room and told me my fiancé had called him and decided he couldn't go through with the marriage. I was left at the altar. The best man thought the solution was for him to marry me—no, really, it was his idea—so my father wouldn't be disappointed.

"The best man walked out front and gave a ridiculous story about being on a secret mission and having just got back and that my fiancé was actually a stand-in for him and that he'd been sent off on a secret mission himself the night before the wedding. I married the best man, and, fortunately, my father was too sick to realize the truth. Out of three hundred people at the wedding, I believe he was the only one who believed the story. We had planned on staying married until my father died and then getting divorced. There's not many bachelors that would do that. My father passed away almost two months later, and we discovered that we had fallen in love with each other. We decided to stay together because we were truly in love. He is my lover, my knight in shining armor, and my hero ... would you like to meet him?"

Every woman in the place was obviously moved, and they collectively nodded. Jessie looked toward the back. "JT darling, would you come up here, please?" JT walked forward. Why he was trembling, he didn't know. He walked up on the dais, kissed Jessie, and turned around to the audience, who was giving a standing ovation. It went on for several minutes before finally quieting down.

Jessie wiped her tears with the handkerchief JT had handed her. "And if you don't think we were meant to be, I want to add that his last name is Logan also. I don't have to have new business cards printed now." The room erupted in laughter and more applause.

They left, and since her nerves wouldn't allow Jessie to eat before a speech, she was now starving, so they went to hotel's the restaurant. They were seated in a booth with no one nearby. They ordered, and while they were waiting on the food, she looked at him. "Thank you for that. Sharing our story was therapeutic, and I really felt a release from some unseen burden, but I suddenly realized a fear greater than any I have ever known though. I don't think I can live without you. What is going to happen when you go out on a job and come back wounded again or dead? I will never make demands on you or ask you to do something you didn't want to do. I just don't know how to look past what could happen."

He half-smiled. "First thing, now you know why I am thirty-eight years old and have never been married. The one edge I have always had over other people is that when I go on a job and put my life, as well as other men's, on the line, I take on a mindset of, 'I'm going to die on this job, so I'm going to do the best that I can and not worry about dying so the others will stand a better chance of coming back alive.' I realized on the last job that I couldn't convince myself I was going to die because I couldn't reconcile that in my mind with not seeing you again. That's what got me injured, and I don't know if I can do that anymore. What I think I'll do is take on a different position in the company, one of planning, and let some of the younger ones do the execution part. It's going to take time though." He smiled. "You've ruined me—I'm no longer able to work like I did."

She reached across the table and held his hand. "Thank you for that." She had tears streaming down her face.

He smiled. "I won't be making as much money, so I may have to live off you like your sisters told you I would. How's that sit with you?"

She smiled through the tears. "That's fine—I told them I was willing to give you my money if that was what you were after." She paused as she dried her eyes. "Can I ask what you do and how much money you make doing that?"

He looked across the room and back. "Trans Global Insurance is a front for a hostage-release business. How much I make varies from job to job. On this last one, we got the target back and picked up a bonus by freeing a woman we didn't know was even there. We negotiated a price for releasing her. We did a side job for the CIA while we were there, so our ride to and from was paid for. We cleared about 8 million for that job."

She had her mouth open. "Eight million ... dollars? How many jobs do you do a year?"

"It varies. We've done as little as one and as many as six, but we also keep track of people who are insured with us. That's worth about $30 million a year."

She smiled. "No wonder you were willing to sign a post/pre-nup. You probably have a hell of a lot more money than I have."

He laughed. "Not as much as you think. There's expenses, like getting everyone to the site, airplanes for insertion, helicopters for extraction, weapons, ammo, and, of course, administration."

She looked confused. "Administration? How big is your home office? I mean, how many big wheels do you have to pay to sit there and make this happen?"

He laughed and handed her his phone. "Here's a picture of the Trans Global Building. It's a huge office building on the outskirts of Paris, and all the offices are rented out to various businesses, except for the top floor. There is only one person in that office. Margaret does all the hard work coordinating, which is the key to our success. I'm the only big wheel that takes more than he should, but ... like I said, I'm thinking of taking on an executive position and doing more coordinating and planning and letting the younger ones do the legwork. I do own the business, though. I'll have to transition in, and it may take a little time."

She was silent for a long time. "That releases me from that great fear I had. I doubt you need my money, but you're welcome to whatever I have. How much travel will you need to do now?"

He thought a minute. "Most of the planning will be done by phone. Background checks and things like that will be done by Margaret and Scottie. I'll just need to go and approve the final plan for whatever we're doing. That's something that's too risky to do over the phone."

"Can I go with you then?"

He shook his head. "No, there's the small danger of being arrested."

"Why? You're just helping someone by saving a life."

He shook his head again. "No, it's against the laws of most countries for foreigners to come in armed, raise a small army, and kill its citizens, even if the citizens are breaking the law. We try to plan from an adjoining country when we can, to confuse anyone trying to trap us."

"It seems like the CIA would know about you."

He smiled again. "They do. They keep tabs on us and even ask us to do a little dirty work for them sometimes. As long as we aren't interfering with work they are doing, they don't bother us. On the last job, I borrowed an airplane and a few helicopters from them in return for ... finding someone for them."

She looked at him with a serious expression. "Have you ever killed anyone doing that?"

He stared at her for a full ten seconds. "I'm not going to lie to you. People die all the time—that's part of it."

* * *

They finished eating and spent the day doing a little sightseeing in Dallas. The next morning, they packed and went back to the private airport. He asked her to sit in the small terminal while he checked to see if the plane was ready. As she was sitting there, she heard two men talking just around the corner from her. One asked the other, "Who owns that Lear warming up? That movie producer over there wants to rent it or hitch a ride to Memphis if he can."

The other man spoke up. "That belongs to a guy named Logan. It's his plane, but he tells people that it's a company plane and company policy won't allow him to take on passengers. He doesn't need the money."

When JT walked in, the movie producer walked up to him. "I was wondering if I could get a ride to Memphis. I'm willing to pay."

"No, sir."

"Why not? You're going there anyway."

JT narrowed his eyes. "You smell like a dirty ashtray. I don't want you in my plane." JT walked off.

A few minutes later, he motioned to her, and they walked to the jet. She looked at him as she climbed aboard. "We're taking a different plane back?"

He nodded. "I was doing a friend a favor by bringing his down, and I needed to pick this one up. We just had an engine overhaul on this baby. Now that's about $300,000 in expense money."

A young, skinny woman in a white uniform with bars on her shoulders boarded the plane. "Hi, JT. We'll be ready in a moment, so go ahead and get buckled up." JT and Jessie sat down in the spacious seats of the jet.

Jessie leaned over to him. "These flight attendants get younger and younger. I would bet she's not twenty-one yet."

He let out a big laugh. "She's twenty-five, and she's not a flight attendant—she's one of the pilots." Jessie dropped her mouth open again, and then she closed it and looked straight ahead without saying anything as another young woman came aboard. That made him laugh again.

* * *

After they were airborne, Jessie said, "I heard two men talking in the terminal. They didn't know I was around the corner. One said some guy wanted a ride to Memphis. I heard the other say that this plane belonged to you, but you told everybody it was a company plane. Is that true—is this your plane?"

He was silent for a few minutes. "I told you I wouldn't lie to you. It's my plane."

"Every day, I am in awe of what I find out about you. Is there anything else I would find unbelievable about you?"

He nodded. "Plenty, but you don't have enough time to hear it all." He smiled but stopped when he saw she didn't. "Remember, I asked you to let me go slow. You want to know things at a fast pace, and I want to tell you at a slow pace. This marriage thing is new to me too." She nodded and said nothing.

After a few minutes, Jessie turned to him. "I almost forgot. Angela is getting a divorce from Billy. This is the funny part—he apparently got in a fight with someone who was tougher than he was and got the living hell kicked out of him. I mean broken ribs, fractured skull, both arms and one leg broke. I don't wish anyone a beating like that, but if anyone deserved it, he ..." She looked at JT and narrowed her eyes. "You don't know anything about that, do you?"

"Me? I know I couldn't whip him in my condition, and when would I have had the time?" She didn't say any more, but he could tell she was still suspicious. Surprised, he admired her intuition. He realized that she had sharp mind that processed every detail not because she was a doctor or lawyer but because she was highly intelligent.

When they got back to Memphis, JT spent the next two months in therapy three times a week. He had gotten his strength back and was working with free weights again.

CHAPTER 5

Jessie came in one afternoon. "I have to go to Los Angeles to testify in a court case Wednesday. It will last three days, maybe more. You need to spend another week in therapy, and I'll be tied up all day, every day, so you'll need to stay here on this one, okay?"

She looked surprised when he nodded and said, "Okay. Call me if you need me. Are you going to need a ride to LA?"

She smiled. "No, they are paying my way, first class hotel, meals, and everything is paid for. You don't mind staying here?" She followed that up really quickly with, "You are staying here, I mean in Memphis, aren't you?"

He smiled. "Yes, Mother. I told you I wouldn't do anything without letting you know."

She sat down next to him and kissed him. "Please don't be mad at me for caring and worrying about you."

He kissed her back. "I'm not mad at you—I appreciate you."

JT took her to the airport on Wednesday and kissed her good-bye. "Call me when you know your return plans."

She nodded and waved as he drove off.

He got back to the house and Skyped Scottie. "How are we doing on the new business?"

Scottie replied, "We've done the background, the logistics, and have a ride to and from. We've rehearsed it and are ready to move tomorrow. Do you want the details so you can make any changes?"

JT shook his head at the image on his computer screen. "I'm not going to start second-guessing or micromanaging you. How many students are studying under you?"

Scottie looked back behind him and then back at the camera. "This is best done with a minimum of people. One group of students is all." JT knew that meant he was taking eight men with him.

"Okay, let me know as soon as you have completed the course and when you pass the test."

"Roger that, boss. One other thing—we got a hit on a simple child grab. The father took the kid to the desert. They've been located and wouldn't expect anyone to come after him. You're not here, but I can put Bad Billy on it. He can handle it. What do you think?"

He knew that by mentioning the desert Scottie meant it was in the Middle East. "Make it happen. It'll be good training for him in case he needs to be in your spot someday. Make sure you have the final approval of the operation."

"Ten-four, boss. When are you coming back?"

"I'll see you in a couple of weeks. I'm still healing up from my fall."

He ended the call, stood up, and walked around. He was restless. He figured it was because there was action out there and he wasn't there. That feeling was what was referred to as "being on the jazz," and it made him feel useless.

The following Monday, on their daily phone call, Jessie said that she would be arriving Wednesday at noon. "I'll call you when I get off and get my luggage."

On Wednesday, when he pulled into the cell phone lot at twelve thirty, his phone rang. "Well, that's perfect timing—I just pulled in. I'll be right there." He pulled up to the curb, got out, grabbed her, and kissed her so long that the airport police had to ask him to move on. He put her suitcase in the back and got in. He kissed her again briefly and drove off.

He asked about her case, and they chitchatted until they got home. He kissed her again, and when they went into the bedroom to put away her suitcase, he grabbed her, and they started undressing each other. They made love, and then she got up and took a shower. When she came out, she went into the kitchen in her bathrobe. "What smells so good?"

"I picked up some Corky's Barbecue, and I just heated it up. There's coleslaw, baked beans, and some of their famous banana pudding for dessert."

She tasted the barbeque. "You didn't get any onion rings. I love their onion rings."

He sat down. "Nah, they don't sell onion rings at the drive-through. You have to dine in to get those."

She sat down, and they ate. When she went to the kitchen to put the dishes away, he grabbed her from behind. He pulled her robe up from the back and made love to her again, standing in the kitchen. A few minutes later, they both heard, "Oh my God, let's go." They turned and saw Lenore trying to pull Hazel away from the glass. Hazel wasn't shy; she wanted to watch.

Jessie laughed with a red face. "I'm embarrassed, but that should teach them to snoop around. I didn't hear the car pull up, did you?"

He looked at her with a mischievous grin. "Hell, with all the noise you were making, a freight train could have pulled up, and we wouldn't have heard it."

She laughed and hit him on his sore shoulder. He winced.

"I'm sorry, sweetie. Are you okay?"

"Yeah. It's still a little tender, but I'm fine."

She got dressed, came back into the kitchen, and sat down at the table. "Can we have a talk?"

He looked at her as he wiped the counters down. "Uh oh, sounds like I'm in trouble."

She frowned. "I wish you wouldn't sound like that. I'm not your mother, and I don't want to sound like it. Anyway, will you sit down and let me tell you about something weird that happened?"

He pulled a chair out and sat down. "Sure." He reached back, got a bowl of grapes, and started eating them.

She hesitated. "Well, when I got to the airport in LA, there was a van for the Hilton, but there was only one seat left, and it was in the fourth row. I didn't want to crawl over a bunch of people, so I took a cab. When I got in, the driver was a Middle Easterner, not surprisingly. I don't know what country, but he looked Egyptian, Arabic, Pakistani, something. Anyway, his first name was Ibrahim, and his last name had about fifteen letters in it, all consonants. We drove on, and I noticed he had his radio on a Christian station. I thought that strange, since most people from that region are Muslim. Then I noticed he had a cross hanging from the rearview mirror. The radio was louder than I would have liked it, but I figured that maybe he was a recent Christian convert.

"A commercial came on, and they announced a big revival at the Mt. Olive Christian Church outside LA starting Sunday. It was going to be led by twin brothers, CD and JW Logan. I know Logan is not that uncommon of a name, but knowing somebody named Logan that goes by initials rather than a first or middle name piqued my interest."

JT stopped chewing his grapes. "Then what?"

"I didn't give it another thought ... until I got to the hotel, and there was a billboard about forty feet tall and eighty feet wide on top of the building next door. They were advertising the revival, and the twin brothers were standing side by side. It looked like two pictures of you ... now, tell me I'm crazy and they're not your brothers."

He put another grape in his mouth and started chewing again. "So, did you go to the revival?"

"Yes, and please quit eating grapes—it's driving me crazy."

He put the grapes he had in his hand back into the bowl and set the bowl on the counter behind him. He looked at her. "So?"

"I went to the revival Sunday and got there early so I could sit near the front. When they came out, I almost fainted. They are duplicates of you. Well, they don't have the shoulders and chest you do, and they have a little stomach, but in the face you look just alike." She waited for a reply.

"Did you talk to them?"

"No. I wouldn't do that without talking to you first. They're not twins, are they? Ya'll have to be triplets, identical triplets. Am I right?"

He finally nodded. "Yeah, though the only thing we have in common is looks."

She pursed her lips as though not sure whether she should pursue it anymore, but then she said, "Tell me about your family and what all this is about. I'm ashamed that I haven't asked before, but it's probably better that I didn't. You would have lied to me, wouldn't you?"

"Yeah, probably."

"When was the last time you saw your brothers?"

He thought about it for a moment. "About twenty years ago." He stared out the window.

Tears came to her eyes. "What happened? Three people who should be as close as you three, and you don't even talk. That's ... I don't know what to call it."

He was still staring out the window. "My father was an old-fashioned hellfire-and-brimstone preacher. When he had three sons at once, he was convinced God wanted all three of us preaching the gospel. He herded us in that direction, and my brothers were preaching by the time they were fourteen years old. My dad was pissed that I wouldn't preach as much as my brothers did."

She opened her mouth. "You used to preach?"

"Yeah, a little—youth revivals and midweek services and things like that."

She shook her head. "Why am I surprised?"

He looked back at her. "Anyway, the day after we graduated high school in May, Dad told us to be downstairs on Monday morning so he could take us to enroll in the seminary. I sat down with him and asked if I could apply to the military academy, and he blew his top. 'No son of mine will be killing people for a living. Trust me on this, son. God has a plan for all three of you.' I thought about it and decided I wasn't going to the seminary. If he wouldn't help me get in the military academy, I would just join the army," JT said and then sat there in silence.

"JT?"

He shook his head and glanced at her; he'd been lost in thought. "Anyway, Monday morning, CD showed up in a gray pinstripe suit, JW showed up in a dark brown suit, and I showed up in blue jeans and a shirt with my duffle bag packed. Dad gave me a look that could kill, and then he stared at me for what seemed like an hour. His face was red, and he finally said, 'I'll give you five minutes to get back upstairs and get changed.' I looked him in the eye. 'Dad, you always said that to preach, you had to be called by God. I haven't been called. God has not told me to preach. If these guys want to, great, but it's not what I want to do.' My father told me that if I didn't hear God's call, it was because I wasn't listening. He told me God had revealed to him what I was to do. Anyway, he asked for my car keys, and as I started out the door, he said to me, 'If you go out that door, don't ever come back through it.' I hesitated a minute and walked out and hitchhiked to the recruiting station."

She seemed frozen. "That's the last time you spoke to them?"

He thought a minute. "No, I was in Germany on assignment in the field years later. When I got back, I called my mother, which I did on Sunday afternoons between two and three thirty because I knew Dad and the boys were at church. Mom had a bad heart, so she had to rest a couple of hours each day. Anyway, I called, Dad answered, and I asked to speak to Mom. He said, 'If you cared enough to check on her, you would know she died two weeks ago. CD said he called, but you were never in and he hung up the phone.'"

Jessie went around the table and pulled out the chair beside him. She put her hand on his, and he could see the tears in her eyes. "Go on, tell me the rest."

He stared out the window again. "I called CD and asked him why he didn't call me when Mom died. He lied and said he tried several times. I told him that they always had someone taking messages, and I asked why he didn't leave a message. He said the number just rang and nobody answered. I knew we had a person manning the phone in the day room twenty-four hours a day and that he was lying. Then I told him he needed to change his ways or change his fucking church." JT lifted his eyebrows. "You can imagine that that didn't go over well. Before he hung up on me, he told me to never call him again and that I was dead to him." He looked her in the eye without saying anymore.

She blinked a tear away. "What about JW? Did you have a falling out with him?"

"JW is anybody's old dog that will hunt with him. He was so used to Dad and CD telling him what to do, he just went along with CD. There's no telling what CD told him, but I never called either one of them back again, and, of course, they never called me back."

She lowered her head for a minute and then raised it back up. "Is your father still alive?"

He shook his head. "No, but I made my peace with him before he died. I had an aunt that worked admissions at the hospital, and she would call me each time he was admitted. I would fly to California and wait until midnight and take pizza or doughnuts up to the nurses on that floor. I told them the family wasn't speaking to me and I wanted to see my dad. Dad and I made peace, but I refused to make peace with my brothers. I was with him when he died, but neither CD nor JW know that."

She stood up, sat in his lap, put her arms around him, put her face in his neck, and sobbed. "My sisters are crazy, and I could kill them sometimes, but we love each other and keep in contact, as you've seen." She smiled. "I don't understand your brothers, especially being preachers. How could they do that to you?"

He shrugged. "There's always two sides to every issue, and the truth usually lies in the middle. If you talked to them, I'm sure they would tell you a different story."

"Are you going to stay estranged from them all your life?"

JT thought a minute. "It's worked out well for the past twenty years, so I don't see a need to change it."

"No, JT. It's just not right. It's wrong in so many ways; you need to mend this fence, somehow."

He looked her in the eyes. "Jessie, you can't fix this. It takes two sides to want it. They don't want it, and I don't want it. You're fighting a battle you can't win, and you'll only make it worse, if it can get worse, by trying. Leave it alone, please. I'm sorry you found out."

She stood up. "I'm not, but I wonder how many other secrets you're keeping from me. It hurts, JT. Do you understand that?"

He stood up too. "It was never my attention to hurt you, but something like this is beyond fixing."

She shook her head. "Never, it is never beyond fixing. Maybe we can get an intermediary to get both sides together."

He laughed. "You mean like a preacher? Hell, we're up to our asses in preachers now. One more will simply muddy things up worse. Are you thinking a lawyer? Lawyers have to take the side of whoever is paying them, and none of them will do it for free. Forget it."

"I will." She waited for a response.

"No, you won't, because you can't be impartial. This is another 'we' and 'they' thing. You're a 'we' this time. Let's drop it and move on, okay? We don't need to discuss it anymore."

"It's on my mind, and I can't stop thinking about it."

He smiled. "You'll lose your mind if you give it a lot of thought."

No more was said about it that week. When she came to the breakfast table the next week, he sat down across from her. He reached around behind him, picked up the bowl of grapes, and set them on the table. He picked one up and started to put it in his mouth, but when he saw her looking at him, he put it back in the bowl and put the bowl on the counter behind him.

She laughed. "You can eat grapes if you want."

He smiled. "I need to go to the home office for a planning meeting." He held up his hand as she started to speak. "Please trust me. I'm not going to do anything where I can get hurt. I'm not going out on a job."

She stared at him. "You'll not do anything to get arrested either, will you?"

He shook his head. "No, I won't get arrested either."

She thought to herself, *This would be a perfect time to go to California and come up with a plan.* What plan? She thought she would figure one out. "I have to make a trip to Sacramento and maybe El Paso. I was hoping you would come with me, but my travel plans aren't set yet, so I can't ask you to wait."

He shook his head. "This can't wait—too many people are waiting on my input—but promise me this: if you go anywhere near LA, you won't contact my brothers, okay?"

She hesitated but then nodded. "I won't. You have my promise on that."

CHAPTER 6

The following week found JT on a private plane to Belgium and Jessie on a commercial jet to LA. She landed and took a rental car to a hotel she knew was within five miles of the Logan brothers' mega-church. She had to come up with something without contacting either one of the brothers.

The third day, she had about given up when she saw the wife of one of JT's brothers walk into the shop across the street. She had seen both of them at the revival but said to herself, *I don't know if this is Carla or ... what was the other's name? Wanda. That's it, Wanda, but which one is this?*

She walked down to the corner, crossed at the light, and made her way to the shop that was directly across from the hotel entrance. When she walked into the very expensive shop, the woman was looking at some dresses. Jessie finally got up the nerve to walk up to her. "Excuse me. I saw you at the revival awhile back. Are you Carla or Wanda?"

The woman turned to face her and smiled an ambassador's smile. "I'm Wanda Logan. Did you enjoy the revival?"

Jessie nodded. "I enjoyed it very much. Oh, I'm Jessie Logan."

Wanda's eyes widened. "Well, isn't that a coincidence."

Jessie smiled and shook her head. "It's no coincidence—I believe we are related. Will you let me buy you a cup of coffee, and I'll tell you all about it?"

Wanda seemed unsure of herself. "I suppose so. You have piqued my curiosity." They walked down to the corner and went into a coffee shop. After they ordered, Wanda asked her, "Well, why do you think we're related and how?"

Jessie pulled up a picture of her and JT on their wedding day, with her in her wedding dress and JT in his dress blues, but didn't show it just yet. She looked over at Wanda. "I'm your sister-in-law. I'm married to your husband's brother."

Wanda frowned. "You're not my sister-in-law. Is this some type of scam?" She started to get up.

Jessie handed her the phone with the picture on it. Wanda's eyes got big, and her mouth dropped open. Jessie watched the shock spread over her face as she sat back down. "Oh my God, Wanda. You didn't know there was a third brother, did you?"

Wanda looked up at her and back at the picture. "Is he younger or older? He's identical in the face, but he has a different ... body."

Jessie took her phone, opened the wedding album, and handed it back to her. As Wanda went through the wedding pictures, her mouth remained open. When she finished, she looked up at Jessie.

Jessie smiled. "As I understand it, CD is the oldest, JW is four minutes younger, and JT, there, is seven minutes younger than JW."

Wanda's head snapped up. "Triplets!" Everyone in the coffee shop looked in their direction.

Jessie smiled as she glanced around. "Shh. Yes, triplets. Not only that, but identical triplets. Do you know how rare that is? You obviously didn't know, so let me tell you the story." She started with her trip to LA and seeing their husbands on the billboard, and then she told Wanda the tale JT had told her.

After she was through, Wanda's eyes were wet. "I can't believe my husband or CD would do that. It's not in their nature ... they're both dedicated Christians, not to mention preachers."

Jessie nodded. "I know. It shouldn't be in their nature. It could be in my husband's nature—he's in the insurance business. Really, Wanda, JT told me there's two sides to every story, and the truth is somewhere in the middle. I propose we don't become adversaries on this but allies. None of the three brothers want this resolved, but I do. What do you want?"

Wanda was silent for a minute, gazing out the window. "I need to talk to Carla about this."

Jessie frowned. "You know, JT told me CD was the driving force and decision maker and JW was a follower. I suspect the same between you and Carla, her being the decision maker and you being the follower." Wanda looked hurt and adjusted her seat. Jessie smiled. "You know, I see a bit of fight in you every once in a while. You might want to try and develop that if you want to survive in this man's world. Now, what's it going to be? Are you coming in with me, or do we need to talk to Carla first?"

Wanda appeared to pull herself up with all the authority she could muster. "I'm in."

Jessie nodded. "Call Carla, and let's see if we can get her on board."

Wanda picked up her phone. "She's getting a pedicure this morning. I don't know if I can get her down here until after, and, oh, she had Pilates at noon."

Jessie narrowed her gaze at Wanda. "Well, we certainly have to have our priorities straight, don't we?"

Wanda looked peeved. "Hello, Carla? I have something that is going to be earthshaking to you. I mean this is something that will be life-changing, and I hope you don't faint when I tell you. No, I can't discuss it on the phone. I need you to come down to the CK Coffee Shop by the Hilton on Louis Street. Fine, then, go get your pedi, but this is the last opportunity I'm giving you to hear this. Bye." Wanda raised her eyebrows as she hung up. "She'll call back any second. If she's anything, she's nosy."

As though on cue, her phone rang. "Yes, dear? Yes, that's it, Carla. I've met another man, and I'm planning on running off with him. This is a plea for you to save me from myself. Jessie and I are here waiting. Are you coming or not? Okay. I'll see you when you get here."

Jessie smiled. "Now, that's the kind of fight I like to see in a woman."

They sat and made small talk while they waited. "How long have ya'll been married, Jessie?"

"A couple of months. I'll tell you the story sometime—it's unique. What do you do, Wanda? Are you a stay-at-home mom?" Wanda was a pretty woman with a good figure. She was immaculately dressed and manicured.

"Well, yes, but so much of my time is taken up with the church—being a preacher's wife has certain responsibilities. This is the first time I've had to myself in months, so I thought I would do some shopping. What do you do, Jessie?"

Jessie thought a minute. She didn't want to overshadow the issue, but she didn't want it to be a shocker when they needed to be concentrating on the issue at hand. "Well, about forty per cent of the time, I'm a neurosurgeon at the main campus of Baptist hospital in Memphis. Another forty per cent of my time is tied up in court—I'm also a lawyer. The remaining time has been spent getting to know my husband lately. Every time I think I know him, I find something mind-boggling about him, like this."

Wanda sat there with her mouth open. "You're a doctor and a lawyer?" Jessie just nodded.

Carla walked up an hour later, stopped, and looked at Jessie with a confused expression. Wanda patted the seat beside her. "Sit here, girlfriend. First, let me say that I'm highly insulted that you think I would run off with another man. I'm lucky you're as nosy as ... heck. Second, I want you to meet our sister-in-law. This is Jessie Logan, Dr. Jessie Logan."

Carla looked at Jessie and then at Wanda. "Dear, have you been drinking?"

Wanda narrowed her eyes at Carla. "First you think I'm a slut, and now you think I'm a drunk. What's wrong with you?"

"What am I supposed to think? You're talking crazy. How is she supposed to be our sister-in-law when we're married to the only two brothers in the family?"

Wanda said to Jessie, "May I borrow your phone, please?" Jessie opened the album and handed it to Wanda, who in turn handed it to Carla. "Scroll through those for a minute." Carla squinted at the image, and Wanda rolled her eyes and said impatiently, "Put your glasses on."

Carla glared at her and pulled a pair of glasses out of an oversized purse. She looked at the picture, and her jaw dropped. "I can't tell if this is CD or JW."

Wanda patted her on the shoulder. "Here comes the life-changing news I have for you. That's JT. He's the third of a set of identical triplets. We're married to the other two."

Carla stared at the phone. "No way."

Jessie and Wanda said at the same time, "Way."

Jessie looked at both of them. "Have you seen family pictures when they were young?"

Carla shook her head. "No, they were lost in a fire and ..." Wanda and Carla looked at each other.

Still looking at Carla, Wanda said, "Well, what's the answer?"

Carla was staring at the phone again. She finally said, "The answer? What's the question?"

Wanda responded before Jessie could say anything. "Jessie and I think this needs to be fixed, and we're going to try and do something about it. Are you with us?"

Carla eyed Wanda. "Are you sure about this? It sounds like some type of—"

Jessie nodded. "Scam? You found me out. I Photoshopped your husbands in, and I'm going to extort the church. Carla, if you don't want in, we'll do it ourselves. Of course, now that you know, we'll have to kill you."

Wanda broke out laughing. Carla didn't change her expression, which was part shock and part surprise.

Wanda took the phone and held it up for Carla to look at. "Dear, look at the shoulders and chest on this guy. He's got more muscle on him than our two husbands put together. They are three brothers, identical triplets. Is this soaking in? Let Jessie tell you what she told me, so you'll be up to speed."

After Jessie related the story, Carla narrowed her eyes at Wanda. "Okay, what's the plan?"

Wanda looked at Jessie.

Jessie shrugged. "If I had a plan, I wouldn't be here with you two. One thing, though, when I told my husband I had to come to California, he made me promise not to contact his brothers. I didn't promise anything about you two, so I'm open to suggestions."

Carla seemed to be deep in thought. "Well, first, I think we are going to have to confront our husbands. I don't see any way around that."

Wanda looked concerned. "How? What are we going to say?"

Jessie cleared her throat, and they turned to her. "I would suggest you do it in a public place like a restaurant so they are less likely to make a scene. What about this? I get reservations at a restaurant. I'll reserve a table for the four of you, and I'll get a table next to you. Your husbands won't know me. You drop the bomb and, if it seems like it's the right thing to do, introduce me. If not, pretend I'm not there. What do you think?"

Wanda pointed to Jessie's phone. "Can you e-mail me some of these pictures?"

Jessie nodded. "I can do better than that—I'll air-drop them to you." Wanda appeared confused, so Jessie held out her hand. "Give me your phone." She loaded her up with three pictures. "What about you?" Carla appeared to still be dumbfounded. She nodded and handed her phone to Jessie. "Let's exchange phone numbers and e-mails, okay?" They both just nodded.

* * *

Two nights later, Jessie was sitting in an Italian restaurant waiting for the two couples to show up. They finally walked in and sat at the table next to Jessie, the men holding their chairs for the ladies. After they ordered, CD said to the two women, "Okay, what's so important that it requires a fine dinner to discuss?"

Carla looked at Wanda and smoothed out the red and white checkered tablecloth but didn't say anything. Wanda leaned forward. "Well, there's no way to ease into this, so let me just jump right in. We want to know why you haven't told us about your brother. You know, the third person in a set of triplets ... Well?"

CD's face got red, and he sputtered, "That's none of your business, and we are not going to discuss it."

"*Au contraire*, dear brother-in-law, it is our business. This is not behavior worthy of a preacher, and as preachers' wives, it is our duty to let you know when you're not practicing what you preach."

CD's face got redder, if that were possible. He raised his voice. "I said we are not going to discuss that. Do you understand me?"

Wanda raised her voice above his. "Keep your voice down, preacher. You're not in church, and I'm not your wife." That seemed to take some of the steam out of CD as he looked around to see who was listening.

He glanced at Wanda and then back at his wife. "I don't want to discuss that here."

Wanda looked at Carla, but she just sat there, so Wanda asked CD, "Why not here? I can guarantee your wife is going to discuss it when you get alone, and my husband and I are going to definitely discuss it, so why don't the four of us talk about it together?"

CD's gaze moved from her to Carla and back to her. "How did you find out about him?"

"Please don't answer my question with a question. We can get into that later. Right now, tell us what has gone on for three brothers to not talk for twenty years. The two preacher brothers are the ones I'm mainly concerned about."

Jessie liked the new boldness in Wanda.

CD said, "You don't know what he did to our father. It broke his spirit when JT refused to follow his wishes."

Wanda shook her head. "Pop-Pop was a hellfire preacher until the day he got too sick to preach. He died of a coronary disease, not a broken spirit. You're going to have to do better than that, CD."

He muttered, "I just don't like the way he treated our father. He walked out on us when we needed him the most."

Carla narrowed her eyes. "I heard he went into the army instead of the seminary, and he was told not to come back. Is that true?"

JW stepped into the conversation. "Where are you getting this information from?"

Wanda glanced at Carla with raised eyebrows, and Carla nodded her head. Wanda said, "His wife came to LA on business." She told them the story Jessie had told them. "She happened to see me from across the street from the hotel she was staying at. She promised her husband that she wouldn't contact you two, but she didn't say anything about your wives. We need some answers."

The conversation paused when the food arrived, and then CD said, "We haven't spoken for twenty years, and it's worked out okay. He hasn't bothered to contact us in all that time."

Wanda nodded. "How many times did you try and contact him?"

"Dad told him if he walked out the door to not ever come back. That was good enough for me. I really don't want to open this can of worms."

Wanda sort of laughed. "It's a little late for that isn't it, CD?"

CD looked back at her. "Well, how about you have this woman come talk to me. We can settle this matter then." He sat silent.

Wanda turned toward Jessie and said, "Jessie, you want to join us?"

Jessie stood up and walked over, bringing her chair. Wanda said to the two men, "CD, JW, this is JT's wife, Dr. Jessie Logan. Be careful what you say—she's a lawyer besides being a surgeon."

Jessie stuck out her hand to CD. He took it and shook it. She turned to JW, and he stood up and shook her hand. "Nice to meet you, Dr. Logan. Please, sit down."

She pulled up her chair between Carla and Wanda. "Please call me Jessie. I didn't mean to upset your happy homes, but your wife is right—this can't go on. Brothers not speaking is not right by anybody's standards, especially church standards. Now, are you two ready to meet and see if we can get through this without killing each other?"

JW turned to his brother and said, "We really need to end this, CD. It has become a way of life that we haven't spoken to him. I can put it behind me, I think."

CD shook his head. "I don't think I can, not just yet."

Carla surprised everybody when she said, "You've had twenty years, CD. If not right now, when?"

CD leaned back and thought for a long time, and it appeared he couldn't think of another argument against it.

"Okay ... set it up, and we'll see how it goes, if you can get him to come."

Jessie nodded. "That's the next hurdle I have to overcome. He's as stubborn as you are, CD. You don't get along because you're so much alike."

CD gave her a sideways look and appeared to grit his teeth, but he didn't say anything.

After a minute, Jessie said, "I'm going back to Memphis tomorrow. I'll be in touch with your wives and see if I can get JT out here."

CHAPTER 7

JT arrived in Belgium and was met by Scottie. They drove to an isolated farmhouse out of the city, and Scottie went over the plan. "We've located the woman in Marrakesh. It's not going to be hard to get to her, but people are definitely going to have to die on this one. She's in the city, and we can't storm in and rescue her. We're going to have to go in quietly, eliminating anybody in the way, and then get the hell out. We'll have to kill witnesses too. The hard part is getting in and out of the country. Any questions?"

JT studied the map. "How are you going to get everybody into Morocco?"

"Fake passports, bogus business meetings, and so forth. We'll go in one at a time, staggered over five days so as not to draw attention. We'll meet at a safe house here, get equipped, and move out in a covered truck. Hit the house just after dark and be back out in less than fifteen minutes. We'll disperse and meet back at the safe house individually. We have fake credentials for her and hope to get her on a plane quickly before an airport lockdown. We'll take ten days to get out one or two at a time because they'll be looking for a group of people. We'll all get back here and get debriefed."

"What's the payoff?"

Scottie smiled. "Five point five million dollars, half of the ransom demand."

JT nodded in approval.

Scottie handed JT a photo of a man in hunting gear. "We also have a hit on a survivalist in the woods somewhere in Pennsylvania. The cops can't catch him, and he's killed several people. A leading businessman who lost a daughter to him contacted us. We have the people with the skills to find him. Bad Billy led a hunter/killer team in the army, and I would send him. It'll be a $400,000 payday. Billy said he wanted to go alone."

Scottie walked him out of the map room. "We have three other jobs in the wind. We could get paid big if we do them all. All three are kidnappings for ransom. Problem is, I need another leader for the third one. I can take the first, Dutch can do the second one, but the third will need to kick off before we can reconnect."

JT shook his head. "I think we're overextending ourselves. I hate to miss the money, but I'd hate to lose men. I still want you leading every extraction when you can. I owe it to my wife not to get involved, and I've lost the ability to convince myself that my dying won't matter—it'll matter to her." JT hesitated in deep thought. "Of those three, pick two, and let the third one go."

Scottie shook his head. "Man, we're sure going to miss you out there."

JT smiled. "I have the confidence you'll do a better job than I can do."

"That means more to me than I can tell you." Scottie's tone was almost emotional.

JT slapped him on the shoulder. "Get it done, man. I'll be leaving, going back to the States tomorrow. Oh, by the way, warn the team if they come across an eighty-year-old lady in their retreat path, they should waste her." Scottie smiled and nodded. "Seriously, use that as a training tool."

The next morning, Scottie knocked on JT's door. "We have a problem."

"What is it?"

"We need another pilot to pick the target up and fly her out. It's too far for one pilot to do it all. We can get her on the plane manifest if we send our own plane. The main airport is already on high alert from some other ruckus. How about it?"

JT grimaced. "Damn. Okay, but if I get killed doing this, there's going to be hell to pay from my wife."

Scottie laughed. "Come on. I'll show you the route. It will take a while because we need to take an ancient DC-3 in, so there'll be several refueling stops."

Two days later, JT had a fake passport and a fake pilot's license. After being dropped off at the airport, he lifted off and made his way to the Mediterranean Sea and then across to Morocco, landing outside Marrakesh. The militia came and inspected his plane to make sure he wasn't bringing anything illegal in. The next day, men in a cargo truck brought some big crates out and loaded them on the plane. One was marked in French and Arabic, "Poisonous snakes, for research only." The militia did not insist on inspecting it.

When they got airborne, JT let the co-pilot take the controls, and he went back, took a crowbar, and opened the end of the crate. A woman crawled out from the little room in the interior of the crate. "Thank you. I was getting claustrophobic in there." She had a British accent. JT and the co-pilot alternated flying and sleeping, and the woman had to get back in the box each time they landed for fuel.

When they landed at their final destination, the militia was waiting for them. They got on the plane and opened each crate after the drug dog went through it. They opened the crate with the snakes and, sure enough, found glass terrariums with snakes in them. They closed it back up quickly and told them they could unload. After they left, JT got the woman out and gave her a uniform like theirs with the fake name and emblems on it. She stepped behind the box, stripped off her clothes, and put on the pants and shirt. He gave her a jacket to match, and they walked out the side door of the plane. They got in a truck with some of the boxes from the plane. The boxes were opened at a checkpoint, but no questions were asked about the woman being with him. They arrived at a warehouse, and a man came running up and hugged her and kissed her.

After several minutes of that, he came over and shook JT's hand. "I am eternally grateful. If there's anything I can ever do, please let me know." JT nodded, and they walked into an office on the side of the warehouse. The husband sat down at a laptop and typed. He looked at JT. "You have an account number?" JT typed it in. "Five point five million dollars. It's complete." He stood up, shook JT's hand again, and walked his wife out to a car.

JT got on a plane back to the States. He had to go through Mexico and then to Dallas before finally getting back to Memphis. When he got back home, Jessie came running up to him, and they kissed for several minutes.

She walked him into the house. "Well, tell me about your trip." She looked at him and froze.

* * *

"JT, what did you do?"

He frowned. "Who says I did anything?"

"I do—I can see it in your eyes. What did you do? You went on a job, didn't you?" He walked over and took her hands, but she pulled them back. "Don't try and sweet-talk me. I want to know what you did."

He sighed. "Scottie did the extraction, and I flew a plane in and picked up the hostage. One, it was a last-minute necessity. Two, there was nothing dangerous about it. It went like clockwork, and I won't do it again."

She frowned. "What country were you in?"

"You don't need to know that."

She sat down, and he sat by her and asked, "Did you take your trip?" She nodded. "Where to?"

Since he had been honest with her, she decided to be honest with him. "I went to Los Angeles and met your brothers and their wives."

He looked at her with a serious frown and stood up. "You promised you wouldn't do that."

"I promised I wouldn't contact your brothers, and I didn't. I met with Carla and Wanda. They didn't know you existed, and they agree with me that this has got to end."

"It's still the same thing as contacting them."

She nodded. "I suppose there's a fine line there, but it's done. They are willing to meet if you are. What about it?"

He walked to the window and looked out the back. "I wish you hadn't done that, Jessie."

She was silent for a minute. "I may end up wishing I hadn't either, but I did it. I didn't mean you any hurt over this—I just know this is not right. Will you go to LA with me and sit down and talk to them? Please, if you don't, they'll be right in that ya'll don't speak because of what you did, and that's refusing to meet with them." She had tears running down her cheeks.

"Let me think on it for a while. I can't get past his not notifying me when Mom died. I missed my mother's funeral, and I didn't get to say goodbye, all because he was being an asshole."

She nodded and went in the bedroom.

* * *

JT sat out on the couch until it grew dark. He didn't turn on any lights; he just sat there in the dark. He didn't want to see his brothers again, especially CD. He knew Jessie was right, but he didn't want her to be right on this.

She finally came in and turned on the light, sat down beside him, and took his hand. "Please come to bed—I need you."

He looked over at her. "You shouldn't have done that, Jessie."

She sounded mad. "I know that, and you shouldn't have participated in that job or extraction or whatever you call it, but you did after you promised me you wouldn't. What's done is done. Can we move on to what's next? Please come to bed."

He got up and went into the bedroom. The lights were turned down low, and soft music was playing. He took a shower and crawled in next to her. She was naked, so they made love and went to sleep in each other's arms.

The next morning, JT woke up and noticed Jessie looked sad. "What's wrong?"

She said, "You tossed and turned so much, you almost threw me out of bed. I'm sorry, JT, really I am, but then again, I'm not either. I don't know what to say." She looked at him. "I'm sorry for the hurt."

He smiled and kissed her. "I'll go, but CD should have started this reconciliation attempt because he started this mess."

She kissed him again, picked up her phone, and walked into the kitchen to call Wanda.

JT's phone rang. He looked at the caller ID; it was Robert. He said out loud, "This ought to be good." He walked out the back door, went to the deck, and sat down in a lawn chair.

"Hello?"

There was a brief silence, and then he heard Robert's voice. "JT, this is Robert."

"I know who it is, Robert. What do you want?"

"Man, I feel so bad about what I did to you and Jessie. I'm really and truly sorry. Let me ask you a question. Are you going to have me killed over this?"

"Well, I had plans to have you and your team taken out. I didn't have time to do it, and I didn't want to farm it out. That's the only reason you're still alive."

"I wish I could express how sorry I am, and if there's some way to make it up to you and Jessie, I'll do it. Look, I was drunk that day, and when I got to ... where we were going, I realized what a fool I was. I still love Jessie and would do anything—and I mean anything—if she would forgive me and take me back. She'll probably never forgive me for letting her dad down. I know he wanted to see her married before he died."

"He did."

There was a long pause.

"He did what?"

JT leaned back and propped his feet up. "He saw her get married."

"She's married? When and to who?"

"She got married the day you were supposed to marry her. She went on with the wedding."

"Without me? Who in the hell did she marry?"

"Believe it or not, she married me—or I married her so her dad wouldn't be disappointed, and we were going to get divorced after her dad died, but something happened."

Robert's voice had a tremor to it. "Ya'll married? That was ... awful nice of you, but what happened to the marriage?"

"I hope you're ready for this, Robert. We fell in love, and we're still married, and we plan on staying that way. As for her forgiving you, Robert, you got to know, she wouldn't piss on you if you were on fire."

Robert's voice was trembling. "I can't believe you would do that to me, man. I still love her."

"Robert, you must still be drunk. I had planned to take you out, you and your posse, but considering how things turned out, I'll let you live, but don't push me. Don't try and get in touch with my wife. On second thought, come on over if you're in town—I would love to see that. If you come, come alone—leave your boys behind."

There was another long silence on Robert's end. "Jay and Zangwill were killed ... down south. Charles was shot up pretty bad and will probably never be any use anymore. Carl is not physically hurt, but he's pretty shook up, being Zangwill's brother and all. He may not have the nerve to do another job."

"Robert, your sad tale is breaking my heart. I don't really give a shit that they're dead or wounded. Don't give me any crap, or you'll regret it. I won't kill you, but I'll make you wish you were dead. Do you understand me? You're not in love with her; you just want someone who will support you."

The silence seemed awfully loud on Robert's end, and then all of a sudden he said, "Buddy, you better watch your back. You'll never see me coming."

JT smiled to himself. "I'll look forward to your trying to get to me. You aren't half the man I am on your best day. You watch your back too, now that you've pissed me off."

The phone went dead as Jessie came out. The leaves were rustling in the wind, and the sound of traffic drifted up from the street. "Who were you talking to? I couldn't hear, but watching you, it must have been serious."

JT smiled. "It was Robert. He told me he was still in love with you and would do anything to get you back. When I told him we were married, I'm not sure but I think he shit himself. Anyway, he didn't know we were married. We threatened to kill each other and then hung up."

She sat down beside him. "Is there a chance he might come after you or me?"

"Nah, he's probably making plans to leave the country. His team is dead or wounded, and he's not man enough to do it by himself. He knows I have the talent to hunt him down and kill him or could pay someone to do it."

She nodded and looked at him. "I've made flight reservations to go to California so we can have a sit-down with your brothers. Will you go? I don't want to have to defend you by myself. Wanda and Carla know we're coming ... or at least that I'm coming. Will you go with me?"

He sat silent for a minute and saw a tear form in her eye. He reached out and touched her face. "Don't cry. I'll go, but I don't want to and wish you had never done this, but let's get it over with."

She hugged and kissed him. She sat there with her arms around his neck and rocked from side to side, enjoying the breeze. They were still like that when Lenore and Hazel pulled up. They got out, and Lenore looked at them. "I'm about to believe you two did fall in love. I'm not fully convinced, but it's close." Jessie stood up, and JT did too.

JT started for the house but stopped and turned to Lenore. "I married her for her money, you know—somebody to take care of me so I don't have to work." He went in the house.

Lenore looked disapprovingly at Jessie. "He admits to being after your money."

Jessie walked up to Lenore. "He's in the insurance business. He has about ten times the money I do, maybe more. Give it a rest, and stay out of my marriage."

* * *

The next Saturday morning, they boarded a first-class flight to LA. They didn't talk much for most of the way; JT seemed lost in thought, and Jessie didn't want to push him away. She had gotten him this far, but that didn't mean he would attend the meeting. They landed, and Jessie had a Range Rover waiting for them. They got in and went to the hotel Jessie had stayed in before.

When they got settled in the room, JT asked her, "Okay, when and where is this meeting supposed to take place?"

She pursed her lips. "At church, tomorrow morning during the morning worship service."

He frowned. "Whose idea was that?"

She was determined to go through with this and raised her eyebrows. "Mine. I had to convince Carla and Wanda to go along with it, but I want them to see you in church so the congregation will know who they really are by the way they react toward you, if it's unchristian-like. Plus, they are less likely to make a scene in church."

JT nodded. "That might be a good plan, if they don't know I'm coming."

She smiled. "Wanda and Carla do, but CD and JW don't. It'll be a surprise. By the way, I know what JT stands for, but what about CD and JW?"

JT smiled slightly. "Charles David and John Walter, four distant uncles I believe."

She frowned. "Who are you named after?"

"My dad."

"The youngest of the three, and you got your dad's name?"

"Yeah, Mom said when he looked at us, he saw something special in me. That's when he was convinced God had plans for all three of us. That's another burr under CD's saddle."

* * *

The next morning, JT was very apprehensive. He dressed and glanced worriedly at Jessie, and she walked over and looked him in the eye. "Don't back out on me now—we're almost there. Please?"

He nodded and kissed her, and they got in the Range Rover to drive to church. They drove up close to the front where there was some empty parking places marked "Visitor." JT looked at her. "That's us, I guess," he said, pulling in. JT had gone for a neat, GQ style in his blue, double-breasted suit. It was well fitted. Jessie was wearing a gray, pinstriped business suit; she looked like a lawyer.

When they walked in church was about to start, so they sat down in the back row. They were so far back they had to watch what was happening at the pulpit on a big screen hung high up. There was another one on the other side. There was a prayer and a hymn, and then they saw Carla and Wanda walk up to the pulpit. Carla stepped up to the microphone. "If you are visiting our church, you may not know us. I am Carla, CD's wife. This is Wanda, JW's wife. We want to welcome all visitors this morning. In a minute, we're all going to stand, as is our tradition, and shake hands with the people around us, but first we want to give a special welcome to our brother-in-law and sister-in-law. Dr. Logan, will you and your husband come up here, please?"

Jessie stood up, grabbed JT by the hand, pulled him to his feet, and started down the pew. When they got to the aisle, Jessie gripped his hand tighter as though afraid he was thinking about going out the door. As they walked up the aisle, people turned and looked, and some had their mouths hanging open. Halfway up, applause broke out. CD and JW sat in obvious shock. Jessie and JT walked up the steps spanning the front of the church, and Carla and Wanda met them and hugged them. They turned to their husbands, who were clearly dumbfounded.

Carla's look made CD come over, and JW followed. CD walked over, shook JT's hand, and then hugged him. It was a wimpy hug, and JT figured he'd rather not have done it but would have been embarrassed if he hadn't. JW hugged them both and seemed genuinely glad to see JT. The three wives walked the men to the podium and arranged them with JT in the middle.

Carla took a hand-held mic from a stand and walked up beside them. "Friends and visitors, this is JT Logan, and standing over here is his wife, Dr. Jessie Logan. Looking at the men, we have to apologize for telling you they were twins when they are obviously a set of triplets. It was easier to explain because JT has lived overseas for some years, but he and his wife live in Memphis, Tennessee, now. Now, if you would, please stand and shake the hands to the people around you, and if you don't know them, then introduce yourself."

A murmur settled over the congregation for five minutes. "Ladies and gentlemen, please return to your seats so we don't cut in to the worship service any more than we already have. They will be down front after the service if you want to meet them."

Carla and Wanda took JT and Jessie down and seated them in the front row. It was empty because nobody sits in the front row in a Baptist church.

Everybody returned to their seats, and the choir director stepped up and led the choir in a hymn. CD then stepped up to the pulpit. He seemed to be shaken, but he started his sermon, though he didn't seem to be into it. Afterward, JW led them in a final prayer, and a closing hymn was sung.

Carla led Jessie and JT to the middle of the church at the bottom of the steps. It seemed everybody in the church wanted to meet them. CD and Carla were on their right, and Wanda and JW were on the left of them. People were coming in both directions. The three brothers were the same height, but JT was quite a bit thicker in the upper body. They didn't have the shoulders, chest, and arms he had, but the three of them were identical in the face.

JT and Jessie said thank you about three hundred times. The only sticky part was when the little old ladies wanted to chitchat forever. JT knew there was no way to say, "Nice to meet you too—now, move on," but he thought it several times. After two hours, they were finally alone, and Carla turned to them. "Now, we're going to our house for lunch."

They arrived at what JT figured was a $400,000 house. He looked at Jessie. "Preaching the gospel must pay awfully well."

She smiled. "Don't start, please."

He smiled back. "Okay."

They got out of the car behind Wanda and JW and walked into the house. There were several people in the kitchen, and the aroma of the food seemed to permeate the entire house. They sat down in the dining room at a table big enough to seat ten people easily. Carla brought a young man up. "JT, Jessie, I want you to meet our oldest son, Wesley. Our youngest son is on a mission trip to Chile."

JT stood up and shook the boy's hand. "It's nice to meet you, Wesley." The slim boy with brown, curly hair looked back at him. JT said, "You must be eighteen by now, right?"

Wesley nodded and then looked at his mother. "Can I sit next to Uncle JT?"

She smiled. "Sit across from him, and then you can see him and talk to him better."

JW brought his two girls in and introduced them. As each pixie-looking girl stuck out her hand, JT took it and kissed it. They seemed in awe.

While they were eating, JT looked at the food down the table. "I haven't seen this much food since I was in the army."

Wesley stopped eating and looked up. "Were you in the army, Uncle JT?"

JT looked at him and smiled. "I was and I am. I'm inactive with the First Air Cav."

Wesley's eyes were wide open. "The Air Cav! Then do you fly helicopters?"

"The army trained me as a pilot. I started out flying 'slickers' and went to the Apache later, but that was some time ago."

"Was the slicker a Huey Iroquois UH1C made by Bell Helicopter?"

JT smiled. "You know your helicopters—I'm impressed." Wesley sat there with a proud expression on his face. JT glanced at CD and could tell CD didn't like the conversation.

"Uncle JT, did you fly the Apache in combat?"

"Yeah, I did, a couple of times."

Wesley looked at the rest of them. "Did you know the Apache has a machine gun mounted under the nose of the helicopter, and the gun fires in the direction the pilot is looking? If he looks right, it points right. If he's looking left—"

CD interrupted him. "I think that's enough talk about helicopters and the army. If you're through, son, aren't you supposed to be at the youth council meeting at three?"

"Yes, sir, but I would much rather stay here and talk to Uncle—" His father's look cut him off from saying anymore.

Wesley stood up. "If you'll excuse me, I have to go. Will I see you before you leave town?"

JT nodded. "Sure. If not today, tomorrow."

Wesley reluctantly left. JW's girls had to be somewhere too, so they left as well. It left the three couples there alone making small talk, steering clear of the impending conversation that was sure to come. They finally finished eating, and Carla stood up. "Let's go in the den and let the ladies clear the table."

* * *

When they had all sat down, there was an unnerving silence in the room. JT looked at his brothers. "I guess we should talk about our differences. Isn't that what this meeting is about?"

Carla seemed to want to head off any adverse conversation. "Well, I was hoping it was a reconciliation meeting where we could all be reunited and ..." The look on everybody's faces told her she needn't finish.

JT said to CD, "The part I'm having trouble with is you not calling me when Mom died. Dad said you did, but if you did, you didn't leave a message, and please don't sit there and tell me you did."

CD looked down at the floor and then to the left. Jessie frowned; she knew from selecting jurors that was body language for guilt.

CD glanced at her and then JT. "I did call several times, but I didn't leave a message. I figured if you were not in your BOQ by eleven or twelve at night, you were too busy to check on your own mother."

JT glared at CD. "CD, I was in the field the two weeks before Mom died. If you had left a message that she was near death, they would have brought me in. I shouldn't have had to hear the hate that I did from Dad when I called that Sunday, and for your information, I talked to Mother every Sunday between two and three thirty because I knew the three of you were at church. We did that for years."

CD sat there silent and then finally said to JT, "What about Dad? You didn't know he was sick or when he died, and you certainly weren't at the funeral."

JT replied, "You know Aunt Billie worked the reception at the hospital, didn't you?" CD nodded. "Every time he was admitted, she would call me, and I would come to town and see him. I made peace with Dad a long time ago. I told the nurses my family wasn't speaking to me, but I wanted to see my father. I was holding his hand when he died, and I was at the graveside service. You just didn't see me."

CD frowned. "Why didn't you call us when he died? We didn't hear about it until hours later."

JT's expression was determined. "Isn't that what you did with me and Mom?"

"You mean we missed saying goodbye to our father so you could have that time all to yourself? That's pretty selfish, don't you think?"

"No difference with you two and Mom, is it?"

CD sat silent.

JW looked at JT. "He's right, JT. That was the wrong thing to do. You shouldn't have denied us that privilege, no matter what anyone else did." He cast a quick glance at CD.

JT stared back at his brother. "There's a lot of things we shouldn't have done ... but we did them, didn't we?"

CD said quietly, "I'll never forget the hurt on Dad's face when you walked out that door to go join the army."

"CD, he gave me no choice—I had to walk out or go in the ministry. I wasn't called to preach. I'm glad you two were. Just because we're triplets doesn't mean we want the same things in life. I was hurt too, because he made me choose. Dad was a manipulator and a control freak. He told me that God revealed it to him that I was supposed to go into the ministry, but God didn't reveal it to me. I asked God on several occasions, CD." Tears began to flow from JT, and then CD and JW. The women had been crying since the talk first began. "You're in the ministry because Dad told you to go, not God. JW is in the ministry because he can't exist without you for some reason. That's why you're at the same church."

Jessie spoke for the first time. "The question is, where do we go from here? Do you like being estranged from each other, enough to want it for the next twenty years, or are you going to forgive each other and get on with your lives?"

CD stood up. "I need to sleep on this."

JT stood up and just nodded. He then turned and walked to the back door and out. Jessie hugged Carla and Wanda and then grabbed CD, turned him around, and hugged him. After hugging JW as well, she walked out and got in the car with JT.

When they got back in their room, Jessie pulled her clothes off in front of him, and he went to her. That was the only way she could comfort him. They lay there, and after an hour, Jessie turned to JT. He had his back to her. "JT, are you awake?" She almost whispered it.

She was surprised when he answered without hesitation, "Yes."

"I'm sorry for the pain, but I'm not sorry I did this. Will you ever forgive me?"

"There's nothing to forgive. You're right—this has been festering long enough and needs to be out in the open.

Whatever happens, I can walk away knowing I said my piece and did my part."

She had tears in her eyes again. "You haven't told them you forgive them. Are you waiting on them to do it first? You may wait another twenty years if you do."

He didn't answer.

* * *

They got up and got dressed, and JT said to Jessie, "I saw a park a few blocks from here. Let's walk down there. I need to walk some of this food off." She nodded. They walked to the park, where there were couples walking and children playing.

Jessie's phone rang. It was a local number. She answered it and heard Wesley on the other end. "Aunt Jessie? I got your number from Mom. Can I come talk to Uncle JT?" Jessie handed JT the phone.

JT listened and said, "Do you think your dad would want you to?"

"Probably not, but it's what I want to do."

JT smiled. "We're at the park near the hotel. Do you know where that is?"

"Yes, sir. I'll be there in about ten minutes." JT smiled again because he knew Wesley had been on his way to see them to be that close.

JT and Jessie were sitting on a bench under a tree watching kids play soccer when Wesley came walking up about ten minutes later. JT stood up, and Wesley hugged him tightly. He hugged Jessie too and sat down next to JT.

"Uncle JT? I was wondering if you could help me get into the military academy."

"Why do you ask me, son? Your father would be the one to do that."

Wesley shook his head. "He wants me to preach, but I'm like you—I have my own mind. The military fascinates me, and I will confess I did some research on you at church. You received the Congressional Medal of Honor. A recommendation from you would go a long way."

JT hesitated before answering. "Son, you're going to have to get this straightened out with your father first. You're pitting us against each other, and this is a bad time for that. If you get your father's permission, I'll be glad to do that, but I can't go against him right now."

JT's phone rang, and he saw it was Margaret. He stood up. "Excuse me—I have to take this." He walked away, and Jessie scooted over by Wesley and put her arm around him.

"Hello, Margaret. What's up?"

"Trouble in the wind. You are being accused of murdering men, women, and children at a village in Iraq two years ago. Word is they have a picture of you in front of all the dead."

JT gritted his teeth. "That's bullshit. Where's it coming from?"

"A Democrat congressman who's up for reelection."

"Who's behind him, do you know?"

"Not yet, but I'll look into it. Any ideas in what direction I should search?"

JT thought a minute. "My first look would be at Robert Mason."

There was silence on her end for a minute. "Nah, I don't think he has the balls to mess with you."

"I didn't either, but we had a 'death threatening each other' phone conversation a few days ago. He said he was coming after me, and I told him I would be ready. The only way he could stop me from killing him would be to have me put in jail. Check into it, please."

"Will do, boss." The phone went dead.

JT went back over to the bench. Jessie had obviously had a talk with Wesley about what he was asking. JT said to Jessie, "You need to get with Carla and Wanda and get this meeting set for tomorrow. I have to get back to Memphis. I have some trouble in the wind that needs my attention." She nodded.

Wesley looked at JT. "If you enlisted in the army, how did you get to be an officer without going to college or the academy? Did you go through OCS?"

"I got a battlefield commission," JT said. "I was a five-stripe sergeant, we were in a battle, and we were overrun. When the smoke cleared, I was the ranking man on the ground. General Harry Edmenson landed in his Deloatch and told me I was the acting company commander and I was now a lieutenant. His XO looked at me and whispered to the general, 'Look how old this guy is.' The general took another look and told me I was now a captain."

Wesley's eyes were big. "Wow, you went from being a staff sergeant to a captain?"

JT nodded. Jessie smiled and told Wesley he probably needed to get back before his dad missed him.

They hugged Wesley. Then they walked back to the hotel, and Wesley went home.

When they got back, JT felt exhausted all of a sudden. He went into the bedroom, lay down, and went right to sleep.

* * *

Jessie shut the door as she went back into the sitting room. Then she went out onto the balcony so she wouldn't disturb JT. She got Carla and Wanda on a conference call.

Carla started first. "CD wants us to set up another meeting for next Thursday. He has a full schedule this week. Can you do it?"

Jessie answered. "JT says he needs to get back to Memphis. We need to meet tomorrow if possible; otherwise, it may be postponed for a week or so. I hate to lose the momentum we have."

Carla agreed, as did Wanda. "Let us talk to our husbands, and we'll let you know as soon as possible."

Jessie went back in, and when JT woke up an hour later she told him what CD wanted to do about meeting.

JT quickly answered, "No, business requires me to leave for Memphis tomorrow. If I'm that far down on his priority list, then there's no reason to have this meeting."

Jessie froze; she couldn't let this fall apart now.

Carla called back as Jessie and JT were getting ready to go out and eat. "CD wants to meet right now. He's going to let JW lead the service so he can meet with you. Will you come back to the house?"

JT nodded, and Jessie told them they would be there in half an hour.

When they got there, CD had a bad look on his face. As they sat down in the living room, CD stared at JT, and JT stared back. "Go ahead, CD—get it off your chest."

CD stood up and stepped toward JT. "Did you talk my son into going into the army?"

JT stood up and stepped in front of CD. "Don't stand up like you're going to do something. I will knock you on your ass if need be." Carla and Jessie stood up and pulled on both of them until they sat back down. "I didn't talk to him about the army. He talked to me, and I told him he would have to clear it with you first."

CD was fuming. "How did he get your number in the first place?"

Carla said quickly, "I gave Jessie's number to him. I thought he wanted to talk about helicopters, and I didn't see any harm in it."

CD glared at her. "Do you see any harm in his getting killed in a war?"

Carla's face took on a mean expression to match his, and she said with gritted teeth, "That's not fair, CD."

CD got back to his feet. "I don't see any reason to renew this kinship. He's already turning my son against me."

JT stood up also. "If that's the way you want it, CD, it's your call."

CD said, "Please leave my house."

JT turned to CD, and Jessie knew he was fixing to swing. She took his hand and started out, saying to Carla and Wanda, "We'll stay in touch, okay?"

The two women nodded, but CD turned to his wife and said, "You will not! I forbid you to talk to this woman again."

Carla narrowed her eyes at her husband. "You don't have a say in the matter, husband. You need to start thinking about another career, because you stink at this one that requires forgiving." She turned and walked out of the room. Wanda followed Jessie and JT out.

They got a flight back at eight o'clock the next morning to Memphis. On the way back Jessie put her arm over his. "At least I know this wasn't your fault. It's been CD all along."

He smiled at her. "Thanks."

* * *

Once in Memphis, Jessie had to see patients at the hospital the next few days and study some legal briefs. She knew she could concentrate better in her office at the medical center, but she also wondered what type of trouble JT was looking at.

Jessie being gone was fine with JT because he had a lot of phone calling to do. He Skyped Margaret to find out what she'd learned.

"Hey, boss, I have some news. You were right. It is Robert Mason—not that I could prove it in court, but I'm confident enough that I wouldn't feel guilty about having him wasted. I have the picture of you supposedly standing over the dead. I'm sending it now. They leaked it themselves, so they must not be sure about it, but I'll admit it looks like you."

The picture came up on his screen. It showed a man standing over a pit with obviously dead bodies of men, women, and children. It was slightly out of focus. The picture showed the back of the man, who was turned slightly turn to the right and looking back over his right shoulder toward the camera. The man was wearing Iraqi peasant pants and shoes to blend in, but he was not wearing a shirt. He was muscularly built like JT, and he had a one-inch-long beard that concealed most of his face, a pair of wraparound sunglasses that concealed the rest, and a black cowboy hat. It did look like him. He clicked back to Margaret.

"Yeah, it does look like me, but I would never go without a shirt over there because I would be toasted in about two minutes. That was a posed picture. Next, I wouldn't wear a black hat in that heat, and, finally, I would never wear my unit hat if I were trying to go unnoticed. I've been set up. Does the congressman have a date as to when this supposedly happened?"

"Yeah, he says sometime between May and August of 2013."

"They won't be able to prove it. Better yet, I'll be able to prove it's not true, but I want this to go to trial to expose everybody and maybe wreck the congressman's chance for re-election. Keep digging; let me know when you get something. Have you located Robert?"

"No, sir. He's holed up in some third-world country the best we can tell, but I'm working on it. We checked his family's place in Kentucky. He's not there. What's next?"

JT thought a minute. "Maybe have someone warn them about Robert's bad behavior." She took his meaning to have someone put a shot through the window of the house. Word would get back to Robert, and it might flush him out of hiding.

JT hung up, sat there, and thought about his options.

At noon, he turned on the news. Sure enough, there was a news conference by the congressman, saying he had uncovered information about a murder. The announcer said, "It's about this man." It showed the picture that Margaret had sent him. "This is believed to be Colonel JT Logan, US Army. He is now a civilian, and sources says he heads up a mercenary group of people that will kill anybody if paid enough." They then put up a picture of him in his gym pants and long-sleeved T-shirt, in about the same stance as the man in the other picture. He knew it was a recent picture of him crossing the street to go to the gym downtown.

Margaret texted him that Arian would be arriving in Memphis from Atlanta in three days. That Thursday about four o'clock, Arian came driving up. She got out of the car, and he hugged her. "I want you to stay here at the house with us. It'll be easier to work on this."

She looked at him with a serious expression. "As your lawyer, I know we have to find a high-profile lawyer to defend you."

"Can't you do it?"

She shook her head. "No, this is going to take some big guns. Your wife and I aren't in that league. I suggest Will Garret from LA. He would jump on something like this. He's defended all types of people for things far worse than this, he has a tendency to intimidate anyone who goes up against him, and he loves publicity."

JT nodded. "Okay, talk to him."

"Let me take some notes, and I'll call him." They sat for two hours and talked while Arian took copious notes.

Jessie came in and hugged Arian. Arian stood up. "I need to go make a few phone calls. Is it possible to sit out on the patio? The weather's so nice right now."

Jessie hugged her again. "Sure, and I'll turn on some music in here so you'll have complete privacy." Arian nodded her thanks.

Jessie turned to JT. "I'm beginning to worry, JT."

"Don't. I can handle this. Please have faith in me that I know what I'm doing."

She nodded and then walked up and kissed him. "I have a meeting at the courthouse at four, so I have to get going."

He grabbed her as she started to walk away. "Get your stuff, and I will drop you off and pick you up when you're through. I don't want you in that parking system downtown, especially after dark."

She picked up her briefcase, put some folders in it, and checked to see if she had her laptop. They went out, told Arian they were leaving, got into JT's car, and left. He dropped her at the front door of the courthouse and waited until she walked up to the door and the security guard opened it for her.

As JT drove toward Germantown, his phone rang. It was a local number, but he didn't recognize it. "Hello."

"Uncle JT?"

"Wesley? It's good to hear from you, my man. What's up?"

"I was wondering if you would do me a favor."

"If I can, I will."

"Will you pick me up at the bus station?"

JT paused. "In Memphis?"

"Yes, sir, and hurry. There's some guys that look like trouble."

"I'll be there in a few minutes."

He sped down the interstate and got off on Airways, glad that he was already downtown. He pulled up on the sidewalk in front of the bus station because he knew there wouldn't be any parking within two blocks. When he walked in the door, Wesley was backed up against the wall by two gangbangers. A security guard was standing nearby but apparently wasn't doing anything about the threat to Wesley.

JT walked toward them as if he were going to walk by them. When he got even with the two gangbangers, he punched the nearest one in the side of the head hard enough to knock him into the second thug. JT could hear their heads crack as they hit, and they both dropped.

JT turned and saw the security guard halfheartedly go for his gun. JT pulled his and pointed it at the guard. "You didn't want any of this when they were threatening him, so stay the fuck out of it now. Do you understand me ... bro?"

The guard froze with his weapon halfway out. JT walked up to him, took his gun, and then yanked his badge off his shirt. Everybody in the station heard the guard unload in his pants. The guard simply stood there in a gray rent-a-cop company shirt and cap, maroon sweatpants, and dirty white sneakers.

JT walked back to Wesley, who hugged him and clung to him. JT pushed him back. "Come on, son. Let's get out of here."

The second gangbanger was moaning and holding his head while trying to sit up. As he walked by, JT clubbed him with the guard's gun, and he dropped back unconscious.

Before they made it out of the station, they heard the security guard say, "I quit—they don't pay me enough fucking money to put up with this shit."

JT put Wesley in the front seat, and as he went around to the driver's side, the guard came out. "Sir, I can appreciate what you did. However, I was wondering if I could get my gun back. I still owe my brother $185 for it."

JT felt sorry for a man trying to make a living doing that, as well as having to face gang members to do his job, and he pulled the clip out of the scarred and abused Glock 9. He pulled the bolt back, ejecting the shell, disassembled the weapon into four different pieces, and handed the gun back to the guard. Then he got in the car and drove off, keeping an eye in his rearview mirror.

When JT drove up the ramp for the interstate, he looked at Wesley. The boy had tears in his eyes.

"Uncle JT, I was so scared. I thought I was going to die."

JT suppressed a smile. "You need to learn to take care of yourself in those situations. I can teach you that, but what are you doing here, young man?"

"Same thing happened to me as it did to you. I tried to talk to Dad about going to the military academy, but he wouldn't listen. He wouldn't give me a chance to tell him I just don't feel called to go into the ministry. When I left, he took my car keys and cell phone. I was lucky I had already cleaned out my bank account in case he did this. I got a friend to take me to the bus station."

"How did you call me if you didn't have a phone?"

"I paid a woman five dollars to let me make a call on her cell."

JT headed for the house, and as he got off the Germantown exit he asked Wesley, "Hungry?"

"Man, yeah, I haven't had anything but snack machine food."

"What do you want to eat? Steak, hamburger, anything you want."

Wesley looked out through the windshield. "Will you pull into that IHOP?"

JT pulled in, and they went in. JT drank coffee as Wesley ate three eggs, bacon, biscuits with sausage gravy, and a stack of pancakes with strawberry syrup. He had two glasses of milk. JT smiled as Wesley belched.

The boy looked at JT. "Excuse me—that was rude of me."

JT laughed. "I'm just glad it came out this end." Wesley laughed with him. "Do your mom and dad know where you are?"

"No, sir, and I don't want him to know, and I don't care if he's worried. He probably won't be, but I don't care."

JT was quiet for a minute. "What about your mom? She'll be worried sick. Don't you care what she's going through?"

Wesley had tears in his eyes and nodded as he looked out the side window, no doubt hoping JT wouldn't see him cry.

"Look, son, I'm going to have to call your parents and let them know you're okay and safe. Remember, he's my brother, and we're trying to heal a twenty-year fight. This is not helping any."

They got in the car and drove off. A few minutes later, his phone rang, and he could see it was CD. JT put his earpiece on and answered the phone. "Hello, CD. He's safe. I just picked him up at the bus station."

"You son of a bitch, you planned all this, didn't you?"

"CD, do you kiss your wife with that dirty mouth?" He saw Wesley smile.

CD's voice was trembling. "I want my boy back, JT."

"I'm not holding him against his will; he can walk out anytime he wants. Is Carla there with you?"

"Yes, you are on speaker phone with her and two police officers who are going to arrest you."

"I don't think so, CD. First, you're in California, and I'm in Tennessee. Second, your son is over eighteen, so he can do pretty well what he wants. Those officers will tell you that."

Carla cut in. "JT, where's my boy? Let me speak to him." JT turned his earpiece off and pushed a button on the steering wheel.

"Talk to your mom, son, and be aware that your father and two police officers are listening."

"Mom, I'm okay." They could hear her crying.

CD started to say something, but Carla cut him off. "CD, I'm not finished. Wesley, please come home."

"I can't, Mom, not right now."

Carla began crying hysterically.

They heard CD's voice again. "JT, you weren't going to call me and tell me about this, were you?"

"CD, I just got a call from him telling me he was at the bus station. I got him something to eat, and we were discussing the need to call you when you called me. Let me ask you a question. Did you take his cell phone away from him?"

"Yes, but that's none of your business."

"You dumb bastard, you could have tracked him with that and not had to go through all this. Besides that, you put him in danger by him not being able to call for help. When I got to him, two gangbangers were going to wreck him."

Carla's voice came back. "Wesley, are you hurt? Did they hurt you?"

"No, Mom. You should have seen it. Uncle JT knocked them both out and took the gun away from the security guard that refused to help me, but I'm fine."

"Why didn't you call me the minute you heard from him?" CD demanded. "You weren't going to call me, were you?"

"I was busy listening to him, CD. That's something you ought to try. He's got a lot of heart and feelings. You should hear his side."

"He's just like you, going against everything I have tried to do for him."

JT laughed. "You're just like Dad. It's going to be your way or the highway, so guess what, CD? He's on the highway. Carla, he's okay and safe. I will take care of him until you get that idiot brother of mine to start thinking straight."

CD's voice shook with emotion. "JT, put my boy back on a bus home tonight. Do you understand me?"

"I understand you, CD, but if I was going to send him back, I would put him on a plane. However, I'm not going to send him home. He has to decide that himself. Carla, I'll get him a cell phone tomorrow, and he'll call you when he gets it, okay?"

"Thank you, JT. Thank you so much." The phone went dead.

Wesley said, "Dad hung up, didn't he?"

"Maybe." JT shrugged his shoulders. "Wesley, you got to have a plan to make something work. I'm not going to tell you what to do. I'll tell you if I disagree with you, but you have to make the ultimate decision. You can live with me, and I will take care of the same needs your dad did, but ... you need to do something soon, because if you don't, you're going to find yourself twenty years from now with nothing having been done. The hurt you cause your mother will be ten times the hurt your father will be feeling. There's a bond between mother and child no man will ever understand."

"What do you mean?"

"Your dad has limits for you, and if you don't stay inside those limits, he says stupid things like never come back. He still loves you even though he doesn't show it. Your mother will always show her love for you, even if you killed somebody."

Wesley seemed to be thinking hard. "Uncle JT? My plan is to go in the army—that's the only solution I can come up with."

JT pulled into the driveway. He turned off the car and then turned to Wesley. "How about you having a sit-down meeting with the two of them—hold on, let me finish. Make it a condition that he has to hear you out and not interrupt. When he talks, you do the same. Tell him what you want and why it's important to you, and be sincere."

Wesley looked out the window and back at JT. "That won't work, Uncle JT. First, I can't go back—if I do, I'll never be able to get away again. He'll probably lock me in my room, even though I'm eighteen. Second, my mom is a good Christian wife. She won't argue with my dad or even state her opinion. He's the head of the family, and she backs him whether she agrees with him or not."

JT chuckled. "I bet she will now. Your father has done stepped on the mother's love for her son. She'll listen, she'll talk, and she'll tell CD if she thinks he's wrong—believe me. Now, as far as your going home, invite them here. Ya'll be on neutral turf, so to speak. Tell him what you want and why you want it. If he refuses, I'll try to get you in the military academy, but don't tell him that. Let him think you're going down to the recruiting station as soon as he leaves. One other thing: Uncle JT is a mouthful—call me JT."

Wesley grinned widely. "Thanks, JT."

JT introduced him to Arian, explained the situation to her, and then took him in and put him in a bedroom. "Take a shower and get in bed. I have to go pick up Jessie when she calls, but I'll be back. Get some rest; you look like you need it."

Jessie called as JT shut the door. "I'll be ready by the time you get here."

"I'm on my way." He drove back downtown to the courthouse, and she walked out and got in the car.

Her expression serious, she said, "There's big trouble brewing. Wesley has run off, and they don't know where. CD blames you for this."

"Hold up a minute. Wesley is at our house asleep. He called me, and I picked him up at the bus station. I've talked to CD and Carla, and they know he's safe. He does blame me, but I don't really give a ... hoot, because I didn't do anything wrong. I'm taking him tomorrow to get a cell phone. Did you know CD took his cell phone away from him?"

Jessie shook her head. "It seems like he would want him to have it in case he might call."

"The dumb bastard didn't think that far ahead. He thought Wesley would go down the street, get lonely, and come back and submit to his will. He's just like my father."

Jessie smiled. "Wesley's just like you. That's what's got CD's panties in a wad." JT smiled too. Jessie paused and then said, "More trouble on the horizon. Sunday, JW got up to make announcements and asked Wanda to come up and stand by him. He told the congregation he was resigning as associate pastor of the church effective immediately. He told them it was a personal decision and asked for their prayers. Do you know who he didn't tell he was going to do that? CD."

"Did Wanda say what brought that on?"

"Yeah, she said the remark you made about CD following his dad and JW following CD made him realize he was under CD's control and totally dependent on him. Wanda just said it was a realization that came late, but better late than never. A church search committee wants him to come look at a preaching job in Owensboro, Kentucky."

JT thought a minute. "I need to call him, I guess, and apologize."

"According to Wanda, he's going to thank you."

* * *

The next morning, Arian told JT that his new attorney, Will Garrett from LA, would be in that night. "He's staying at the Hilton downtown and wants us to meet with him first thing in the morning. Can you do it?"

JT nodded. "I have things to do tomorrow. It won't be an all-day affair, will it?"

"Shouldn't be. We should be out by lunch I think, or at least you will."

In the afternoon, JT took Wesley to the phone store. He told him to pick out a new iPhone 6 plus. Wesley grinned and told JT, "The only phone they would let me have is an old flip phone of dad's—it was embarrassing." Wesley looked at him as they rang up the phone and protector cover. "How much will this cost, JT?"

"Don't worry about it. It's on my plan. I'll pay for it and the monthly bill, and you have unlimited data, even if you go back home. Now, let's see about a computer." They spent the afternoon buying Wesley the few essentials that he needed, and JT even bought him an iPad that he didn't need. Then they went to the mall and bought him some clothes.

The next day, Arian followed JT downtown to meet with Will. She wanted her car there in case she needed it.

Will welcomed them in. "Let's get started. I get $5,000 a day plus expenses. Is that suitable to you?" JT nodded. "Next, I won't need your lawyer here—I have my own team." Arian appeared disappointed.

JT said, "Will, I know how big of a big shot you are, but if I'm paying you $5,000 a day, I will have some say-so in what's going to happen. She stays, if for nothing else the experience of watching you work."

"My associates pay dearly to have the experience to work with me."

"I figure hers will be covered by the five thousand a day. If she can't help, she can help you keep up with your expenses. Do you want the job?"

"How serious are you about staying out of jail, Mr. Logan?" Will was clearly trying to intimidate him.

"Damn serious. I have this case won, and I could put an end to it today, but I want it drug out in the public to discredit those accusing me. I can prove that's not me in the photo and will, when the time is appropriate, so I can do this without you. You can have the glory for winning, and I'm willing to pay you money I don't have to spend. Do you need me for anything else?"

Will shook his head. "No, the preliminary work will be done by Arian and myself for now. We might be calling you from time to time with questions. One thing—are you a mercenary that will kill anyone for the right money?"

JT smiled and shook his head. "Arian will explain what I do."

When JT got home, Wesley was playing with his computer. "How's it going, sport?"

"Good, JT. Everything is great."

"Call your mom yet?"

"No, sir. I can't bring myself to get yelled at by my dad, even over the phone."

JT smiled. "Let me have your phone a minute." Wesley gave it to him, and JT dialed a number.

"Hello, Carla? Is CD around? No, I wanted to talk to you anyway. You need to do something about CD, or you're going to lose this boy. He's willing to sit down with you and CD, but he has some conditions." JT paused. "I'm getting to that. First, CD and you are going to have to let him have his say, without interrupting him, and he will give you the same courtesy. Second, you're going to have to come here. He's not coming home until this is settled one way or another. If ya'll agree on something, then you can go from there. If you don't, he's going to the recruiting station." He paused for a few seconds. "Yes, I heard about JW. Not my problem. CD can get someone to substitute for him. You can't swing a dead cat in that church without hitting a preacher of some kind. If CD won't come, you come, but that's the only way you'll get to talk to him. Okay, this is Wesley's new cell number. I'm putting him on, and good luck with CD." JT handed the phone to Wesley and walked into the bedroom to give him some privacy.

JT lay down and took a nap. An hour later, Jessie, kissing his ear, awakened him. Without opening his eyes he said, "Leave me alone, lady. I'm married."

She laughed. "That's a good comeback, sleepyhead." Her face turned serious. "JT, this has hit the TV, and it's getting a lot of coverage. The hospital is concerned about the publicity and me."

He looked up at her. "Can they fire you?"

"They can, but they won't. They know I'm a lawyer also, but, still, it can make for a rocky relationship. I'll stand by you no matter what comes. I trust you."

"Thanks for that, babe. CD and Carla may be coming soon. That's the only way they'll get to talk to Wesley. When I find out when, I'll let you know, or Carla will."

"She's already talked to me about your conversation with her. She and I have become good friends, and Wanda has too."

CHAPTER 8

There was much haggling over whether it would be a military or civilian trial since JT was detached from his unit. It was finally determined it would be a civilian trial because the military wanted nothing to do with prosecuting a Medal of Honor recipient. The lawyers went through the hoops and hurdles of the legal jockeying without JT's help.

Apparently, the shot through the family home got Robert out in the open. In a news conference he admitted he was the source of the picture. JT watched it on TV with Will, Arian, and two members of Will's team. JT said to Arian, "Pretty smart move on his part."

Will frowned. "Why?"

"Because I can't afford to kill him now."

Will stood up. "You said you weren't a mercenary."

"I'm not—nobody would have to pay me to kill him. I would do it for the sheer pleasure of doing it, but I would kill him." He smiled and walked to the door after looking each of them in the eye so they'd realized he wasn't one to be messed with.

That afternoon Jessie came in and stood in front of JT. "CD and Carla will be here at five o'clock this afternoon. I told them I would pick them up and take them to the hotel, and, no, they don't want to stay here if that's what you're wondering. Carla would, but CD won't."

"That's probably good, because if he pisses me off enough, I may have to lay him out."

Jessie grabbed his ear. "No, there will be no hitting of any kind. I mean it, JT."

"Okay, but you need to keep CD in check. If he jumps up and starts toward me, my instincts and training are going to tell me to knock him on his ass."

She looked at him again. "I figured we would leave the three of them by themselves to talk, won't we?"

"Hell, no. That would be two against one, and Wesley wouldn't do it. I'll sit back out of the way and keep my mouth shut. You need to be the facilitator, since you started this whole thing. Make sure they both get their say and no one hogs all the conversation. You know my brother can talk the ears off of a wooden Indian."

She smiled, and they got up and went into the den. "How'd the talk with your mom go, Wes?"

"Good. I can talk to Mom, but Dad is another story."

JT smiled. "You can talk to your dad too, but you really need to listen to him if you want him to listen to you. You need to hear what the other person is saying. When he talks, listen, and don't be formulating what you're going to say back to him when he finishes, understand?"

"Yeah. Why is it I can talk to you but not him?"

JT smiled. "You can. Try, okay?"

Jessie left and returned an hour and a half later. When they entered the house, CD's expression was somber, and Carla looked scared. She ran, hugged, and kissed Wesley when she saw him. CD walked up and shook Wes's hand. "Good to see you again, son."

"You too, Dad"

JT got up and walked to the dining table. He was still in the same room with them, but he was as far away as he could get and still hear.

Jessie stood up. "CD, if you and Carla don't mind, I will be the facilitator for this meeting. Simple rules: don't interrupt the other person, and listen to what they are trying to tell you. Okay, who's going first?" No one said anything. "Okay, Wesley, I want you to start. Tell your dad what you want him to know. Be polite and kind. Go ahead."

Wesley looked at the floor and then at his father. "Dad, I've never felt the call to preach. I know you want me to, but it would be wrong. I have been fascinated with the military a long time. Growing up under you, I think I would do well in a regimented society. I am ... I would like to go to the military academy at West Point, and I would like to be an officer. I want your and Mom's support in this."

There was a long silence.

CD stood up, and Jessie quickly said, "CD, would you mind if I asked you to stay seated? I know you are a preacher and are used to talking and walking, but you are not going to be preaching tonight, and it's less intimidating if he doesn't have to look up at you." CD sat back down. "Go ahead, CD."

"Son, I have spent my whole life serving God. I just wanted you to do the same and glorify His name. I'm afraid you will get killed if you go in the army or, worse, wind up killing people like my brother." He glanced back at JT. "We were accosted at the airport by reporters who thought I had killed women and children. Please, reconsider this."

"Dad, I can glorify God by being a soldier. Actually, I want to go to Army flight school. I want to fly helicopters. It may not necessarily be a gunship; there are other aircraft I want to fly. And I wouldn't mind being like Uncle JT—I admire him. He stands up for what he believes in, and no one messes with him or gets in his way. He told me about ya'll trying to mend a twenty-year split, and I don't mean to intrude or cause problems there. He didn't know I left home or that I was coming until I called him. He saved me from a beating at the bus station, and I want to be able to stand up for myself just like that. Do you know why I came to him? Because I knew he would listen to me. He will let me make my own decisions and support me in anything I choose. He may not agree with me, but he won't stop me. Will you let me to go to West Point? I'm going in the military, one way or the other."

There was another long silence. CD started to stand up, but sat again as though thinking better of it. "I cannot support your going in the military, and I wish you would reconsider. If you don't want to attend seminary, then pick another career. I'll pay for you to go to college, any college you can get into, but not the military. I'm sorry, but I would never forgive myself if anything happened to you." CD's eyes were getting moist.

Wes looked at his mother. "Mom, I value your opinion also. I want to know what you think, and I don't mean to be disrespectful, but I want to know what you think and not what you think Dad wants you to say. Will you tell me honestly?"

With tears running down her cheeks, Carla cleared her throat. "I would rather you go to seminary or college at home ... but I will support you in anything you decide to do." CD gave her a startled glance, but she ignored it. "I just want you to be happy, son. If this is what you want to do, I'll be behind you all the way." She got up and walked across the room, Wesley stood up, and they hugged and cried. CD just sat there staring at the floor.

CD finally stood up. "I think we should go." He walked out, Carla kissed Wes and followed him out, and Jessie drove them back to the hotel. Wes went to his room.

JT walked to Wes's room and knocked lightly. "Son, are you okay?"

Wes opened the door. "Will you help me to get in the academy?"

JT stepped up and hugged the boy. "I'll help you, and you'll make me proud the day you become an officer." Wes hung onto him and cried. After a few minutes, JT pulled back and shut the door.

The next day, JT got Wesley to start lifting weights and drinking a protein drink every day.

JT called Margaret. "Marge, I need some footwork done."

"When did you ever not want some footwork done?"

JT smiled. "I need to find out what it takes to get my nephew into West Point. He has the grades. Will my holding the CMH be any good in this?"

"I'll find out and let you know, boss."

He turned on the TV to watch the news. He was surprised to see CD explain to a news crew that he wasn't JT Logan, though he admitted to being JT's brother. The news once again showed the picture of the man at the death scene with JT's picture beside it.

When the trial started a month later, there was much posturing by both sides. Will brought in a forensic specialist who testified that the man in the picture was five foot ten, with a margin of error of one inch. The prosecutor brought in a forensic specialist who testified that the man in the picture was closer to being six feet with a margin of error of two inches. Will asked him if the two-inch margin of error was in the negative, would that make the man five foot ten, the same as the other testimony? He agreed that it would.

Robert took the stand but never looked at JT. JT stared a hole in Robert; he knew Robert could feel his stare and knew it made Robert super-nervous. Robert testified that he was in Iraq during the time and had, in fact, taken the picture of JT looking over the dead. He said he never turned it in because he was afraid JT would have him killed.

To JT's surprise, Arian got up and walked toward Robert. "Robert, had you planned on marrying Jessie Logan, JT's wife, last November?" He seemed surprised, as did the judge and prosecutor, at the question.

The prosecutor stood up. "Relevance, Your Honor?"

Arian said, "It goes to show cause." The judge allowed it. "Yes, I was."

"Was it your or her idea to break off the marriage?"

"Mine, I just couldn't see myself getting married because I traveled a lot back then."

Arian just looked at him for a minute, and it clearly made Robert uncomfortable. "You, in fact, left her at the altar, got on a plane, and flew out of the country, did you not?"

Robert shrugged. "I did, and it was the worst mistake of my life."

"Your worst mistake? People decide to not get married all the time, but you call leaving her at the altar and not even calling her—"

Robert raised his voice. "I said it was a mistake."

Arian was silent for a few seconds. "Robert, are you a mercenary?"

"No, I am a troubleshooter, for government contracts mostly."

"For the government? Funny, I can't find anybody at the state department or anywhere else to corroborate that. Why is that?"

"Okay, I am a mercenary, just like JT Logan."

"So you lied to me, didn't you?"

"Yes, but I corrected it."

She nodded her head, started to walk away, but turned back. "As your best man, JT married your fiancée so her father could see her married before he died." She looked at the jury. "They fell in love—you really ought to hear the story. As I said, they fell in love and are still married today." She looked back at Robert. "Did you call JT later and apologize for what you did and, not knowing they had married or were still married, express your desire to get back with her and make it up to her?"

He sat there for a few minutes until the judge told him to answer the question. He looked at Arian and said, "No, I did not."

"You already lied once. Are you sure you're not lying now?"

"Objection, Your Honor!"

Arian looked at the judge. "Withdrawn. No further questions." She sat down at the table with Will, and he patted her hand and nodded.

JT leaned over to Will. "Why bring all that in?"

Will whispered, "Because it gives cause to why he is making this up, and because there are nine women on the jury." He winked at JT as he sat back.

Court was dismissed for the day and was to convene at nine the next morning. They walked out, and Will got in a limousine with his two associates, Arian, JT, and Jessie. When it pulled away, Will looked at Arian. "You did great. That will put a doubt in the jury's mind." He looked at JT. "Now, I have to know what your ace in the hole is before we return to the courtroom."

JT nodded. "I'll tell you at the hotel."

The next three days, the prosecutor tried to build his case by showing photos of the dead. He rested, and the judge told Will to call his first witness. Will stood up. "I call my first and only witness, Colonel James Thomas Logan, US Army."

JT got up, walked to the witness chair, and was sworn in. Will looked at JT. "How tall are you, Colonel Logan?"

"Six foot four."

Will nodded and repeated in the direction of the jury. "Six foot four."

Will looked at the judge. "Judge, what I have to say is long and tedious. If I may conduct a small demonstration, I can get through this to everyone's satisfaction in a few minutes."

The judge raised her eyes. "By all means, counselor. Let's take the fast road on this one."

Will had his assistant walk to the side of the courtroom opposite the jury. She stood up a life-size cardboard cutout of the man in the picture. Will looked at JT. "Would you mind standing next to the cardboard man, Colonel?"

JT walked over. Will had purposely made the cardboard cutout five foot nine as a contrast to JT's six foot four.

"Now, Colonel, would you strike a similar stance as the figure in the picture?" Will had told JT that calling him Colonel would make his high rank stick in the jury's minds. JT assumed a similar stance. Will said, "Hmm, something's not right." He picked up a pair of tan, baggy pants, walked over, and gave them to JT. "Put these on if you will." JT put them on over his pants, and he looked more like the man in the picture. Will then picked up a sack and pulled out a pair of tan boots. "Will you put these on, please?" When JT had done so, Will picked up JT's shoes and took them back to the desk. "Something is still not right. Mr. Logan, will you take off your coat?"

He did, and one of Will's assistants walked over quickly and took it from him. JT was wearing a dark green, short-sleeve, T-shirt-type dress shirt, and it showed his physique quite well. He looked even more like the man in the cutout.

Will nodded at the other assistant, who walked over with another sack and pulled out something dark. "Mr. Logan, will you allow my assistant to put this fake beard on you?" JT leaned forward so the man could stick it on his face. It looked like the beard on the cutout. The man then pulled out a black cowboy hat and sunglasses and gave them to JT, and he put them on. Will stood back and looked at JT, as did the judge and the jury. The prosecutor appeared to be getting nervous; he obviously knew Will wasn't going to prove his own client guilty, but that seemed to be exactly what he was doing.

"Your Honor, would it be all right with the court if I have Mr. Logan pull his shirt off?"

"Absolutely, if that's what you want."

The assistant came over and held JT's cowboy hat while he reached back and pulled his shirt over his shoulders. A murmur floated over the courtroom when they saw the whip scars on his back. JT put his hat back on and looked over his shoulder. He seemed to be a copy of the poster, except for the scars and being seven inches taller. Will walked forward. "Mr. Logan, how long have you had those scars on your back?"

"About four years."

"Did you receive them in service to your country?"

"Yes, sir, I did."

"Is that in your military medical records, Colonel Logan?"

"Yes, sir."

Will walked up and said to the judge, "I would like to enter Mr. Logan's medical record as evidence."

The prosecutor objected on the grounds that he had never been given this information in discovery.

Will looked at the judge and said, "It just came to us last night. I have over a one hundred witnesses who will testify that he had those scars four years ago and especially two years ago when that picture was supposedly taken. How many would you like me to call up, Your Honor?"

The judge looked at the prosecutor. "None. I'll allow it."

Will got up for his closing argument. "Ladies and gentlemen of the jury, the two facts I want you to concentrate on are these. One: two forensic scientist say the man in the picture could have been five feet, ten inches tall, give or take. Colonel Logan is six four. Two: Colonel Logan was hung by his hands and whipped with a bullwhip while a prisoner of war. Never mind the fact that he escaped and freed other prisoners and received this nation's highest award, the Congressional Medal of Honor, which was presented to him by the president of the United States. He didn't kill anybody except in defense of his life and those of fellow soldiers. You must find him not guilty. I see no other outcome."

The prosecutor made his closing arguments after Will finished his. He commented on casualties of war and emphasized that many of the dead were women and children.

The jury was out for less than an hour and came back with a "not guilty" verdict.

They went outside to a press conference, and Will spoke for a few minutes about people abusing the justice system at the peril of heroes like JT Logan.

JT stepped up to the mic. "All I have to say is remember the congressman that started all this, as well as the Democratic Party in general, when you vote next election. Many have already sent me a note of support, and I'll probably see a lot more now that the jury has spoken."

They all went home; JT wrote a check to Will for over $1.5 million. Arian went back to Atlanta, and Jessie and JT went back home. It was good that it was over.

* * *

JT got a call that afternoon from his congressman. "Mr. Logan. I received your request to have your nephew in the military academy, and I will gladly endorse it."

Wesley was ecstatic when he received his appointment.

JT was going to fly him to West Point, New York, to enter the academy. Wes's mother was flying out, and they were going to stop on the way and pick up Wanda and JW. CD wouldn't come.

When the time came, they went out to the Gulfstream at the airport next to Memphis International Airport. They flew to Owensboro, Kentucky, and picked up Wesley's aunt and uncle. Soon they were airborne again and then landing at a private airport in New York. They went through Reception Day, or "R Day" as they called it, and took plenty of pictures. On the return flight, JT sat by JW.

"JW, I owe you an apology for what I said—"

"No, brother, stop right there. I owe you a debt of gratitude for making me realize how dependent CD had made me. Thanks for saving me. I don't know how CD is going to do without the twin-brother gimmick. I suppose he's going to have to rely on God and his sermons, just like I am."

They had swapped seats to talk to each other, and after they had left JW and Wanda in Kentucky, Jessie came back to sit by JT. Carla was asleep in the front.

JT leaned over to Jessie. "Want to join the mile-high club?"

She grinned at him. "What if I'm already a member? Have you considered that?"

He shook his head as he laughed. "I don't think you had sex in an airplane with anyone else, and I don't think you're going to do it with me."

She laughed out loud, trying to hold it down so she wouldn't disturb Carla. "You're right on both accounts." She leaned over and kissed him.

As she nuzzled his neck, she said, "Wanda said that Carla has given some thought to divorcing CD, but her conscience wouldn't let her."

JT pulled back and looked at her. "Now, if there was ever a time for you to butt into my family business, it's now."

She laughed again. "Wanda and I are working on it."

JT glanced around the darkened plane. "I think CD needs some professional counseling."

Jessie nodded. "Carla says he looks upon himself as the ultimate counselor in the church, and he would seem weak if he went and got some for himself."

"He's going to lose that church if he doesn't do something. Maybe Carla can shock him into something if she tells him she will divorce him if he don't get some help." Jessie nodded.

When they got home, Dutch was sitting in the driveway waiting for them. Jessie and Carla went in the house, and JT and Dutch went to sit in the backyard. Dutch said in German, "Hey, boss. Margaret said you were due here tonight. Robert contacted me and asked if you were going to have him killed. He said he didn't blame you if you did but asks you to spare his family. I'll do it for $4,000." JT stared at him a minute. Dutch spoke again, still in German. "I have a family medical thing, and I need $4,000."

JT nodded. "I'll give you $5,000 to take him a message. Tell him I'll spare his family if he kills himself. He must do it in a public place, in front of people, to make sure they don't suspect me. If he doesn't do it, then you do it."

Dutch nodded, and JT went in the house, opened his gun safe, and took out $5,000. He went back out. "If you need more for medical problems, just call me, okay? Here's a .223 Robert left here. If you have to do it, kill him with his own rifle."

Dutch nodded. "Thanks, boss."

* * *

Jessie had a busy schedule between being a surgeon and a lawyer. JT felt he needed something to keep him occupied, since things were slow at the office. Jessie's house had acreage behind it with a greenbelt behind that, and he thought he might build a gym out there for his personal use. He talked to Jessie about it, and she said, "Yeah, go ahead. We can move if you want to, if you don't feel like this is your house."

"Nah, I wouldn't want to have to move all your clothes. That alone would take weeks, maybe months," he said, smiling at her.

She put her hands around his neck as if she were choking him. "You have to admit, I got rid of most of those clothes."

He pulled her close. "Yes, you did. This house is fine with me. I'll get a contractor, and we'll design it and get it built."

JT included a bathroom with shower in the man cave and had also discreetly built an underground shooting range beneath it. When it was done. JT enjoyed the gym, and he got Jessie to lifting weights. He also had an elliptical and treadmill installed.

One day, when JT was watching the national news, the reporter announced that Robert Mason, the man who'd accused Colonel JT Logan of genocide, had committed suicide in front of courthouse in the little town in Kentucky he lived in. JT raised his eyebrows. "Hmm, I'll be damned. He did it."

* * *

Two months later, JT received a special delivery letter from a special prosecutor appointed by some congressional subcommittee. She asked him to visit her at the Memphis Federal Building. The letter said that if he did not come of his own volition, she would have a warrant served on him.

Jessie had business at the Federal Building, so she went with him. When they walked in and asked for the prosecutor, the receptionist directed them to an office upstairs. They sat down and waited. After thirty minutes, JT went over to the woman at the desk. "Tell the special prosecutor to issue a warrant for me. If she thinks I'm going to sit at her beck and call, she's crazy as hell."

The woman stood up. "Just a minute, sir. Let me check." She went through the door behind her and was back in less than a minute. "This way, sir. She can see you now."

JT said to the woman as he passed, "I figured she could." They walked in, and a pretty woman in her early fifties stood up and greeted them with a nod. She wore a tan skirt and matching coat over a white blouse. She introduced herself as Colleen Broward from Washington, D.C. Then she looked at Jessie. "Who might you be?"

Jessie said, "I am JT's wife, Dr. Jessie Logan, and I am also an attorney. Is there a problem?"

Colleen raised her eyes. "A doctor and a lawyer ... what is your doctorate in?"

"Medicine."

Colleen turned back to JT. "Let me tell you why I asked you in. A Congressional sub-committee has appointed me to look into your kidnapping, raising-arms-against-friendly-nations, and other mercenary crimes. I don't know how you pulled off getting out of the genocide charge, but I am going to nail you to the wall. Mr. Logan, I'm going to put you in prison for the rest of your life, and I have enough evidence to jail you until you're past the age of dying. Do you have anything to say?" She sat there with a big smile on her face.

Jessie stood up. "Let's go, JT."

JT stood up and looked at Colleen. "You haven't got shit. If you did, you would have me arrested. All you can do is threaten and run your mouth."

Jessie grabbed his sleeve. "Let's go, JT. Don't say any more."

Colleen stood up. "You pushed Robert Mason too far. He gave me dates and details. I don't know how you pushed him into killing himself, but I'll find out."

When they got home, he called Arian, and she contacted Colleen and told her to route any inquiries about JT Logan through her office.

Arian kept JT informed of what they were doing. Three weeks later, she texted JT and said she would be in town the next day because they had a meeting with Colleen at ten thirty. She arrived at the house at nine o'clock and sat down. Jessie had canceled her appointments so she could be there.

Arian looked at them. "I don't know what she's got. She doesn't have Robert, that's for sure. Unless she has someone else, nothing she contends that you did is substantiated in any way. I think this is coming from that congressman that lost his ass in the polls. He needs to get something stirring until after the election. It should quiet down until just before the election. We'll see when we meet with her in the morning."

The next morning, the three of them drove down to Colleen's office. Colleen didn't keep them waiting this time. They went in and sat down. Colleen drummed her pencil on her desk before saying, "Mr. Logan, I have irrefutable evidence of your kidnapping three adults in three different countries and a child in Saudi Arabia. This is going to be a long and drawn out, so I would prepare for it."

Arian spoke up. "If you will give us the information, we will answer it in due time. If you've called us up here to talk about what you might have, this will be the last time we will come in voluntarily."

Colleen looked at Arian and then back to JT. "Now, can you tell me if you were in Morocco anytime last year?"

Before JT could answer, Arian said, "He can't say anything because he is a contract agent for the CIA. He can't tell you because it might damage national security."

Colleen narrowed her eyes at him. "Is he saying—"

Arian interrupted. "He's not saying anything. You know that information on national security is protected by—"

"I know what it is protected by, counselor. Does your client have anything to say?"

Again before JT could say anything, Arian responded. "No. Let's go, JT. We're through here." They got up and left.

When they got in the car, JT looked at Arian. "What was that about? She didn't tell us anything."

Arian smiled. "She just wanted to get your reaction to her statements about having evidence. You didn't give one that I could see—good job." JT thought about it on the drive back as Jessie and Arian talked.

When they got back to the house, Jessie offered to let Arian stay with them. "No, thank you, Jessie, I'm going to try and catch the eleven-thirty flight back to Atlanta."

After she left, JT went out on the porch and dialed Scottie.

"Hello. What's up, boss?"

"Scottie, I have a special prosecutor after me saying some really stupid things. She says she has evidence of me kidnapping people, raising arms in foreign countries, and so forth. She's getting it from somewhere. I know Robert's not doing it, but she's getting information from someone. Are all the goats in the pen?" Scottie would know JT was asking if there'd been any personnel changes.

There was a long pause. "No, boss. One goat got out. I would have a hard time believing ..."

"Check it out anyway, and let me know."

"Sure, boss. Right away."

It was two weeks before JT heard back from Scottie. "Hey, boss, we found the goat that got out. It was dead. Looks like some wolves or something got it before we could get there. We couldn't hardly recognize it."

JT knew the man who had left had turned for personal profit, and Scottie had killed him or had him killed. That would also send a message to the rest of the team.

"Thanks, Scottie. Let me know if you hear anything else."

"Sure thing, boss."

Nothing happened on the case until one day JT heard tires squealing in the driveway. He grabbed his gun and started to the back door. A car squealed to a stop, and Colleen jumped out, followed by what he assumed were two investigators working for her.

JT dropped his gun in a magazine rack by the door. He opened the door and stepped out, and Colleen slapped him before he could stop her. She looked at him with fire in her eyes. "You bastard, you had Robert killed so he wouldn't talk, you had Johnny Webster killed so he wouldn't talk, and now you've taken my daughter. I'll have you jailed for the rest of your life if I don't kill you myself."

JT stood there with blood running down his chin from his mouth. He turned so the security camera could see it. He let her stand there and saw her chest heaving with heavy breathing. "First, Ms. Broward, I think Robert committed suicide. That's on a video if you want it. I didn't know Johnny Webster was dead and don't know why he would be dead. Next, I realize your privileges of being a special prosecutor, but I don't think hitting someone you're trying to prosecute is legal, nor is threatening to kill them."

One of the investigators smiled at him. "We didn't see or hear anything."

JT replied coolly, "Thank God for security cameras, huh?"

The smile left the man's face as he looked up and spotted the camera.

"Now, I'm going to tell you something you're not going to believe, but I have no knowledge of anything about your daughter. I didn't take her."

"Liar!"

"You had better leave, Ms. Broward, and take your two guard dogs with you."

The FBI showed up the next morning to ask him questions. They came in and sat down, and the one who introduced himself as Terry Bradford said to Jessie, "Ma'am, if you will excuse us, we need to talk to your husband alone."

She stared back at him. "Mr. Bradford, I am an attorney, his attorney when his is not available. Speak your mind in front of me, or leave my house."

He raised his eyes and nodded. "Okay. Mr. Logan, Special Prosecutor Colleen Broward says you had her daughter kidnapped. Any truth to that?"

JT stuck pressed his lips together and shook his head but said nothing.

Observing him carefully, Terry said, "This looks pretty bad. If you did have something to do with it, we'll find out, sooner or later."

JT nodded his head. "You're welcome to look."

Terry looked a little peeved, probably because he couldn't read JT. "You haven't bothered to deny it. That seems strange."

JT yawned as though he were sleepy. "I didn't kidnap her daughter."

Terry nodded and then said, "I understand Ms. Broward assaulted you in her rage last night. Do you want to press charges? She can be held accountable for her actions."

JT looked over at Jessie, and she nodded slightly and wrinkled her brow. He then said to Terry. "No, sir. I understand her news about her daughter made her act irrationally."

Terry nodded again. "That's awfully nice of you. She'll be happy to hear that. Well, Agent Jenkins, I guess we're through here. Sorry to bother you folks." They got up to leave, but Terry turned back before he got to the door. "We'll be in touch if we have more questions."

JT didn't hear anything else until two days later his phone rang. "Hello."

"Mr. Logan, this is Special—"

"What do you want, Colleen? We're wasting a lot of time using titles and last names."

There was a pause. "First, I want to apologize for hitting you the other night. Second, I want to thank you for not charging me with assault. You can still do that, and you might want to. I'm not letting up on this. Also I want—"

"Colleen, I didn't have your daughter taken, and I don't know where she is. I'm considered a bad person and cold-hearted sometimes, but that would be low, even for someone like me. By trying to pin the disappearance of your daughter on me, you're allowing whoever took her to get away with it. I don't do things like that, and I don't do the things you're trying to charge me with. Go on with your prosecution, but you're going up a dead-end ally, and you're going to be disappointed."

JT could tell she was sobbing. "Someone told me that you freed kidnapped people. Is that true?"

"That's something you're going to have to address with my attorney."

"JT, I'm just seeking information that might help my daughter."

"Colleen, did you not just get through saying you were going ahead with this investigation?"

"Does that mean if I drop the investigation, you'll help me?"

"No, Colleen, I'm not going to help you under any circumstances. Can you understand that? I don't know anything about your daughter." JT hung up the phone.

Jessie walked up behind him and put her arms around him. "You should have had her charged for hitting you. I looked at the video on that—she drew blood."

JT turned around and put his arms around her. "Honey, I hope you believe me when I say I didn't have anything to do with her daughter. I can't help her because that would be considered an admission that I had her daughter kidnapped, and I didn't. Besides, if I put her in jail, they would just get another prosecutor."

She kissed him. "I believe you because you can't lie to me worth a damn. I can see it in your eyes when you're not totally forthcoming with me." He was glad she was the only one.

Two weeks later, Arian called and told him there was going to be a hearing the following Friday. "Word has it that Colleen has a witness that saw you in Morocco on the date the woman was kidnapped."

JT thought a minute and said, "We'll see."

He called JW. "I was wondering if you would do something for me."

"Sure, if I can."

"I am being accused of something I didn't do. I need you to come help discredit a man that's going to lie about me."

"How can I do that?"

"Just sit behind me in the courtroom. He has to positively identify me, or it won't mean anything, and I promise you I haven't done anything he says I have. I'll send a plane for you Wednesday night and take you back anytime you want. Bring

Wanda and the girls with you if you can. We would like to see you all again."

"I'll see what I can do, JT."

That Wednesday night JT and Jessie were sitting at the airport when the Lear came up to the hanger and cut its engines. JW and Wanda got off, followed by their two daughters, and they all hugged.

As they drove back to the house, JT asked the girls, "What do you want to do while you're in Memphis?"

The older one, Brenda, who was sixteen, said, "I want to see Elvis's house."

JT laughed. "I wouldn't mind seeing that myself."

Brenda's mouth dropped open. "You live in Memphis, and you've never been to his house?"

JT shook his head. "Nope, but he's never been to mine, so I would say we're even." They all laughed.

The younger daughter, who was twelve, said she wanted to see the Peabody ducks and the Mississippi River.

Jessie smiled. "We can take care of that."

* * *

On Friday, JT walked into the courtroom and sat by Arian. JW sat behind him. When they called the witness to the stand, he wouldn't look at JT.

Colleen walked up to him. "Do you mind if I just call you Mr. Abdul? I can't pronounce your last name." She smiled at him.

He smiled back. "That is most certainly permissible."

"Mr. Abdul, do you recognize the man you saw in Morocco in this courtroom?"

Abdul glanced at JT, and when he saw JW behind him, he looked panicked. Colleen turned toward JT and saw JW at the same time. She turned to the judge. "Your Honor, this is outrageous. It's trickery and shouldn't be allowed."

The judge looked down at her. "What are you talking about, Ms. Broward?"

"They have brought in a look-alike to confuse my witness."

The judge asked JW, "Sir, what is your business in this court?"

JW stood up. "I'm here for moral support of my brother, sir."

The judge gazed at him a moment. "Are you twins?"

JW shook his head. "No, Your Honor."

The judge said to Colleen. "There's nothing illegal about that. A little suspicious maybe, but not illegal."

Colleen turned back to Abdul. "Can you point out the man you saw?"

Abdul began to sweat. He looked at the two men and pointed at JT. "That one."

Colleen said to the judge. "No further questions."

Arian got up. "May I call you Mr. Abdul also?"

"Oh, yes."

"Mr. Abdul, how can you be certain it's this one?"

"Because he is sitting at the table."

Arian frowned, and Colleen closed her eyes and winced as though she had a headache. Arian walked over beside him and turned back toward the two men. "Can you tell if you can spot which man it is, just by his looks?"

Abdul looked at her. "Oh, no. That's impossible. They look just alike to me."

Arian suppressed a smile. "Mr. Abdul, were you promised asylum if you testified for Ms. Broward?"

"Oh, yes, I—"

"Objection, Your Honor."

The judge smiled. "Sustained, counselor, sustained. Ms. Broward, are you through with this witness?" She nodded, and the judge told Abdul he could step down. "Next witness, Ms. Broward?"

She looked at him for a few seconds. "May I have a brief word with my associate?" The judge nodded and looked at his watch.

Finally Colleen turned around. "Your Honor, we're dropping the charges against JT Logan for lack of ... credible witnesses. Two have mysteriously died, and this one has been compromised by deceit."

The judge hit his gavel on the bench. "Then this hearing is dismissed." They got up and walked out. Jessie hugged JT, and JW shook his hand. They walked out front, and JT's car was brought around.

Colleen walked up to them. "That was pretty shrewd, Mr. Logan, but I could get your brother on perjury. You two are obviously twins."

JT shook his head. "He wasn't under oath, and we're two-thirds of a set of identical triplets, but I was saving that for the next time you tried to railroad me."

She acknowledged his barb with a rueful smile and then said, "Can I talk to you alone about an unrelated matter?"

"Not alone," JT said. "I think I prefer to have counsel present."

Colleen nodded, and she, JT, and Arian walked a few feet away from the car. She looked at Arian and back at JT. "I was told that you did, in fact, rescue kidnapped people. I looked into Trans Global pretty closely."

JT nodded, but kept his expression solemn. "Obviously you did, if you could get one of my men to lie about me. I don't appreciate that."

She looked down and back up. "I need help to locate my daughter. If you are an expert at that, I need you, and I'll pay whatever you ask."

JT shook his head. "There's no way I can help you. I would expose myself to future prosecution all my life. I don't trust you, and I can't help you."

She had tears running down her face. "Can you give me any advice, any help at all?"

JT knew he should walk away but said, "How long has she been gone?"

"A month."

"Have you received a ransom demand?"

"No, I would have paid it."

"Where did she disappear from?"

"She and some friends went to Rio for the carnival."

JT told at her, "She was probably kidnapped and sold into the sex trade if there's no ransom."

Colleen sat down on the steps as she hyperventilated. JT looked at Arian and said, "Give me paper and something to write with." She handed him a notebook and pen. He wrote something down, tore the sheet out, and handed it to Colleen. "Here is the name and number of a man who does that kind of work. Maybe he can help you, but I can't." He helped her up, turned, and walked away.

Since the court session had ended so early, they went back to the house to pick up the girls and took them to Graceland and then to the Peabody. Afterward they drove down to the river, and the girls stood there in awe. They must have taken three dozen pictures each of the rushing water.

On the ride back, JT asked Brenda, "Where are you going to college?"

She shrugged. "I want to go to Yale, but Mom and Dad says that's out of our reach, so I may just go to UK."

JT shook his head. "No, don't compromise your goals. Shoot for Yale." She smiled.

Later that evening, Jessie and Wanda were in the kitchen, and JT and JW were in the den. JT looked at his brother. "I appreciate what you did today."

JW smiled. "I owe you ... a lot."

JT smiled back and said, "I'll pay for your girls to go to college, wherever they want to go. Encourage them to reach for the stars. I'll send you $240,000 for each of them."

JW's eyes got moist. "Thanks, brother. I appreciate that."

In the next few weeks, Scottie conducted two more extractions, and they netted another ten million. JT approved the plans without going to Europe.

* * *

Jessie and JT were sitting in the den a month later, curled up in a blanket together in front of the fireplace. The back doorbell rang, and JT got up and saw it was Colleen.

"Shit, I thought I was through with her." He opened the door and invited her in. It was just before Christmas, and the weather was cold. She walked in, and JT told her to go over by the fireplace to get warm. She looked drawn and ten years older than when he'd last seen her.

She said to them, "I know I'm the last person you expected to see, but I'm desperate. I need your help."

JT took in a deep breath. "Colleen, the only way I can prove I didn't take your daughter is to not help you. I'm open to prosecution for the rest of my life if I do. Did you contact the man I told you about?"

"Yes, and he asked why you would recommend him since you had a hundred times the resources he has. He said everything looked suspicious, so he turned me down."

JT stood up. "Wait here; let me make a phone call." He walked into the bedroom, shut the door, and dialed a number. "Pathfinder? I have a situation I need to get out of." He gave Pete the details of being prosecuted and why he couldn't take the case even though he knew he could find her if she was still alive.

Pete was quiet for a few minutes and then said, "If you want to help the lady, you only have one recourse—do it for free. You're right; she can bring charges if you ever take a nickel in payment."

JT thanked him. Pete was quiet for a second. "Say, boss, whatever happened to that situation with that girl I told you to marry?"

JT smiled. "I married her, fell in love with her, and we're still married."

"Well, I'll be damned." The phone went dead.

He walked back into the den. "Colleen, I'm having someone find out all the information I can on these girls. I need names, pictures, and anything else you can get me. I can't promise you anything."

She nodded. "I'm going to Rio over Christmas to show her picture around and see if I can find anyone who recognizes her."

JT shook his head. "Don't do that. You will run people underground that can give us information. Don't go down there, okay?"

She looked at JT. "Then I'm going back to Alexandria, Virginia, where I live. Call me the minute you hear anything, please."

After she left, JT called Scottie. "I have another extraction. Come see me."

"Will do, boss."

Three days later, Scottie drove up. He and JT shook hands. "What's up, boss?"

JT motioned with his head. "Let me show you my workout room." He took Scottie into the garage. They walked through to the area where his man cave was. It had a couch, a couple of chairs, and, of course, a big-screen TV.

JT sat down and turned to Scottie. "Here's the thing. We have six eighteen-, nineteen-year-old girls abducted on a trip to Rio a month and a half ago. The parent hasn't received a ransom note, so you can guess what that means."

"Sex trade?"

"I need someone down there immediately, sniffing around. We have to locate them if they're still alive. This will be a civilian operation because military gear would stand out like a candle at midnight. A girl named Broward is the main one I'm looking for. The others are extra if we get them out."

"What's the pay-off?"

JT looked down at the floor and back up before answering. "Base it on five million. I'm paying for this one because I can't take a dime for the Broward girl."

Scottie frowned. "Why?" JT explained how if he ever took money and she was released, he could later be charged with the abduction because it would appear he'd staged it to get paid.

"It would be circumstantial evidence, but people have been convicted on less."

"Okay, boss, I'll get Dutch down there today."

"What's Dutch's family medical problem?"

"His little girl, eight years old I think, has leukemia."

"Make sure her bills are paid, and let me know if you need the money."

"Will do, boss. He's too proud to ask, and he's almost broke due to the bills."

Four days later, Scottie sent a text. "Located, in 3, <>." JT knew he had located the girls in three separate places, but there was a problem he couldn't discuss.

JT sent a text back. "Solution arrival imminent, wait." He was telling Scottie he was on his way.

Jessie cried when he told her he was going to Rio. "Sweetheart, I don't intend to get involved if I don't have to, but they have run into a problem, and I need to go. Six girls down there are being sexually abused and may be in danger of dying if they're not dead already. I'll be careful."

She looked up through her tears. "If you get killed, I'll kill you again when you get back."

He smiled and kissed her. "I'll send a message or call you when I get a chance. Don't call or text me."

* * *

Thirty-six hours later, his commercial flight touched down in Rio. Scottie was waiting. "What's the problem?"

Scottie answered after they got in a dilapidated old car and drove off. "They've been sold off and split up. Four girls are in two separate places in the red-light district, and two girls are out in the boonies a few hundred clicks. The bad guys are in constant communication with one another. We have to hit all three at once. I'll lead one team. The other teams will be split between Bad Billy and whoever you recommend to lead the third team." He looked at JT.

JT narrowed his eyes. "So you need a team leader, is that it?"

"Yes, boss. We are stretched with one full team going on one and the other team being split in half. Dutch would normally do it, but he ain't thinking straight because of his little girl being sick."

"Why one full team on one?"

"That's the one that's out in the bush. We may have to fight our way out."

JT nodded. "Where is the Broward girl?"

"Don't know, boss. We have to get them all out to see."

"Okay, which team do I take in?"

Scottie asked, "Are you sure you want to do this?"

JT looked at Scottie and said dryly, "We don't have a choice. If we did, you wouldn't have sent for me, correct?"

Scottie nodded. "Sorry, boss. I want you to take the A team in. We don't need to be in contact with each other until we get back. We just need each team member in contact. These radios are set up for the A team, these for the B team, and these for my team. We leave in various delivery trucks that will be stolen literally minutes before we need them. They frisk everybody at the door, so we have to go in shooting, locate the targets, and move out. We will have a 'customer' go in and put invisible ink on each girl's forehead. It can only be seen when you shine one of these lights on them. Every team member will have a light. Any questions?"

JT studied the part of the map that covered the area where his team would be. "I assume this is the easiest and safest one by virtue of the fact you gave it to me. Where do I really need to be, the C team?"

Scottie shook his head. "Team A and Team B have a 60 percent chance at success. Maybe 70 percent now that you're going. C Team has a 40 percent chance of success, and I'm the extraction leader, so that's the one I'm taking. Good luck, boss."

JT said, "If I get killed, you better die too, or my wife will be looking for you."

Scottie laughed. "Nobody dies on this one, trust me."

JT smiled. "I do. I feel good about this. Get the A team in here and let me go over it with them."

JT met with the men and was glad to see Dutch on his team. He suspected Scottie put him there to watch out for him. JT looked at the group and then pointed at a map. "From what I see, we have armed guards here, here, and here. Are they in uniform or civvies?"

Dutch replied, "Civvies, but they're easy to spot. They're armed with .223s."

JT snorted. "I'm glad our government isn't letting the Russians arm all the bad guys in the world. At least our weapons are being put to good use. Dutch, I'm going to take out this man and this one. You take out these two, and, Charles, you and Gunter take out the one out back. Come in the back and take out anybody between the back door and these rooms, whether they be bad guys or customers. We'll come in the front and take out these four, or is it two?" JT looked at Dutch.

Dutch shrugged. "Sometimes it's two, and sometimes it's four."

"Let's plan on seeing four," JT said. "We'll move down the hall. Remember, take out every man you see. If he's a customer, he needs killing for being in a place like that, and that will ensure us that no one is behind us. Make sure we don't shoot each other. Have your lights on your heads, and grab every girl with ink on her head. Any questions?"

Charles held up his hand. "There are a few girls in there to control who does what, and they can easily be mistaken for the dolls doing business. How do we handle them?"

JT pursed his lips. "If there's not any doubt, kill them. If there's any doubt, kill them anyway. I'm not losing anybody because we're trying to separate the sheep from the goats. What else?"

Charles held up his hand again. "What if we know for sure some of the girls are captives like ours? Do we leave them? Take them? Kill them?"

JT looked at him. "If you are 110 percent sure, I'll leave that up to you. If you're 1 percent wrong, you may die and cause others to die. We can't take very many more than the ones we're after. Understand?" Everybody nodded.

The next afternoon, a half hour before sundown, a covered truck pulled into the warehouse. Written in Portuguese were the words "Soap & Cleaning Supplies." Dutch looked at it and laughed. "That may give us away, because I'm pretty sure they're not going to be expecting cleaning supplies. That's the nastiest place I have ever been in."

JT smiled as Charles and Gunter got in the cab of the truck. JT and Dutch sat on opposite sides near the back. A cloth hung from top of the truck cover to the floor; it was tied to the tailgate keeping it from flying open and revealing their cargo. The truck drove out of the warehouse and down some of the roughest streets known to man. The road got so rough that occasionally JT would peek out the back to see if they were on paved roads.

Eventually, JT gave Dutch the signal to saddle up. He pulled out a ten-round magazine, shoved it into the handle of the .40-caliber Glock, and racked the bolt. He ejected the magazine and replaced the round in the magazine that he had put in the chamber. He then replaced the magazine and put the silencer on as he watched Dutch do the same. Finally, the truck came to a stop in a ghetto-looking neighborhood. The houses were built next to each other, and the street was narrow. Before JT could pull the curtain aside, it was torn open by someone on the outside. JT found himself staring at two men armed with automatic rifles. He shot each of them in the forehead and jumped out. When he looked around the side of the truck, the two men Dutch was supposed to take out came running. JT shot them both in the head, and they dropped like four hundred pounds of mud.

Dutch jumped out, and he and JT walked in the front door. JT shot the bartender and two men with guns on their belts. As he was doing that, he heard the *zip, zip* of Dutch's silencer and saw two men drop. Dutch then shot a man sitting at a table having a drink. They moved immediately to the curtain covering the hallway to the back. Dutch stepped ahead of JT, Dutch's silencer went off twice, and then they both heard a silencer go off in the back. He knew Charles and Gunter were in the back door.

A door opened suddenly, and a man came out swearing in Portuguese. JT stuck the silencer barrel under his chin and pulled the trigger. The bullet exited the top of the man's skull, leaving a splatter of blood on the ceiling. The dead man stood there, JT pushed him back, and he collapsed into the room. Three men sat at a table counting money. JT shot two of them of them, and they hit the floor. JT saw his bolt was open and was lucky the third man was in shock and just raised his arms instead of reaching for a weapon. JT ejected the magazine, slammed another in, racked the bolt, and shot the third man as he sat there with his hands up. JT went over to clean up the bodies by shooting all three in the head.

As he turned to leave the room, plaster exploded from the wall, and a sharp pain and warmth spread under his left arm. He felt the area with his right hand; there was blood, but it wasn't a lot. He left the room and saw Charles herding five girls. Two of them had ink on the foreheads. Dutch turned and made the sign for Gunter and Charles to take them to the truck. JT nodded, pointed at Dutch, and motioned him to follow him. They went back into the room and found a duffel bag on the floor full of US currency. JT raked everything off the table into the duffel bag and motioned Dutch out. Dutch stopped and looked in another bag that was full of powder JT was sure was cocaine. Dutch raised his eyebrows.

JT motioned with his head and said, "Bring it."

Dutch grabbed the bag with the drugs and took point as they put five girls in back of the truck. They were the last two in, and JT was startled by Dutch's gun going off by his ear. He looked out the back and saw two men collapsing in the street. Dutch glanced at JT and shrugged his shoulders, telling him he didn't know who they were, but he wasn't chancing it. JT nodded in approval. JT gave the bag, which JT estimated had about $600,000 in it, to Dutch. "A bonus for your little girl." Dutch said nothing but got misty eyed.

They took off for the warehouse, and as they drove, JT immediately started throwing bags of cocaine out the back. Some burst, and some didn't, but all of a sudden there was a sea of people blocking the road for anybody who might try to come after them.

The ride back to the warehouse seemed to take forever, especially since his wound was starting to hurt. He could feel blood soaking his shirt. Finally, they pulled in and the door came down. When they got out, B Team was already there. Bad Billy came up. "Anybody hurt?"

JT said, "Yeah, me, dammit." They took him over to the area they had set up for first aid. Billy cut his shirt off and examined the wound that was slowly seeping blood. He looked up at JT. "The bullet went through your lat. It's an in and out and didn't hit a rib, so Conrad will stitch you up and put a bandage on it. You'll live."

Conrad held up a syringe, but JT shook his head, so he stitched him up with just a local anesthetic. He gave him an antibiotic shot, put a good bandage on the wound, and gave him another shirt.

JT asked Bad Billy, "Did you get your pigeons?"

He nodded. "Two of them and one extra."

JT walked over, looked at the girls, and asked if any of them were named Broward. They all shook their heads. As he turned to go back, he heard the *zip* of a silencer. He instinctively pulled his gun up. Dutch had shot the extra girl they had brought with them.

JT looked at him. "What was that about?"

"I was watching them. These others had fear in their eyes, and the fifth one smiled like she was happy, so I knew she was dirty." He turned to the girls. "Was she a bad guy?"

The girls, all looking relieved, nodded.

JT told Dutch, "Start interviewing the pigeons and see what you can come up with."

JT walked over to the door behind Billy, who was looking out a peephole. "When are they due back?"

"Twenty minutes ago."

"When are they going to get here?"

"Right now. Raise the door." The door went up, and the truck came in. Scottie's team unloaded three girls. Two had the ink on their heads. JT went up to them. "Are any of you Broward?"

"Who are you?" one of the girls asked.

He smiled. "I'm the guy that your mother sent to bring you home." She started crying.

Scottie walked over and said, "Okay, let's get these stolen trucks out of here in ten-minute intervals."

After the last truck left, Scottie came up to JT. "You did okay I see. Anybody hurt?"

JT opened his shirt, and Scottie saw his bandage. "Oh shit, that means we're in trouble with your wife, doesn't it?"

JT smiled. "I am, at least."

Dutch walked over. "How did you get hit? I didn't hear a gun go off."

JT said, "Either one of the bad guys was using a silencer, or I was shot by one of my own men."

They all looked around at the rest of the team, knowing the bad guys didn't have silencers, and then at each other.

"Don't worry about it—it's minor." It had to have been a case of accidental friendly fire, since all team members were more than capable of a kill shot if that had been the intent. "The fallout from my wife is going to be a different story." They all laughed.

They gave the girls some decent clothes to put on, and they all stayed in the warehouse. They could hear sirens screaming throughout the night, but none came near the warehouse.

The next morning, three of the men slipped out, returning an hour later in cars. They pulled in at five-minute intervals so they wouldn't attract attention. Scottie stepped up and said, "Listen, everybody. We're going out in fours. JT is going to be the first one out because he's been shot, and he's taking the Broward girl with him, Dutch, and Gunter. The cars will be back, so don't get antsy. Let's go." JT walked the Broward girl over to the first car, helped her into the back seat, and then crawled in behind her. They gave her a hat to pull down over her face. Gunter was driving, and Dutch was up front beside him. The car headed out of Rio and eventually came to a small airport that had a twin-engine Cessna. They all four got in, and a man gave JT an envelope with fake passports for him, the Broward girl, Dutch, and Gunter.

JT told her, "You're going to have to be calm at all times. The authorities are looking for someone who's nervous. We are father and daughter here on vacation. Let me do the talking. In fact, when we come up on anybody, just put your head on my shoulder and pretend you're asleep." JT texted Colleen and asked her to come to his house, saying he had some information for her.

* * *

Thirty-six hours later, the plane touched down in Memphis, after several stops in South America and Mexico. The Range Rover was waiting for them. JT's side was really hurting, and he was a bit light-headed. He figured it was psychological because he was afraid to tell his wife he had been shot.

When he got out of the car, Jessie bolted from the open doorway and kissed him. He winced as he felt her weight in his arms. She pulled back. "What's the matter?"

"Nothing serious ..."

The Broward girl looked at Jessie. "He's been shot."

Jessie took on a mean look. "Where? How serious?"

He opened his shirt and glanced down; red bloomed against the white bandage. He could feel the fire shooting from her eyes.

He leaned down to kiss her, but she pulled back. "Don't kiss me. I'm mad at you. You said you wouldn't participate. You said you wouldn't go on another extraction. You lied to me." She pulled back and hit him in the stomach with her fist. She then hit him on the right shoulder with her fist. She stepped up and drew back her fist again, but she stopped, put her arms around him, and kissed him as she cried. He just held her.

He gently pushed her back. "This is Colleen's daughter. She needs something to eat and some rest."

Jessie went over and hugged her. "I'm sorry. What is your name, dear?"

"Kathleen, but most people call me Kate."

Jessie smiled as she hugged her again and then led them both inside. "What would you like to eat? If we don't have it, I'll go get it."

Kate's eyes got big. "I would really like a pepperoni pizza."

Jessie smiled and picked up her phone. She pushed a button and ordered a pizza, cheese bread sticks, cinnamon sticks with icing on them, and a three-liter bottle of Coke.

JT raised his eyebrows. "You have the pizza company on speed dial?"

She shot him a "you're not out of the woods yet" look, and he decided dietary advice could wait.

Jessie took Kate into a bedroom and gave her a gown to sleep in. She smiled as she pushed the young girl's hair back. "Take a shower, and the pizza will be here by then."

JT walked into their bedroom and suddenly felt drained and a little dizzy. He lay down across the bed and dropped off to sleep. He awakened to Jessie unbuttoning his shirt. He held his arm over his head as she pulled the bandage off.

He winced. "Damn, are you taking the skin off too?"

"Shut up, or I'll really hurt you. Have you been given an antibiotic?"

He felt weak again. "One with the stitches."

"Did they put you to sleep?" He nodded.

She went to the refrigerator and came back. She swabbed his shoulder and gave him a shot. She gave him a second shot, but before he could ask her what it was for, he was unconscious.

It was light when he awoke; he had apparently been asleep all night. He got up and half-showered, careful not to get his bandage wet. He saw under the tape signs that iodine had been applied.

Jessie came in as he stepped out of the shower. He looked at the wound in the mirror. "When did you put the iodine on it?"

She crossed her arms, still looking mad. "In the middle of the night you bled a little, so I redressed the wound."

He asked, his expression serious, "You're not going to divorce me over this, are you?"

She broke out laughing. "Quit saying things that make me laugh. I'm trying to be mad at you."

He smiled. "You deserve to be, and I deserve whatever punishment you have for me." He held up her chin. "Honey, there was no other way. I had to do it or leave her down there, I promise you."

"I believe you," she said, smiling even though tears filled her eyes. "I need to quit thinking about what might have been and be thankful you're alive." She kissed him again.

* * *

He got dressed and went into the kitchen. Jessie was preparing his favorite: scrambled eggs, bacon, sausage gravy, and cold cantaloupe. She even had ketchup on the table.

They saw Colleen drive up, and Jessie went to get Kate. JT opened the door, and Colleen rushed in. "I came straight from the airport. Do you have any information about my daughter?"

Before he could answer, the second bedroom door opened, and Kate stepped out. Colleen looked at her and covered her mouth with both hands as tears ran down her face. She finally ran to Kate, who met her halfway. They hugged, kissed, and cried, and then Colleen said to JT, "I owe you—"

JT interrupted. "You don't owe me anything, remember?"

She smiled through her tears. "I was going to say a debt of gratitude, but that seems so little. This wasn't free, so who paid for this?"

"I did. Let's leave it at that."

She nodded. "Did any of the other girls get out?"

Kate nodded. "All of them. They rescued all of us, and Mr. JT got shot during the rescue."

Colleen looked at him in shock.

Jessie walked to JT's side, pulled up his shirt, and said, "He'll live—if I don't kill him myself." Then she waved them all toward the kitchen table. "Come sit down before it gets cold."

Kate ate like there was no end in sight. Colleen and Jessie drank coffee. Kate and Colleen watched JT put ketchup on his scrambled eggs, and Jessie looked at them and winked.

Colleen ran her hand down the back of her daughter's head. "Get your things; we need to catch a flight to DC."

Kate looked somewhat sheepish. "This is all I have. I didn't have this much until Mr. JT gave me some clothes." A tear escaped.

Jessie said to Colleen, "Get her home and have a thorough exam done. Do you want me to give her an antibiotic shot now?"

Colleen nodded. "That would be nice of you."

Jessie walked out and came back with a syringe.

Kate's eyes got big. "Have you done this before?"

Colleen laughed. "She's a doctor, honey. She's done it many times before."

As Jessie gave Kate a shot, JT walked up to Colleen and said, "What I did for your daughter is what I do for a living, nothing else, okay?"

Colleen nodded, and then she and Kate said their good-byes and left to go buy some clothes before they got on the plane for home. As they walked out the door, he heard Kate say, "I saw them kill some men. I've never seen anybody die before."

Within minutes, Jessie's phone rang, and JT heard her say, "Well, CD, that's a choice you're going to have to make." Her gaze drifted up and met JT's cold stare. "Well, he's standing right here. Hold on." She handed JT the phone.

He heard CD's voice on the other end. "JT? Look, I don't want to be difficult, but Wesley said he wants to spend Christmas at your house if you'll let him. I want my boy home for Christmas."

"CD, that's between you and him. Whatever you decide is good with me."

CD was silent for a minute. "If you give him a choice, he'll stay with you. I want him here—it's important for his mother's well-being. Please make him come home."

"I'll see that he comes to your house for Christmas. He might come here for a day or two, but I'll make sure he's home for Christmas."

"Thanks, JT." The phone went dead.

The next day JT's phone rang; it was Wesley. "Hey, cadet," JT said, "what's up?"

"Nothing, JT. I'm going to be a little forward here, but can I spend Christmas at your house?"

"No ... you can come by for a few days, but you need to spend Christmas with your family."

Wesley was quiet for a few seconds. "I guess Dad has already called you, huh?"

"Wesley, you know your dad doesn't tell me what to do. It's only right you should be there. Do you realize how hurt your mother will be if you don't come home?"

There was another long pause. "Yeah, JT, you're right. I'll be there on the twentieth."

"Good enough, cadet. I'll send your ticket to your iPhone."

On the twentieth, Wesley arrived at Memphis International. He looked good in his uniform. JT hugged him and took his bag, and they got in the car and drove off. They got home and talked into the night. Eventually, Wesley said to JT, "I know I need to go home, but I dread it so much. I want to see my mom ... and even my dad some. I don't want to hash this over about the academy. I'm there, and I'm going to stay there."

JT nodded. "You may have to tell him that, but I think your dad has changed some. Give him another chance, okay?"

JT took Wesley to the airport the next evening. He had him in a first-class seat. Wesley promised to come back to Memphis on his way back.

Jessie and JT started decorating the house for Christmas that night, and Jessie said, "I never did this before. I just took gifts and spent time with each of my sisters. If you weren't on speaking terms with family, what did you do for Christmas?"

He smiled as he looked down at her from the ladder he'd been using to hang a garland. "The last six or seven years I spent my Christmas aboard a cruise ship. All the food you want, gym, and a nice bed to sleep in."

"That's the saddest thing I've ever heard. You spent every Christmas alone?"

JT smiled. "I didn't say I was alone."

She narrowed her eyes as she tried not to smile. "Did you find a different person each year, or did you have an annual thing with someone?"

He looked at her out of the side of his eyes. "I am good friends with a couple, and seven years ago, he got a chance to go hunting during the Christmas holidays in Alaska for bear, caribou, wild chickens, or something. He was in a dilemma—go hunting, which he loved to do, and spend the first Christmas in twenty years without his wife, or stay home. She wanted him home but knew what an opportunity this was for him. I suggested she go on a cruise with me, and they both agreed to that. I told them it was a double-occupancy cabin, but we would have two beds. That didn't bother him because he knew me, and he certainly knew her.

"That went on for five years until he had a knee replacement year before last and couldn't go hunting. He told his wife that he looked forward to spending Christmas with her. She looked at him and said, 'Maybe you can't go hunting, but that won't stop me from going cruising.' She went with me that year, and last year I talked him into going. I think they will be spending all their Christmases on cruise ships now."

Jessie asked, "Were you ever tempted with your friend's wife?"

"She was my friend too. In fact, I knew her before she married him. She told me once that he asked her if we ever got physical, and she looked him in the face and said, 'If we had, I'm the kind of person that wouldn't say anything.' She never did tell him otherwise."

"So, did you ever mess around with her?"

JT shook his head. "Nah, we really were friends. That's all."

They spent the next two days decorating, shopping, and buying food. She was going to have her sisters and their kids over for Christmas for the first time.

* * *

Christmas Eve, JT went to work out in the gym. As he was coming back to the house, he saw Jessie standing in the kitchen, crying. He rushed in, and tears were pouring down her face. She tried to talk but couldn't.

JT grabbed her by the shoulders. "Jessie, what's wrong? Tell me."

She regained a little bit of composure. "Wesley ... killed ... in a car wreck. A drunk driver ..." She collapsed, but JT caught her before she hit the floor. He laid her on the couch and sat in the chair staring out into the cold gray of the winter. His ears rang, and his vision was blurry. He sat there for what seemed like an eternity. Jessie finally got up but couldn't seem to stop crying.

JT called Carla Christmas Day "Carla, do you feel like talking?"

"Yes, JT."

"What happened?"

"Wesley got home, and he and CW seemed to get along fine. They had a nice long talk. I was so happy for both of them. Yesterday, Wesley decided to go meet some of his friends at the mall, drove my car, and a man ran a red light and hit him broadside. JT, the man had nine previous DUIs, and he was on his way to a work-release program for repeat offenders. He was drunk and speeding when he hit Wesley."

"Carla, let me talk to JW and see what plans they can make, but Jessie and I will be there as soon as we can, okay?"

"Please do. Please hurry."

JT called JW. "JW, I know how many commitments you must have as a pastor and it being Christmas, but as soon as you can, you need to see CD. I'm afraid he's going to feel Wesley's death is his fault."

"Why would he think that if it was a drunk driver?"

"Wesley wanted to come here for Christmas, and CD wanted him at home, I think more for Carla's sake than his. He went home and died, and I'm afraid CD will look at it that way. As soon as you know, call me, and I will text you the tickets."

JW said, "Okay, bye." JT could tell he was crying.

JT called his pilots. "I have an emergency trip to LA. Fly us out, and you can come back. I'll be there for several days, and if I can get a commercial back, I'll take it, but you may have to come get me."

"Not a problem, JT. We'll meet you at the airport in two hours. The plane is fueled and ready, but I have to file a flight plan."

"Sounds good."

JT and Jessie packed and then drove to the private airport near the main airport. Jessie called her sisters, explained what happened, and told them to go to the house and take all the food and presents that she had bought for Christmas. Then JT pushed a button on his phone and started speaking in German. "Dutch, I have another side of my house that needs work. Can you meet me in LA as soon after Christmas as you can?"

"Sure, boss. I'll see if they have anything for tonight."

"No, stay there with your little girl for Christmas. That's an order. I'll go ahead and transfer the money to your account."

"Thanks, boss. I could sure use it."

When JT hung up he could feel Jessie looking at him.

"Stop it, Jessie."

"Stop what?"

"Staring at me."

"Are you going to kill the man that ran into Wesley?"

He was silent. He thought she had the greatest intuition he had ever seen. "No, I'm not going to kill him."

"What are you going to do, JT?" She was sounding alarmed.

"I'm going to make sure he never drives again. His walking again may be in question also."

"JT, you wouldn't do that to another human being, would you? You can't do that. Let the law handle it."

"He's not a human being. He's a nine-time loser, and the law can't stop him. They put him in jail nine times, and he got out. If they put him in jail again, he'll get out again and again." He paused, and then said, "I have to do this. That's why I don't want you knowing about this stuff. You don't need to know."

* * *

They touched down at a private airport outside of LA. They got in the car waiting for them and drove to CD's house. When the door opened, Carla fell into Jessie's arms. JT kissed her and went in search of CD. He found his brother in the den, just sitting and staring.

JT walked in. "CD, can I talk to you?"

CD shook his head. "I don't feel like talking right now."

"You need to talk to me."

CD shook his head, and the tears started down his cheeks, which were already wet. "If I had let him go to your house ..."

"I thought you might think that way. Look, CD, there's drunk drivers everywhere. You were right to get him to come home. This is where he belongs. I understand you and he got along when he got here."

CD sort of smiled. "Yeah, actually we did. We hadn't talked like that in forever. I guess it was because I listened like you told me to do. I wish I had done that a long time ago."

JT shook his head. "Don't think about what could have been or what should have been. We should have done things different too, but we didn't. We wasted a lot of good years."

CD just nodded.

JT stood up. "Let me go talk to Carla a minute. JW will be here as soon as he can make arrangements."

He walked into the kitchen. Jessie was sitting with her arm around Carla as she cried. Carla looked up at him. "I should have let him come to your house."

"Don't start thinking like that, Carla. It just so happens that I was going to tell him he had to come here anyway, even if CD hadn't asked me to. I would feel as bad as you do, but I know you can't predict drunk drivers."

She nodded. He walked back in and talked to CD until two in the morning, when Jessie finally came in, saying, "Carla wants us to stay here. She's in bed."

JT stood up. "CD, go to bed and try to get some rest. You're going to need it for the next few days. I know you think you can't sleep, but you'll be surprised."

As CD got up and walked to his room, Jessie handed him a pill. "Here, take this."

The next morning, Jessie and JT woke up around nine o'clock. They jumped up, showered, and went downstairs. CD and Carla were still asleep.

The next day JT and Jessie went with CD and Carla to make funeral arrangements. As they talked to the funeral home director, JT's phone rang. It was Dutch, so JT went outside to answer it.

"I'll be there tomorrow, boss. What do you need?"

"My nephew was hit and killed by a drunk driver that had been cited nine times for DUI already. Look at the papers or the news, and find out who he is."

Dutch was silent for a moment. "Do you want him dead?"

"No, I want him to suffer for the rest of his life. I don't want him to be able to walk again, much less drive, understand?"

"Not a problem, boss."

A few days later they sat with CD and Carla after the funeral, watching TV. JW and Wanda were there by then. The news came on, and the anchor talked about Justin Carroll, the man involved in a deadly DUI accident that had killed a young West Point cadet home on leave. A reporter standing in front of a hospital looked into the camera and said, "Justin Carroll was found badly beaten outside a tavern early this morning and was rushed to the hospital. He's in critical condition, but doctors expect him to pull through. Doctors say his spine was broken, and they don't think he will ever walk again."

CD said, "I know it's wrong to think like this, but I wish he'd been killed. He took my son." He began to cry, as did Jessie, Wanda, and Carla.

JT shook his head. "Nah, he won't be able to walk again, much less drive. He'll spend the rest of his life in misery and pain, sitting in some government housing somewhere. He'll have to be fed baby food and have someone clean him and wipe his ass for the rest of his life."

CD nodded and smiled ever so slightly.

JT looked at Jessie, and she turned away.

They all stayed with CD and Carla another four days and then went home.

On the flight back, Jessie was unusually quiet. JT asked her, "Is this going to change our relationship? I'm sorry, but that's what I do."

She looked over at him. "What exactly do you do?"

Without making eye contact, he said, "I right wrongs that the law or government won't. I'm comfortable with what I do. If you're not, then we need to discuss that and plan accordingly."

"That's not fair, JT. I can't see how you can intentionally cripple a human being. I know something needs to be done, and I know no one else will make it right. I can't see living without you, so I'll have to learn to live with it, but I'm a doctor. I try and heal people, help them mend, and you tear people apart, literally."

He looked at her then. "You make it sound like we are on opposite sides of the same coin. Do you realize he was free in less than a week after hitting Wesley?"

She sat there quietly for a long time. "I realize what you do has to be done. I always thought there was some mystical person or entity that did it, and I never had to know."

They sat silently for a while. Finally she reached over and held his hand, and they sat that way for the rest of the flight.

CHAPTER 9

A month later, JT was at the Wolfchase Mall doing some shopping when his phone rang. A voice he didn't recognize asked, "Are you JT Logan?"

"I am. What can I do for you?"

"I travel quite extensively, and I was in Germany last week talking to an old friend, Freidrick Schell. He told me you could help me."

"Depends. What do you need?"

The man paused and then said, "I live in Memphis. I'm afraid my son-in-law is going to kill my daughter. I've seen bruises, busted lips, and she has had to have dental work done. I've reported it to the police, and they tell me she has to do it. When I confront her, she says it's her fault for making him mad. She won't file charges."

JT thought a minute. "Send me the details—names, pictures, addresses—and let me have someone look into it. I'll let you know."

Sounding somewhat relieved, the man said, "My name is Jonathan Prevost. I'll get this all together for you, but where do I send it?"

"Call me when you get it together, and I'll tell you where."

Jonathan said, "If you can help, you need to hurry, please."

JT shook his head even though the man couldn't see him. "I never hurry in matters like this. The wrong people can get hurt. I won't waste any time, though."

That night, JT called Margaret. "I need a contact in records in the Memphis Police Department."

Margaret was silent for a minute. "Here it is: Rachel Gomez, single mother, four kids. She needs money. I'll text you the number."

"Thanks, Margaret. The next time I get married, I want it to be you."

She laughed. "You couldn't handle me."

He laughed too. "You're probably right."

JT contacted Rachel and asked if she could get him information. He told her he was willing to pay, and she readily agreed to email him all the domestic violence sheets on Jonathan's son-in-law.

Jonathan called, and JT told him to send the information to a post office box. JT picked up the package few days later. He contacted Freidrick Schell and asked about Jonathan. In all his checking and cross-checking, everything seem to check out. He felt sure he wasn't being set up.

JT found the abusive son-in-law, whose name was Glenn Francis, and followed him one morning to work at Kellogg's and then after work to a bar on Winchester Road; it wasn't a good part of town. He sat and watched Glenn, go in, stagger out a few hours later, get into his old pickup truck, and drive home. The next day, JT rented a Mazda with a fake ID Margaret had sent him. He again followed Glenn, who repeated the same routine of work, bar, and home. He lived in a nice neighborhood in Collierville, near the Mississippi–Tennessee state line; JT figured his father-in-law had paid for it.

On Saturday, Glenn's routine changed. He drove out of his garage on a big Harley. The street seemed to vibrate when he thundered by. He went straight to the bar and was in there most of the day. When he came out after dark, Glenn was so drunk JT didn't see how he kept from crashing at every corner.

The next Saturday, JT went into the bar and sat at a table in the back. An hour later, Jonathan came in, slapping friends on the back. The waitress walked up to JT. "Hey, cowboy, I can't make no money off what you're drinking."

JT asked her, "What does a gin and tonic cost?"

"Seven fifty. Want one?"

JT then asked, "What does a club soda cost?"

"Dollar fifty. Want one?"

"Bring me club sodas, and I'll give you seven fifty apiece for each one. You pocket the rest. I'll tip you up front." He handed her a hundred-dollar bill. "Will you do that for me?"

She slipped the hundred in her pocket and looked down at him. "Hell, mister, I'll blow you for a hundred dollars." She smiled and walked away. She kept the club sodas coming until, just after dark, Glenn staggered to the door. JT got up and went out the other door. He drove to an intersection he knew Glenn would go through and killed the lights of another rental car.

When Glenn drove toward the intersection, JT started the car, took off across the street, pulled up beside Glenn, and cut his wheel into Glenn hard. Glenn's Harley jumped the curb and went down an embankment into a drainage ditch. Glenn was thrown from the bike. JT stopped at the curb, turned the rental car off, and jumped out. He looked around while pulling on a pair of leather gloves; no other cars were around, so he ran down the embankment. Glenn was trying to get up in his drunken stupor. JT slugged Glenn, who hit the concrete ditch hard. He had his right leg up on an old tire and wheel. JT stomped it, and Glenn screamed as the leg broke.

JT reached down, took the helmet strap off, and threw the helmet down the ditch. He kicked Glenn, broke his jaw, and knocked him unconscious. JT picked up an old metal fence post and broke Glenn's right arm. He rolled Glenn over on his stomach, picked up a large riprap rock used to line the creek, and hit Glenn in the spine with it. He didn't move.

JT made his way back up the bank and ducked when he got to the top as a car drove by. He got in his car, sat down, and dialed 9-1-1. When the police arrived, he told them that a motorcycle had hit his car and careened down the ditch. The police officer keyed the mic on the applet of his shirt. "I need backup and a bus just east of Winchester and Holmes." He got his flashlight and started down. When the other police car pulled up at about the same time as the ambulance, JT pointed down the hill.

The first police officer finally came back up the hill. "Where do you live, Mr. Logan?"

"Germantown."

"What are you doing here tonight, sir? You're a long way from Germantown."

"I was checking on my plane at the airport and was headed home."

"Is this your car?"

"No. Thankfully, it's a rental. Good thing I took out full coverage."

The police officer wrote up his report and had JT sign it. The other officer came up the hill. "Drunken fool. I don't care that he nearly killed himself, but he fucked up a good-looking Harley."

Nothing else was said, and JT left. He drove off and threw the leather gloves to a homeless man sitting behind a dumpster at a convenience store. Early the next morning he drove down to Regional One hospitalHospital. Many Memphians jokingly referred to the city hospital as the Memphis Knife and Gun Club because it was where people that were shot or stabbed were sent. They were considered one of the best trauma units in the country, though.

JT walked up to Glenn's room, turned on the bright light that the doctor used for examinations, and pointed it into

Glenn's eyes. He slapped Glenn awake, and the man came out from under the anesthetic enough for JT to lean down. "If I ever hear of you hitting your wife again, I'll do worse than this. Do you understand?"

Glenn was in a stupor; he nodded but couldn't focus, so JT walked out. An hour later, he knocked on Jonathan's door; the man was obviously surprised to see JT. He looked back into the house and then stepped out. "Is there anything wrong?"

JT said, "Your son-in-law had a motorcycle accident. He's at Regional One with a broken leg, a broken jaw, and a broken arm, as well as spinal and head injuries. He's been warned."

Jonathan nodded and held up a finger to indicate JT should wait while he went inside. He came back out with a briefcase. He pulled out several clumps of money with paper wrapped around them and handed them to JT. "Three hundred thousand dollars. Is that right?"

JT nodded and looked at him. "He's going to spend the better part of a year recovering, if he can recover. This would be a good time to convince your daughter to make your son-in-law your ex-son-in-law." Jonathan nodded, and JT left.

CHAPTER 10

JT was in a store in Collierville a few weeks later when he overheard one man talking to another. "Our church may have to close. We went through a split in the membership, and half of them left, as did the preacher. We're down to less than two hundred members, we can't afford the note we took out to build the new building, and we certainly can't afford to pay a pastor who's worth his salt. I guess we'll all look for another church."

JT had an idea, and he turned to the man. "Excuse me for overhearing you conversation, but may I ask what church you're talking about and where it's located?"

The man shrugged. "It's not a secret. It's the Locust Valley Baptist Church about three miles east of Cayce, Mississippi."

JT nodded. "Who is the head deacon?" He was given the number of Jim Frazier, and he arranged to meet him at the Cayce Fire Department, where he was a volunteer firefighter.

"Mr. Frazier, I heard about the troubles in your church, and I might be able to help you out. The deal is, I have an older brother that preaches at one of those mega-churches in California. You know, has about five thousand members. I think he's about burnt out and needs a fresh challenge with a smaller congregation. If he met your needs as a pastor, I would pay his salary until the church was built up enough to afford to pay him. I'll buy the church and surrounding land and sell it back to the church when it's financially stable. Does that appeal to you?"

Jim looked shocked. "How could it not appeal to me? You're an answer to prayer, a real answer to prayer."

JT smiled. "I don't think so, but look, here's a folder on my brother, his education, background, and there's a couple of CDs with several of his sermons. Look at it with your deacon body and church family if you wish. My number is on the outside, and if this is agreeable to you, then I have to do the hard part—convince my brother this is a good idea. I can't promise anything." JT smiled.

Jim took out the contents of the envelope. On top was a picture of CD and Carla. Jim looked at it and back at JT. "You're twins, I assume?"

JT smiled. "No, sir. He and I are two-thirds of a set of triplets. I'm not a preacher, but my two brothers obediently followed in my father's footsteps and heeded the call to preach. My father said God called me also, but I was just too stubborn to listen, so I'm considered the black sheep of the family."

Jim looked through the contents and back at JT. "Where does you other brother preach?"

"He has his own church in Owensboro, Kentucky."

The man said, "This is Wednesday, so tonight I'm going to hijack the service and have a business meeting. I'll let you know something tomorrow." They shook hands, and JT left.

He wanted to call CD and Carla, but he knew he had to wait until after the church decided to accept his offer. The next morning about quarter past seven, Jim called. "I hope I'm not waking you, Mr. Logan."

JT smiled, "No, Jim, you haven't woken me, and please call me JT."

"Well, JT, the church unanimously voted to accept your offer, if you can convince your brother that God has a place for him here in Mississippi."

"I'll let you know, Jim, as soon as I hear something."

JT waited until Jessie got home from the hospital. He brought her up to date on what he had done. She stared at him for a minute. "That's perfect! That will revive him and give him a new purpose and may just save his life and his marriage. Call him right away. Can I tell Carla?"

He hesitated and then shook his head. "I'd wait. What if she thinks it's a great idea, and he turns it down? It could hasten the end of the marriage." She agreed.

JT went to his man cave in the garage, sat down on the sofa, and dialed his brother. "CD, I need to talk to you about something." He laid out his plan to CD with all the details and waited for a response.

Finally, CD spoke. "You know, JT, I was just going to talk to Carla about resigning. I'm done here. This sounds like a door God has opened for me. Let me notify the deacon body, resign as pastor, and I'll be there."

"Great, CD. I think you are doing the right thing. Why don't you fly out as soon as you can, and we'll look for you a place to live?"

"Okay, JT, let me run all this by Carla." There was a long silence. "Thanks, JT ... for everything."

"Not a problem, big brother. Look forward to seeing you soon."

CD and Carla moved to Collierville, Tennessee, and pastored the church just across the state line in Locust Valley, Mississippi. Their youngest son stayed in California and attended seminary there. JW came to visit CD with JT the second Sunday CD was at the new church. CD had made no mention of them being triplets. JW walked out to CD's pulpit and made announcements and then looked out over the congregation, saying, "I am not CD Logan. I'm JW Logan, CD's brother, and, no, we're not twins. I didn't mean to deceive you but to remind you to always seek God's purpose for you in life, because the devil will deceive you whenever he gets a chance."

CD came out to the applause of the congregation and said, "I would like to ask my other brother, JT Logan, to come up." JT walked up to the applause of the congregation also.

JT and Jessie continued to attend her church because JT didn't think attending CD's church would be a good idea because of their history.

CHAPTER 11

JT was sitting on the patio when his phone rang. The caller ID said it was Aunt Billie. He answered the phone. "Yes, ma'am?"

"This is your aunt Billie, JT. I understand you have made amends with your brothers. You've missed the last twenty Logan family reunions, so I expect you at this year's reunion. Now I'm an old woman, but I'll still take down your trousers and whip you. Do you understand?"

JT had to struggle to keep from laughing out loud. "Yes, ma'am, I'll be there. When is it?"

"It is going to be on Mother's Day weekend in May at the Hidden Springs Convention Center. I want all three of you there."

"Okay, you can count on me and my wife, but you'll have to threaten CD and JW yourself, though. I can't be responsible for them."

"Oh, don't you worry; I'm going to call them next."

"Say, Aunt Billie, how many people show up to these things nowadays?"

"Well, let me see. My records show there were seventy-eight there last year. I'll know by the end of March. Why?"

"Well, I thought I might have T-shirts printed up with the Logan coat of arms—you know, that red and yellow thing with all the flares and the knight's helmet above the heart with three golf tees through it."

"First, they're not golf tees—they are spikes. Second, who's going to pay for eighty or so shirts? I don't know how big a seller they will be or if you can get your money back."

JT laughed. "I wasn't going to sell them. I'll pay for them and give them away. Is there any way you could guess their sizes?"

Aunt Billie was silent for a few seconds. "I'll send out written registration slips this year. I'll tell them if they want a shirt, I had better have their commitment and shirt size by March fifteenth. That'll get them to commit. You're a good boy, JT, and I take back all those mean things I thought about you all those years."

"Thanks, Aunt Billie. Are you still a size medium?"

"Young man, don't start with me."

JT laughed. "No, ma'am, I won't. Get me the information as soon as you get it because it may take some time to get that many ordered."

On March 18 Aunt Billie sent JT a list of people and their sizes. JT went down to a trophy and sports apparel shop near the University of Memphis to order the shirts. He decided on a summer jersey with the Logan coat of arms on the front and the words *Logan Family Reunion* on the front and back. They were going to be white with the coat of arms in yellow and red and the letters on the front and back in Kelly green. He gave the man a copy of the coat of arms he wanted, plus a list of sizes with a few extras of every size. Aunt Billie had told him that Bubba Logan would take something that would look baggy on a horse. "He weighs four hundred pounds at least," she'd told him.

He asked what the largest size he could get was, and the man told him it would be an eight-X. He ordered it. The man added up the cost and looked up at JT. "You know these jerseys are playing-quality jerseys that a football team would use, don't you?"

"No, but that's what I want."

The guy told him, "This jersey is right at a hundred dollars. We're talking about $8,900."

JT nodded. "Great. Can you get them by May first?"

The man nodded. "I'll have to have the money up front for an order that size."

JT smiled. "Fair enough. Do you make them here or have them made somewhere else?"

"Oh, for this artwork, I'll have to have them printed in St. Louis and shipped here."

"How much more would it cost to have them sent to the Hidden Springs Convention Center in Los Angeles?"

The man shook his head. "I'll ship them there for that price."

JT gave him his credit card.

JT looked up the Hidden Springs Convention Center on the Internet. He went ahead and booked the two best suites they had and noticed they had a heliport. He asked if he could land and park a helicopter there, and they assured him he could.

That spring, JT and Jessie decided to go out a few days early. They arrived at the Memphis-Arlington airport, east of Memphis. There sat a refurbished Vietnam-era Huey painted black. It had the First Cavalry logo painted on the nose. They drove up to it to unload the luggage.

Jessie got out and put her hands on her hips. "Okay, who does this belong to?"

JT smiled. "Me. Is there a problem?"

"You know, there is nothing about you that would surprise me anymore. You never mentioned you owned a helicopter."

JT glanced briefly at her. "Well, it never came up in conversation before, and I bet I can surprise you. We're coming back by submarine."

She looked at him with raised eyebrows. "Seriously? I don't know whether to believe you or not, but if anybody could own a submarine, it would be you."

He was laughing by now. "You know, for a lawyer, you're pretty gullible."

She came around the car as if she were mad, and he grabbed her and kissed her. CD and Carla drove up with JW and Wanda. They loaded the luggage in the wire carrier under the belly, and he helped them in. He slid the doors shut, went around, and got in the left seat. Jessie was in the front beside him. He showed them how to put the headphones on and explained they were voice-activated, though if a control tower called in, it would pre-empt any conversation going on.

He started the rotors and brought them up to speed, he pulled up on the collective, and they lifted off. Wanda said over the headphones, "When we drove up, I saw you kissing. How long are you going to act like newlyweds?"

Jessie replied, "We'll always be newlyweds."

CD's voice came over the headphones. "Say, that would make a good sermon."

JW laughed and said, "I was thinking the same thing."

They flew toward California, stopping to fuel up occasionally. They landed and stayed overnight in Albuquerque. As they flew into the area south of Los Angeles, they heard a voice from the control tower come over the radio. "LA EX to helo niner-three-niner-six, come in."

JT answered, "This is helo niner-three-niner-six. Go ahead, LA EX."

The voice came back. "We have a 1320 heavy that doesn't have a green landing gear light. Could you climb to fifteen thousand feet at a heading of 280 and see if you can see if his gear is down?"

"Sure thing, LA Ex. I'll let you know."

Jessie looked at him and asked, "What's the problem?"

"There's a jumbo jet that doesn't have a green indicator light showing that his landing gear is down. We're going to take a look for him."

Jessie asked, "Is there any danger? Can you fly that fast?"

"Yeah, he'll be going as slow as he can, and I'll be going as fast as I can."

About twenty minutes later, JT spotted the plane. He flew under it and looked up; all the landing gear appeared to be down. He keyed the mic on the joystick. "LA EX, this is niner-three-niner-six. I have a visual on 1320 heavy, and all the gear looks down. I can't guarantee it's locked, but it's down."

"Thanks, niner-three-niner-six. We'll take it from here."

JT replied, "No problem, LA EX. Niner-three-niner-six, out."

Jessie asked, "Why do you pronounce nine as niner?"

"Because a nine and a five sound alike on the radio." She nodded in understanding.

He swung the ship around and headed for the convention center. He came in at a hover, and a man guided him down with flashlight landing lights. He set the Huey down and waited for the main rotor to stop. When it did, an eight-passenger golf cart came driving up. The driver greeted them with a smile. "Hop on, and I'll come back for your luggage." He took them to the registration desk.

Aunt Billie was there arguing with the desk clerk. She was a short, heavyset woman just barely able to see over the counter. JT walked up behind her and interrupted her tirade. "When you get through with this old lady, could you help me, please?"

She stopped talking, turned around, and when she saw it was him, slapped his chest. He stepped up and hugged her. She hugged CD, Carla, JW, and Wanda. She turned to Jessie, and JT took Jessie's hand. "Jessie, this is Aunt Billie. Remember, she's not as gruff and mean as she sounds. She's really a pussy cat."

Jessie smiled as she hugged Aunt Billie. Aunt Billie stood back and looked at her. "Well, you're a nice-looking woman. There has to be something wrong with you for you to become a Logan. I figured he would bring a Puerto Rican midget with a wooden leg or something. I figured that's all who would have him."

Jessie laughed. "I've been a Logan all my life. My maiden name was Logan also."

Aunt Billie turned back to the clerk. "Now, are you going to find me a room, or am I going to have to kill you?"

He smiled. "I'm sorry, ma'am. We have no record of your reservation. Did you receive a confirmation?"

"No, I figured you knew what you were doing. If you don't find me a room, I'm sleeping in the lobby on a couch."

The clerk was clearly trying to keep from laughing. "I'm sorry, ma'am, but we are booked up with the reunion."

She put her hands on her hips and glared at him. "You wouldn't have a reunion if I hadn't organized it, so you better get me a room if you want to see it here next year."

JT asked the clerk. "You don't have anything available?"

The clerk checked the computer and said, "I have a king suite left."

Aunt Billie shook her head. "I'm not paying $400 a night for a room."

JT laughed. "Put her in the king suite, and put it on my bill."

She looked at him. "Thanks, but are you sure?" When JT smiled and nodded, she said, "You must be loaded then; I never thought you would amount to anything."

JT smiled as he finished filling out the registration. "I married a wealthy woman."

Billie walked off. "I wouldn't be telling everyone that if I were you. You have absolutely no shame."

JT took Jessie to their suite. JW and Wanda shared a suite with CD and Carla. When they got to their rooms, their luggage was already there.

They unpacked and started down to eat. They knocked on the brothers' door and then Aunt Billie's.

When they opened their doors, JT said, "We're going down to eat in the restaurant. Do ya'll want to go? My wife's buying." Everybody smiled but Billie.

She shook her head. "Let me get my purse."

JT looked at Jessie and winked. "What do you need a purse for? I'm buying, and if you needed anything out of it, it would take you an hour to find it, as big as that purse is."

She went back into her room, got her purse, and came out. As she shut the door, she told Jessie, "He's about to get on my last nerve. You better control him."

Jessie laughed. "Yes, ma'am. I'll watch him."

JT asked Aunt Billie when they got on the elevator, "Is your room okay?"

She shook her head. "That room is big enough to hold the reunion in there. What do I need two bedrooms for?"

JT smiled at her. "It's either that or the couch in the lobby. If you come across another old lady that needs a place to stay, let her have the other room."

She turned and glared at JT. Jessie stepped up. "JT, quit teasing her—can't you see she's had a rough day?"

Billie looked at her with approval. "Thank you, dear." She turned toward the elevator door. Everybody could see the smile on Aunt Billie's face in the reflection of the elevator door.

They got a table and ordered, and then JT asked Aunt Billie, "How old are you now, Aunt Billie?"

She sat up proudly. "I will be eighty-three on my next birthday, thank you."

JT frowned. "That's impossible. You were eight-three when I was a kid."

Everybody was trying not to laugh, and Billie told Jessie, "I promise you, I'll hurt him." With that, all six of them started laughing, unable to contain it. Billie smiled also. Billie and JT clearly loved to spar verbally with each other.

After dinner, they went over to the convention center. The manager there showed them the registration desk and told them the boxes that had been shipped in were in the storage room behind the desk.

JT looked at the door. "Open it up—I want to see the shirts." The manager unlocked the door, and Billie took the key. JT went in and found that all the boxes were marked as to the sizes that were in them. The shipment included everything from toddlers' and children's shirts up to the single box marked eight-X. JT opened a box marked three-XL. He pulled one out, and it really looked good, so he put it on. "How do I look?"

Everybody applauded with a bit of sarcasm. JW examined the shirt. "These are not shirts, they're jerseys and must have cost a fortune."

JT gave CD and JW a jersey out of the same box, but they were too big. He exchanged them for an XL, and they seemed to fit perfectly.

JT said to Billie, "So you're not a medium anymore. What size are you?"

She looked at him with a straight face. "You get out of here and stand by the registration desk. The sizes are marked, so I'll get my own shirt." She pointed out the door. Jessie got jerseys for herself, Carla, and Wanda, and then they all walked out. Billie locked the door and put the key in her oversized purse.

She looked at the six of them. "I'm going to need help on registering tomorrow. You six have been nominated, and I voted on you myself, so you're hired. We need to be down here by eight in the morning, so don't stay out late. What am I talking about? We have two preachers and a half-wit. Ya'll be in bed by dark."

Jessie was laughing so hard she had to hold onto JT.

JT laughed along with the others. "Okay, but if the room is rocking, don't come knocking."

Billie asked Jessie, "Is he always this vulgar?"

Jessie shook her head. "No, this is one of his good days."

The next morning, JT and Jessie were awakened by someone pounding on their door and calling, "Up and at 'em! We got to go get ready." They got ready and met the others downstairs. It was 7:03 when JT looked at his watch and said, "I'm going for breakfast—ya'll do what you want."

They all walked down and went through the breakfast buffet. Billie finished first and left for the registration desk. The reunion seemed to give her a reason for living. She always started on planning the next year's reunion the day after the last one was over.

Jessie had her laptop with the list of all the family members who were registered. She sat at the desk as family members started to arrive. Carla and Wanda helped anybody who had not registered. JT, along with CD and JW, handed out jerseys. Before long there were white jerseys everywhere with "Logan Family Reunion" printed across the front and back.

JT heard Billie say, "There's my baby boy!"

JT looked around and saw the biggest man he had ever seen. It was Bubba Logan. He was in an old, faded pair of overalls, and JT figured it was because not many clothes would fit him. When JT walked up and shook Bubba's hand, Bubba looked at him with a confused expression.

JT smiled. "I'm JT, and that's CD over there and JW over there." Bubba smiled as he nodded. JT motioned to Bubba. "Come back here with me for a minute." He took Bubba in the storage room and got the box marked eight-X. He opened it, took out the huge jersey, and gave it to Bubba. "Try this one on, Bubba."

Bubba pulled the jersey on, and it was slightly big on him. He smiled and seemed to have tears in his eyes. Bubba looked at JT. "I know you've been helping Grandma Billie out with her house and things. I want you to know I appreciate that."

JT nodded. "Sure thing."

Everybody was registered, including a few stragglers. JT looked at the convention center. It had a stage on the left about three feet in elevation. There were five rows of bleachers across the back opposite the stage, and the floor could be filled with chairs if needed.

The disc jockey was setting up on the stage, and lunch was being set up on the floor in front of the stage. JT saw CD and JW going out the door on the opposite wall in somewhat of a hurry. He wondered what was going on, so he walked over. As he rounded the corner into a small hallway used for bringing catered food into the convention center, he saw CD and JW between a man and a woman.

She had blood running from her nose and an eye that was swelling. CD was telling the man that under no circumstances should a man hit a woman, especially his wife. CD spent five minutes preaching and telling him he needed to get right with God. Then JW took over and told him, as a certified family counselor, he needed help and urged him to let him set it up. He told the man what it would entail.

When they finished, JT stepped up and slugged the man, who catapulted into a stack of chairs and fell to the floor with chairs falling down on him. CD and JW gasped in shock.

"JT, you shouldn't have done that," CD said. They went over and helped the man up as JT stepped up again.

"How do you like getting slapped around by someone tougher than you? I'm going to have family be on the lookout for bruises and busted lips on her, and if I hear of it, I will come back to California, find you, and break both your legs and both your arms. When you heal up from that, I'm going to find you and do it again. Do you hear what I'm saying?"

The man nodded and then tilted his head back, holding a handkerchief over his bloody nose.

JT looked at him just before he turned to go. "Don't ever touch this woman again in your lifetime. I can't stop you from touching her, but I can do something about how long your lifetime will be." The man nodded again.

JT took the sobbing woman by the arm, gave her his handkerchief, and led her out of the hallway. They walked away, and JT stopped when they got to the back near the bleachers. He looked the woman in the face. She looked down at the floor, and he lifted her chin until their eyes met. "This is not the first time this has happened, is it?" She shook her head. "How long have you been married?"

She blotted the blood under her nose. "Eight years."

"This has been going on for the better part of the eight years, hasn't it?"

She nodded. "It's gotten worse lately."

JT said, "I hate to tell you this, but it's not going to get any better. You can have him preached to and counseled all you want, but it's in his nature, and if you don't get out, he's going to kill you someday. Do you understand what I am saying?" She nodded again, and he looked her in the eyes again. "I know this kind of man, and he won't stop hitting you. Get out of this marriage."

CD and JW had walked up and were listening. When the woman walked away, CD protested, "JT, you can't do that. You shouldn't advise her to get a divorce; you should be helping them get through this, and you certainly shouldn't have hit him. That was ... totally unacceptable."

JW looked at JT and nodded. "He's right, JT. This man needs help."

"You two should continue to help him, and I'll help the lady. I bet that punch did more good to correct the situation than your preaching and counseling. Let me know when he calls back and asks for prayer and counseling to heal his marriage, and I will apologize ... to all of you."

* * *

Jessie walked out in front of the convention center; the sunshine felt so good. After a few minutes, she turned and walked up a ramp that led into the convention hall and the bleachers.

Aunt Billie was standing there behind two women. She turned as Jessie walked up. "You're just in time, my dear; these two ladies were admiring your husband's ass."

The two women dropped their jaws and blushed. Jessie stepped up behind them, looked out, and saw JT talking to CD and JW with his back to them. "It's okay, Aunt Billie. There are women admiring his ass every day. It's nice, isn't it?" she asked the two women.

One of them said, "I apologize. I didn't know anyone was behind me." She looked over at Billie with a slight glare.

Jessie smiled again. "It's okay. Just don't look too long. It'll make your panties wet." She winked at them.

Billie sniffed. "You're as vulgar-talking as your husband."

Jessie smiled at Aunt Billie. "Oh, don't tell me you didn't look at a man's ass back in your day."

Billie narrowed her eyes. "I still do, including my nephew's, but I don't talk about it." She turned and walked away as Jessie and the two women laughed.

* * *

JT talked to Billie about the woman who was beaten by her husband, and Billie said she would check on her regularly. Aunt Billie said she was Linda Logan and that her married name was Simpson now.

JT went outside just after dark, looking for Jessie. He saw Linda sitting on a brick wall and walked over. "How are you doing?" She just nodded and looked away. "Where's your husband?"

She shrugged. "He got in the car and left."

He asked, "Where are you staying tonight?" She shrugged again.

He helped her up. "Come with me." He walked back in and ran into Jessie looking for him. He introduced then and told Jessie what had transpired. "Put her in our suite."

Jessie walked her up to the suite and put her to bed in one of JT's T-shirts. Jessie came back down, they walked to the restaurant again, and they sat at a table and ordered. Billie came in and joined them without being asked. JT warned her, "My wife and I were just going to discuss doing some nasty things to each other."

Billie frowned at him. "Talk nasty to each other when I'm not around," she ordered, and they talked about Linda Simpson.

The hotel manager, who had a state trooper with him, interrupted them. The manager had a nametag that read Paul, and the trooper had one that read Brian. Paul said to the trooper, "These are the people you need to talk to." He turned and left.

Brian stepped up. "Do you know a David Simpson?" They all looked at one another, and Billie said, "Yes, he is a member of our family."

Brian looked at them. "I'm very sorry to inform you, but he was killed about two hours ago in an accident about four miles from here. I found a jersey in the back seat that had 'Logan Family Reunion' on it, and I remember seeing the reunion notice out on the marquee when I passed this morning. I thought I would check here first. Would you prefer to notify the next of kin, or would you rather give me the contact information so I can do it?"

JT shook his head. "His wife is up in the room asleep. We'll tell her, but thanks anyway." JT looked at the officer. "Have you eaten, Brian?"

He shook his head. "Haven't had time."

JT motioned for the waiter. "Give him whatever he wants, and put it on my bill. Brian, the steak here is really good, I recommend it."

"Thanks, I appreciate that very much." He moved to sit down a few tables away and ordered.

Billie looked at JT with tears in her eyes. "Are you going to tell Linda, poor thing?" JT nodded. "On another subject, will it cost any more if I let Bubba stay in the extra room in my suite so he won't have to drive here from home every day?"

JT smiled and shook his head. "No, that will be okay, and put all your meals on the room. I'll take care of it."

She looked at him. "You make it hard for me to treat you as the no-good you really are. Is your wife paying for all this?"

I married her for her money."

Billie narrowed her eyes again. "You don't have no insurance job, do you? You're living off of her, and you should be ashamed of yourself."

JT was trying to contain his laughter. "You found me out—I'm a bum. I have no job and no money. I do have a wife that's rich, though."

* * *

The next morning, Jessie was sitting at the registration desk by herself. Billie walked up, sat down, and looked at Jessie. "You must be a very confidant woman to marry someone like him. He doesn't have an insurance job I bet. Is he really living off of you?"

Jessie smiled. "No, Aunt Billie. He does have an insurance job. In fact, he owns the company." Jessie took out her phone and pulled up a picture of The Trans Global Insurance Company building that JT had sent her. "This is his building in Paris. He does have a job, and he's worth many more times than what I'm worth as a surgeon and lawyer. Did you see that black helicopter sitting over past the convention center?"

Billie nodded. "I watched it land."

Jessie said, "That's his, and it doesn't belong to the company like he might have you believe. It's his, he paid for it, and he also owns three airplanes. Please don't tell him I told you all this. He's a very private person, and he loves you dearly."

"Oh, I know he loves me, and I hope you know all the trash talk we do is good-natured. I think the world of him. He paid my house off and pays the taxes on it every year. It broke my heart when he and his father had a falling out when he was young, and I told my brother he was wrong to treat JT like that. When JT Senior got sick and went in the hospital, I called him and told him, and he always came to see him." Billie got a faraway look in her eyes. "I don't know if he told you or not, but he is the youngest, but he was named after his father. My brother told me that he saw something special in JT when he was just a few hours old. He thought it was a sign from God that JT would do great things in the church." She was quiet and looked sad.

Jessie put her arm around her. "He is special, Aunt Billie. I don't know what Pop-Pop saw, but it wasn't to do things in the church, I don't believe. I can't discuss what he does in his insurance company, but he does a lot of good for a lot of people."

Billie patted her hand and said, "I know, dear. I'm sure he does—he's just that kind of guy." She got up and walked out, looking eighty-three years old all of a sudden.

After the reunion, they went back to Memphis and put Wanda and JW on a flight back to Owensboro.

CHAPTER 12

Jessie got extremely busy between being a doctor and a lawyer. She started working twelve-hour days, came home, went to bed, and worked weekends. JT tried to talk to her about slowing down, but she told him she couldn't—she was too busy. He called occasionally to take her to lunch, but she always declined, saying she didn't have time.

JT was getting restless. He approved extractions for Scottie, but Scottie had become very good at JT's job and didn't really require his assistance.

JT was in the gym working out one day when his phone rang. It was his handler at the CIA, Dean.

"What's up Dean?"

Dean paused before he spoke. "JT, I have a job for you if you are interested."

"Dean, you have my attention. Doing what?"

"I can't discuss it on the phone. Meet me at O'Charley's on Poplar, and I'll tell you about it over the lunch you're going to buy me."

JT laughed. "Okay, Dean. I'll see you in about an hour."

JT arrived at O'Charley's about the time Dean did. They got a table in a part of the restaurant that wasn't crowded, so they could talk without whispering.

Dean said, "I need an undercover gunrunner."

JT narrowed his eyes and smiled. "I thought gunrunning was against the law."

Dean smiled back. "We have somebody trying to buy guns, and we don't know who they are buying them for. There is the possibility that they're buying them for a home-grown terrorist cell here in the States. What I need you to do is sell them the guns, but you have to be convincing. We have the serial numbers and a microchip in each one, and we'll see where they go and where they turn up."

JT nodded as he thought about it. "Where is this going to take place?"

Dean smiled. "Actually, it's going to be close enough to get home at night but far enough where you won't be recognized, in Tupelo, Mississippi, near the airport. We'll leak the number of the phone we're furnishing you. When they call, you have to make sure you convince them you are legit."

JT nodded again. "What's the payoff?"

"Name your price."

"Two hundred thousand dollars if everything goes okay and double that if I have to take a bullet or a beating, agreed?"

Dean nodded. "It sounds fair to me. Here's the phone. When you push this button, we will be monitoring your conversation even if you're not on the phone. There will be a Mustang GT waiting for you in Tupelo to show them you're a successful businessman. It's fast in case you need it, and we have cameras in the car. If you get in a bind, we'll send in the cavalry and extract you."

JT considered the plan for a few seconds. "Where are the guns I'm going to sell?"

Dean smiled. "In the trunk. There will be eight automatic .223s. Tell them you can get more if they want them."

JT nodded. "When is this taking place?"

"You'll get the call sometime Thursday or Friday. Remember, we'll be listening, and you must be convincing."

JT nodded and shook Dean's hand. Dean handed him an envelope with instructions as to where the car would be located.

When JT got home that evening, he found a note from Jessie saying she would be staying in a hotel downtown because of the case she was working on. He looked at it, turned it over, and wrote her a note that read, *"I'm taking care of some personal business for a friend here locally, but I won't be home for a few days. Take care and I love you."* He laid his personal phone down by the note so she would know she couldn't call him.

He drove to the Memphis airport and took a twin-engine Cessna, provided by Dean, to Tupelo. He found the Mustang in a storage unit and drove to a safe house in a nice neighborhood. The kitchen was fully stocked, so he cooked bacon and eggs for supper. He looked in the refrigerator and pantry. "Damn, this place has everything but ketchup."

He was sitting there eating when his phone rang. "Hello?"

He heard a British accent on the other end. "I was told that you could get some hard-to-get items that I might need."

JT paused before responding. "It depends on what you want."

"I understand you can get anything."

JT waited about five seconds. "Look, I don't have time for games. State your business, or I'm going to hang up.

The voice came back and said, "I need some automatic rifles. Can you do that?"

"No." He hung up.

He waited, and twenty minutes later the phone rang again. "Sir, I'm told you can get anything I need. I'm willing to pay whatever you're asking."

JT looked out the window to see if there were any cars out front or down the street. He didn't see anything out of the ordinary. "Where did you get my number?"

"From a friend who must remain anonymous."

"Sorry, I can't help you." He hung up the phone again.

It was about two hours before his phone rang again. "Hello?"

"Okay, sir, it was given to me by Darren Billings." JT knew that was the name the undercover agent had used.

"Why didn't you say that in the first place? You could have saved us both a lot of time. Meet me at the Sonic on Highway 78 in one hour. I'll be in a black Mustang GT." He hung up without waiting for a reply.

JT got in the car, drove to the Sonic, and was there in less than twenty minutes. He parked in the back of the building, sat there, and waited to see if any police cars were hanging around. In about an hour, a Mercedes pulled in, and a man got out, walked over, and got in JT's Mustang. He was thin with ill-fitting clothes, sandy-colored hair, and bad teeth, and he smelled of cheap aftershave. He introduced himself as Nigel.

JT said, "You know, if you're not who you say you are, you're going to die."

The man didn't flinch. "I understand. Can you get me what I asked for?"

JT looked out the front windshield and then back Nigel. "If I do, it's not going to be cheap."

"How much?"

JT pretended to contemplate before saying, "Thirty-five hundred dollars each. I can get eight on short notice and more if needed."

Nigel nodded.

JT studied him hard, trying to detect any sign of deceit. "Okay, I want this done quick. Meet me at Warehouse Twelve off Seattle Street at twelve tonight. I'll be around back. Kill your lights before you light up my car so I'll know it's you."

Nigel nodded again, got out, and walked back to his car. JT watched him drive off and turn southwest. JT backed out and headed northwest. He drove around, stopped to buy ketchup, and got to the warehouse at eleven thirty. At twelve, on the dot, a pair of headlights turned up behind him and came up between the two warehouses. Before the lights hit him, the lights went black. The Mercedes backed up to the rear of his car, and two men got out. JT pushed the button on the phone and knew Dean would be listening.

He walked to the back with his hand on the Glock on his belt. Nigel was there with a brown-skinned man. JT squinted at the man. "Who are you?"

Nigel interrupted. "He's with me—don't worry about him."

"I worry about everything," JT growled, "and you should too if you want to stay alive and out of prison." Deciding the gunrunner he was portraying wouldn't be big on cultural sensitivity, he added, "I can't tell if he's greaser or a towel-head."

Nigel's fists clenched at his side. "He is Moroccan. Does that make you feel any better?"

JT looked from one man to the other. "I don't think this is a good idea." He turned and started for the driver's door.

Nigel stepped up. "Please, I need those guns."

JT stopped and looked at them for a minute. "Okay, but the quickest way to kill this deal is to make smart-ass remarks." He opened the trunk and pulled the blanket off the weapons, still in a padded container marked "US Army."

Nigel picked one up and racked it. "Are these stolen?"

"No, you dumb bastard, I bought them at Wal-Mart. Of course they're stolen. Do you want them or not? I've been here too long as it is."

Nigel nodded and handed JT a bag with $28,000 in it. He then said, "You haven't asked me what I was going to use them for."

JT gave him an impatient look. "I don't give a shit what you use them for; just get them the hell out of my car."

JT didn't count the money but waited for them to unload the weapons. When they had gotten seven of the eight rifles out, four sets of blue lights and sirens came blaring through the night. JT slammed the trunk of his car, ran to the driver's door, and jumped in. The other two did the same. JT tossed the bag of money into the passenger seat and threw the car into gear, accelerating up the asphalt toward the police cars headed for him. Nigel's car disappeared in the dark.

JT made a tire-squealing left turn before he got to the police cars. Two cars tried to follow him but spun out attempting the turn. The other two police cars went after Nigel. JT roared through the warehouse district at eighty miles an hour. When he got to the end, he made another sharp turn to the right. Soon he saw there were four police cars after him. He spoke into the phone. "Dean, I think Nigel got away because they're all four after me now."

Dean replied, "Those stupid-ass cops couldn't catch a bad cold, much less a bad guy."

JT hit Highway 78 and headed southeast, reaching speeds of up to 115 mph. When he saw the highway blocked up ahead, he exited the highway and started down surface streets. He didn't know what town he was in, but it wasn't Tupelo. He went around corners in a controlled drift. The tires were screaming as he slid them. He went over a railroad track, and the car went airborne. As he landed on all four tires he looked in the rearview mirror and saw the last of the four police cars—he'd lost the other three at various points when they went airborne and crashed—shudder to a stop after barreling over the tracks with sparks flying everywhere.

The reprieve was short-lived, as almost immediately another cruiser turned in from a side street just behind him. He came to a fork in the road and turned right. When he crested the hill, he could see a barricade across the street; he was on a dead end. When he got near the end, he spun the car 180 degrees and headed straight for the police cruiser. The police opted not to play chicken with him and veered off at the last minute. The cruiser spun out of control and turned over several times in a field.

JT got to the fork again and took the other road this time. He couldn't see flashing lights or hear sirens, so he slowed down so he wouldn't attract attention. He drove the road, looking at the GPS occasionally. Dean came over the phone. "Sounds like you lost them—good job. The main thing is that you led them away from the buyers. We can see on the screen that the guns are headed toward Memphis."

Before JT could respond, blue lights came on from a side road. JT floored it, with all 420 horsepower coming to life. "Dean, they found me. I'll keep them occupied as long as I can so the bad guys can get away."

JT made a controlled drift around a long curve, but the police car didn't make it and slid off the road in a ball of dust. As JT topped next hill, he saw three police cruisers blocking the road. He made a hard right into the field and started cross-country, hoping he didn't tear the undercarriage from under the car. He came up on a newly paved road and took a right turn; the police cars followed. His GPS showed him as still being off road—apparently, the GPS's database hadn't been updated.

He did another controlled drift around a curve, came over a hill, and saw a dead end with a swamp ahead. There were woods on each side of the road now, so he couldn't turn off. He spun the Mustang around 180 degrees, but the road was blocked by three police cars squealing to a halt. "Dean, they've got me. I need to be extracted from the local constabulary."

Dean replied, "We're on the way."

JT was blinded by the spotlights from the police cruisers. He turned off the engine and undid his seatbelt, and then he held his hands out the window.

The police came running up to the car with guns drawn. Each cop was shouting commands at him, often contradicting one another:

"Get out of the car."

"Get on your knees."

"Lay face down on the ground."

"Put your hands behind your head."

"Put your hands out to the side."

He got out and lay on his stomach with his hands behind his head, fingers interlocked. The first police officer to him dropped on him, putting his knee in JT's back. It hurt like hell, and JT wondered if he'd broken a rib. They cuffed him, and the handcuffs were extremely tight; he started losing feeling in his hands almost immediately. One officer finally tried to stand him up but couldn't lift him because of his size. When they finally got him on his feet, an officer said, "Put him in the car."

JT tried to look in his direction. "Don't you want to take my gun first?"

The police officer shouted at the others, "You didn't check him for weapons? What the hell is this, the damn police academy?"

They pulled his gun. Another police officer walked up and said, "Hold it a minute." He hit JT in the mouth with his fist, and JT tasted blood. The cop hit him again in the left eye and then drew back and hit him in the jaw so hard JT knew it was broken. The cop slugged him in the ribs several times and again in the face before the others pulled him off.

As he dropped to his knees and started to lose consciousness, he heard another police officer shouting, "Get off of him—what do you think you're doing?"

The cop who'd hit him replied, "That was my brother that was in the car that rolled."

"We'll charge him with assaulting a police officer, but don't beat him to death."

All of a sudden, it was quiet. JT tried to open his eyes, but the right one was swollen almost shut, and the left one was bad also. He realized he was handcuffed to a hospital bed. His jaw was killing him, and he could tell it was locked.

He felt someone take his handcuffs off and pull him up. He was turned, his arms were pulled behind his back, and he was handcuffed again. As he was being led out, he heard what he assumed was a doctor say, "He needs to stay in the hospital."

"Get out of the way, doc."

He was put in a car, though he was so big he had trouble getting into the backseat of the cruiser. He had to sit on the seat sideways to fit, and it smelled like urine. After a drive of about twenty minutes, they roughly pulled him from the car, and he was walked into a police station and pushed down in a chair.

He raised his head so he could see out of his left eye. There were about six cops in front of him. A sheriff with five stars on his collar walked up to him. "Okay, who are you, where did you get the rifle in your trunk, and how many did you put in the other car?"

JT said nothing.

The officer sat down in front of him. "You have possession of an automatic rifle, a handgun, speeding, reckless driving, assaulting a police officer, felony fleeing, gunrunning, and that's just the beginning. I'm not through making up charges against you. You can make it easier on yourself if you cooperate. Now, here's what's going to happen to you. You are going to be put in jail until we find out who you are, and if you cooperate, we might get you some medical treatment in a day or two."

JT heard Dean's voice outside the door and smiled as best he could.

A police officer came into the room. "Sheriff, we have a situation out here."

"Not now—can't you see I'm busy?"

"But, Sheriff, you need to come out here."

"Goddamn it, didn't I say not now?"

"Sorry, Sheriff, but you have to see this." The sheriff got up and went out the door, cussing.

A deputy with captain's bars on his collar sat down. "You're not beyond receiving more pain if you don't start talking."

JT tried to talk without moving his jaw. "Do you want me to tell you what's going to happen next?'

The captain looked mad but smiled. "Sure, tell me what you think is going to happen next."

JT again strained to talk without moving his jaw. "In a minute, your sheriff and another man will come through that door. They will tell you to take the cuffs off, and then they are going to make you give me back my weapon. Then I'm going to walk out of here."

The captain laughed as the door opened and the sheriff walked in with Dean and another agent behind him.

"Take the cuffs off of him." The sheriff was red in the face.

"Why, Sheriff? We can't—"

"I said take the cuffs off of him, and the next man that hesitates to do what I tell him is going to be on permanent foot patrol. Do you understand me?" He was shouting by now.

They took the cuffs off, and JT tried to stand but started to fall. Dean caught him, as did the other agent. Dean looked at the sheriff in disgust. "You beat a man this bad while he was handcuffed? You are one brave bunch of assholes, I'll give you that." Dean then asked, "Where's his handgun ...? Well, where is it?"

Someone stepped up and handed the sheriff JT's gun. The sheriff handed it to Dean, and Dean handed it back to JT. Every cop JT could see was red in the face.

Dean started helping JT out but stopped. "Sheriff, I want that rifle you found in the trunk, and I want the Mustang brought around and the money. Now, get out of my way."

JT staggered out, and the deputy that had broken his jaw came running up. "He's not going anywhere. My brother is in critical condition, and I will shoot any man that tries to take this man out. I don't give a damn who you are."

Dean pulled his weapon and placed it on the forehead of the deputy. "I am the man who can pull this trigger and get away with it."

The deputy froze. Everybody could see the wet spot in his crotch spread. The sheriff walked between them and pushed the cop out of the way.

They started again for the door, but JT's legs gave out, and he went to his knees. They helped him up and into the sheriff's office and laid him on the couch.

Dean ordered the sheriff, "Get me the hospital wing out of Memphis, now."

JT felt nauseated and tried to swallow. He knew if he threw up, his jaw wouldn't open, and he would drown in his own puke. He remained on the sofa as the sheriff said to Dean, "I don't give a damn if you are the CIA; he's not going to get away with this. He almost killed an officer, and if you were operating in our area, you should have contacted us."

Dean glared at the chief. "Listen to me, and listen to me good, you Mississippi redneck. This is one of my men. He was doing a controlled gun transfer, and we're lucky you're as incompetent as you are, or you would have caught the real bad guys with the other seven assault rifles. Now get out of my way and enjoy this evening as sheriff, because I don't think you are going to be a police officer very long."

JT came to as they loaded him into the helicopter, and he woke again as they took him out. In the emergency room, they cut his clothes off, and he lay there naked with doctors and nurses running in and out. Finally, they laid a warm blanket over him, and he passed out again.

When he came to, a nurse was standing over him. "How are you doing, Mr. Logan?"

JT tried to focus through his swollen eyes. "Where am I?" He realized his mouth was wired shut.

The nurse smiled. "You're in recovery at Baptist Hospital. We'll get you to your room in a few minutes. Are you hurting?" JT shook his head.

They were wheeling him down the hall when he heard Jessie's voice. "Where is he? Where is—"

Dean stopped her. "They're putting him into a room now. Just hang on a minute—he's all right."

He heard Jessie shout, "If he was all right, they wouldn't be putting him in the hospital."

JT winced as they moved him from the stretcher to the bed. His jaw didn't hurt, but his ribs, back, and eyes did.

When he opened his eyes and looked into Jessie's face, she was crying. "I thought you weren't going to do this anymore. You promised me."

JT spoke the best he could. "I got this from a bunch of cops."

"Cops?" Jessie turned to Dean. "What's he talking about?"

"Mrs. Logan, I'm with the CIA, and JT was working with us. It was a simple transfer of some equipment, but the local police thought it was something illegal. They worked him over before we could get to him. I'm sorry."

Jessie said coldly, "It's Dr. Logan." She turned away and walked out of the room. JT could see her as she went to the nurse's station and pulled his chart.

A nurse got up and took the chart away. "Who are you?"

Jessie looked her in the eye. "I'm Dr. Jessie Logan. I'm JT's doctor and wife, and I happen to be a lawyer also. You don't want to mess with me right now." She took the chart back from the nurse.

JT figured she wouldn't be back, so he dozed off again. When pain in his jaw woke him up, Jessie was beside him.

"Are you hurting?" He nodded.

In a few minutes, a nurse came in with a needle. She gave him a shot in the IV. After she left, he looked at Jessie. "Are you going to divorce me over this?"

She didn't smile. "This is not funny. I don't know what I'm going to do, but I can't live like this."

JT blinked as he felt the drugs take effect. "I wasn't trying to be funny. I was dead serious, but this is something we need to talk about when I'm not doped up. You know I love you and will always give you what you want, even if it's a divorce. Let me know."

He woke up and found himself alone. His phone was in his hand. He dialed Jessie's number. She answered and said, "I'm going into court right now. I'll be back up there as soon as I'm through. I love you. Bye."

JT put the phone down as the nurse came in. "How do you feel, Mr. Logan?"

"Hungry. Do you have a steak handy?"

She smiled. "Well, you must be better if you can joke, but you're not going to eat anything for the next three months that won't fit in a straw."

He had forgotten about that. The nurse brought him in a chocolate milkshake, and it tasted good because he was hungry and thirsty.

After a while, the door opened, and a woman in her fifties walked in. "Hi, Mr. Logan, I'm Dr. Margaret Shapiro. I'm the one that operated on your jaw. How are you feeling?"

"Okay, I guess, considering the shape I'm in. When do you think I might go home?"

She looked at him. "Well, you are on some antibiotics that have to be administered intravenously since you can't take pills with your jaw wired shut. As soon as they are through, you should be able to go. Do you have someone at home who can take care of you? I mean, you don't live by yourself, do you?"

He shook his head. "I thought you might know my wife, Jessie Logan."

Doctor Shapiro's eyes got big. "You're Jessie Logan's husband?" He nodded, trying not to talk when he could avoid it. "Let me talk to Jessie, and I'll see. Is she in the hospital?"

He shook his head again. "In court."

Margaret nodded. "That's right, she's a lawyer too. I'll leave her a message, and I'll get back to you." She walked out.

JT felt someone touch his shoulder; he opened his eyes, and Jessie was standing over him. She didn't appear happy. "I talked to Doctor Shapiro; I don't know what to say."

JT looked at her a few seconds. "If you will let me come home and help me get well, I promise I will leave your house and your life if that's what you want."

She seemed to get madder, if that were possible. "I'm so angry at you. JT, I'm scared you're going to die and scared I'll lose you. Why did you do that in the first place?" She crossed her arms.

He stared at her. "Why not? What else do I have to do? You're not at home—you sleep in a hotel. At least when I do this, I know what you are pissed about. The rest of the time, I don't. All I can do is watch you ignore me, but I'll tell you what, you file for divorce or whatever you want to do. If you're not interested in staying in this marriage, I'm not going to fight you." He turned his head away from her and heard her walk out.

JT picked up his phone and dialed. "Scottie, I'm in a bad way. I'm in Baptist Hospital in Memphis, banged up pretty bad. I need out of here and put somewhere I can recover from a broken jaw and bruises."

Scottie said, "I'm on it, boss. I'll see you as soon as I can."

Jessie walked out of court the next morning about ten and drove to the hospital to see JT. When she walked into his room, it was empty. She panicked, fearing he had developed an infection and had been sent to ICU.

She went to the nurse's station and asked where he was. The nurse appeared surprised. "He checked out four hours ago. He didn't call you?"

Jessie shook her head as she fought back the tears. She dialed his number, but he didn't answer.

* * *

In the heat of southern Mexico, Scottie helped JT off the plane and into a car. The air conditioner felt so good against the stifling heat. He was driven to a villa. He went in and looked out at the ocean view. His vision was beginning to return as his swelling went down. He suddenly felt tired, so he went to bed.

Someone lifting his arm awakened him, and he looked up into the eyes of a beautiful Mexican woman.

She smiled and said, "Hi, JT. I'm glad to see you again." Dr. Norma Martinez had taken care of him many times before. "Call me if you need me. You have my cell number."

JT nodded. He looked down and saw that she had put an IV in his arm.

He checked his phone and saw he'd missed Jessie's phone calls. He lay there wondering if he should call her back but decided to wait. He got up with a great deal of pain in his stomach and back and rolled the IV stand into the kitchen, using it as support. He opened the refrigerator and found milk and ice cream. He took them over to the blender, made a milkshake, and slowly sucked it through a straw.

Scottie walked in. "Hey, you're up. What exactly did you do?"

JT relayed the story to him, and then Scottie's phone rang. Holding a hand up to JT, Scottie answered it. "Oh, really? Then let it go. I'll call you and let you know." Scottie put the phone back in his pocket and told JT, "The boys tried to get your clothes, but your wife wouldn't let them in."

JT shook his head. "Don't worry about it."

His phone rang as Scottie walked out; it was Jessie. He answered it. "Hello, Jessie."

Jessie voice sounded weak over the phone. "Where are you? Have Scottie bring you home, please."

JT inhaled and exhaled through his wired-up jaws. "Jessie, you're going to have to make up your mind. Either treat me like you love me or treat me like shit, but this waffling back and forth is driving me crazy."

There was silence for a moment, and then Jessie said, "JT, I need to talk to you. Please come home."

JT closed his eyes. "No, if you want to talk to me, then I'll have Scottie pick you up and bring you to me. I don't have the strength to keep running around the continent."

He could tell she was crying. "I'm tied up in court for the next three or four days, then I have to go to Dallas for three days. I don't know when I'll get free."

JT nodded to himself. "Well, it sounds like you're too busy for me if I was there, so let's do this: when you get un-busy, you call me and I'll have them come get you. Until then, I don't—can't—come home. Prioritize yourself and call me when you get that done."

"That's not fair, JT—it's not a matter of priorities. I have commitments that have to be met."

"I suppose so, Jessie, but I'm not coming back until you see your way clear to the commitment you made to me ... we need to get to where we both want to be. I'll be here for the next three months, so you decide what you want to do and let me know."

She was sobbing. "Are you in town?"

"I'm not even in the United States. If you come to see me, get your passport and plan on taking off a week at least."

"I'm afraid you'll go out on another job, and you'll come back dead."

"Jessie, I have a broken jaw and bruised ribs. I can't get away from the IV pole I'm tethered to. I'm not going to do anything or go anywhere until I am a 100 percent, and that's going to be three months at least."

"Promise me you won't do anything until I get there."

He sighed. "Okay, I promise you I'll be here until you are ready to come here."

She sobbed again. "Okay, I'll stay in touch." There was a long pause. "I love you, JT."

"I love you too, Jessie, but it takes more than love to make a relationship. Call me when you can. Goodbye." He hung up.

* * *

The next morning Jessie walked into psychiatrist Dr. Linda Merton's office, which was inviting with soft green and gold colors on the wall and curtains. Linda, in a black, pinstriped business pantsuit, sat down and looked at Jessie. Linda was a pretty woman about forty years old with short black hair and a nice figure. "What can I help you with, Dr. Logan?"

Jessie told her about how she got married and about the many surprises JT had hit her with. Finally she said, "Sometimes I treat him so mean, and I don't know why. I just get uptight, closed-lipped, and stay away from him."

Linda nodded. "Do you love him?"

Tears started down Jessie's cheeks. "I love him so— that's what hurts. I sometimes wish I didn't, but ... I don't know what to feel or what to tell him. I'm scared he's going to stay and drive me crazy, and at the same time I'm scared I'm going to run him off. This will probably be the last chance I will ever have at love."

Linda took some notes. "Tell me, Jessie, why are you afraid you might lose him?"

Jessie told her what JT did. She talked about him coming in wounded, shot, and beaten up this last time. She told her of the scars on his back from the whip. "I can't ask him to quit because I'm afraid he will resent it someday. I want him to quit, but I want it to be his idea. I get scared and paranoid I think, then I start treating him mean, and he goes out and gets hurt. I feel it's partly my fault."

"Why do you feel it's your fault?"

"He seems to do these things when I'm being mean to him. I don't think he does it to get back at me, but he turns to what he knows best when I treat him mean. Why do I do that?"

Linda slowly shook her head. "Is he a violent person? Have you ever been afraid of him?"

"No, no, nothing like that. He's sweet, gentle, and kind."

"I would like to talk to him, Jessie; will he come in and see me?"

Jessie shrugged. "I don't know. He doesn't know I'm seeing you, and I'm almost afraid to tell him."

"Why?"

Jessie looked over at Linda. "I don't want him to think I'm crazy or psycho."

Linda smiled. "Talk to him, tell him you are seeing me, and see if he will come in to see me. Then I want to see you both together. Let me know, okay? By the way, do you need anything to help you sleep or relax you?"

Jessie shook her head and got up to leave. "You know, Dr. Merton, I know you've heard the old saying, 'if it seems too good to be true, it probably is.' That's how I feel about him."

Linda smiled. "So you think he's too good to be true? The saying says it probably is; it doesn't say it always is."

Jessie got up and walked out. She cleared her schedule for five days the next week.

* * *

JT was sitting outside in the ocean breeze with his eyes closed. He felt a hand on his shoulder and looked up at Jessie. She leaned down and kissed him, ever so gingerly, on his lips.

He smiled at her. "Why didn't you tell me you were coming?"

"I figured Scottie would have told you."

"Nah, he probably thought you were going to tell me. Pull that lounger over here by me."

They held hands and talked. Jessie was looking out toward the ocean when she saw a topless woman with huge breasts walk out of the ocean. She turned abruptly to JT and asked, "Is this a nude beach?"

He smiled. "It's an open beach. You can do what you want."

Jessie noticed that the woman was walking toward them. "Is she coming up here?"

"Yeah, but only because she lives here."

Jessie turned to him and narrowed her eyes. "She lives with you?"

JT was still smiling. "Well, she don't live with me. She stays here, down the hall from my room."

Jessie looked back at the woman. "How long is she going to be here?"

"Until her patient gets well I guess."

Jessie wanted to end the conversation before the woman got there, but she had many questions that needed answers. "Who is her patient?"

He rolled his slightly swollen eyes over and looked at her. "Me."

As the woman got closer, Jessie watched her fasten her top, turn it around, put the straps on her shoulders, and adjust herself. Her top was so small, it barely covered her nipples. When she got to them, JT looked at Jessie. "Dr. Jessie Logan, I want you to meet Dr. Norma Martinez." Jessie shook her hand.

Norma smiled at Jessie as she finished drying what the sun hadn't. "JT told me his wife was a doctor—he's full of surprises."

Jessie smiled back at her. "I know what you mean."

Norma went in to shower. Jessie turned to JT but said nothing. He looked back and held her stare. "No I haven't done anything with her, okay?"

Jessie nodded her head. "I believe you ... JT?" She hesitated. "Will you come back with me? I wouldn't want to leave this place if I were you, but I have this week off, and then my schedule is jam-packed again."

JT frowned. "The packed schedule is what concerns me. When it's packed, it usually means that it is too packed for me. If I have to sit around doing nothing, I would rather do it here and look at Norma's tits." He grinned widely as she hit his arm.

She sat there silently for a few minutes, and they listened to the waves hit the beach. Finally, she said, "I know I'm being selfish, but I need you, and I can't bear to be separated from you. I know I was wrong when I stayed downtown, so I'm going to buy a condo downtown when I get back. When I overnight there, I want you with me. There's a lot to do—restaurants, the Redbirds games, the trolley will take us from one end of Main Street to the other."

He stared out at the ocean. "When are you leaving?"

"I have to be back on Monday, and I have a lot of research to do, so I need to leave by Friday."

JT nodded. "We'll talk about it again on Thursday, okay?"

She nodded. "I need to go in and change into my swimsuit. You want to come in and help me?"

He smiled and got up to go in with her. They made love, and then she changed and went back out with him to the shade of veranda.

That Thursday, she got up early. JT was not in bed. When she went outside, JT was just getting ready to go to the beach. He wore a towel and a Panama hat. She looked at the towel around his waist, walked over, pulled back the fold, and saw he wasn't wearing anything. "Are you going skinny-dipping?"

"Thought I would. I usually do this time of morning. Want to go?"

She scanned the beach and saw no one, so she went back in, stripped down, and put her swimsuit on. They got to the water and JT took his towel off. He eyed her suit and said, "Chicken."

She looked both ways down the deserted beach again and pulled her top off and then her bottom. They held hands as they walked out into the surf. They went in about chest-deep and held onto each other as the waves washed over them. She could still see the bruises where he'd been beaten. They talked about an hour, and then she said, "Ready to get out? Too much sun is bad, especially for redheads."

When they walked back toward the shore, the beach contained fifteen or more people, all naked. There were adults and senior adults as well as children that ranged in age from toddlers to teenagers. He stopped and looked at her. "Are you going to stand in the surf all day or get out?"

She saw she didn't have a choice and walked out holding his hand. They got to their towels, and Jessie wrapped hers under her arms so it would cover as much as possible. JT put his over his shoulders, leaving the lower body exposed. She raised her eyebrows and asked, "Are you showing off?"

He smiled through his wired teeth. "No, I just don't want the scars on my back to get sunburned, and I don't want to explain where I got them."

She nodded in understanding. When they got back to the house, Norma came out with a camera that had a telephoto lens on it. "Hey, I got some great shots of you two from up top. I'll e-mail them to you." She walked off.

They showered and got dressed. When Jessie went back out, JT was already in his lounger, wearing shorts and a shirt.

Jessie sat down and looked over at JT, who was lying back with his eyes closed. "JT, I want to talk to you about several things. First, make damn sure you get all the photos of us from Norma." JT smiled and nodded. "Second, I want to tell you what I've been doing." She paused. "I'm seeing a psychiatrist."

JT opened his eyes. "For your benefit or mine?"

She smiled. "For mine, but she wants to know if you would come in and talk to her. It might help me with my problems. Will you talk with her?"

He squinted at the horizon. "Why are you seeing her?"

She pursed her lips. "To find out why I treat you like I do sometimes. I know it's wrong, but I can't help myself. I'm afraid I'm going to drive you away, or you will go off and do something ... to get yourself hurt like you did with your jaw. I feel terrible about that."

"You didn't have anything to do with it." He paused in thought. "Why don't you ask the doctor if she and her family would like an all-expenses-paid vacation? I'll fly them down, they can stay here, and I'll fly them back. It won't cost them a dime except for souvenirs."

She raised her eyebrows. "That might work; I'll talk to her when I get back and see. I guess this means you're not coming back with me."

He shook his head. "I think I'll stay here—it won't stop me from loving you, though. Also, you don't have to worry about Norma or any other señoritas." He smiled at her.

She narrowed her eyes at him. "I wish I was confident of that."

"Do you think I would do anything like that to you?"

She shook her head. "You know, I don't think you would. I'm not worried about you—it's some of those señoritas that might lose control and come after you." She smiled, as did he.

They went back to the bedroom and made love, and she got on the plane that afternoon to go back to Memphis.

After landing, she called Linda Merton. "Dr. Merton, could you possibly see me for about five minutes or less today? I have some information I think you would want to hear. Fine, five thirty at the Majestic. I'll get a table and be waiting."

At five fifteen, Linda came in and sat down. "What have you got that's so important?"

Jessie smiled. "My husband has agreed to talk with you, but he wants to know if you would do it during an all-expenses-paid vacation to a resort on the Pacific coast of Mexico near Puerto Vallarta, your family included. He'll have you flown down and back. There's plenty of room, and it won't cost you anything except souvenirs."

Linda raised her eyes. "My husband and I have been talking about getting away. When would this take place?"

"Any time you want and as long as you want—a week, two weeks, or more."

Linda nodded. "It sounds great. Let me run it by my husband, and I'll call you when I know something."

Jessie smiled and then dropped her smile. "Will you have kids that will come?"

"Yes, my daughter will want to come for sure, and maybe my son. He wants to go to computer camp, so we may not get him to come. Why do you ask?"

"The resort is on the beach, and it's an open beach, meaning most people walk around naked. How old is your daughter?"

"Eighteen, but this might be a good social experiment for her. I may encourage my sixteen-year-old boy to go to computer camp though. I wouldn't mind him seeing naked women, but, as his mother, I don't want him seeing his sister."

Jessie looked at her. "Or his mother?" Linda nodded.

Jessie and Linda both laughed. They finished eating and parted ways.

CHAPTER 13

Arian, JT's attorney, walked into the county courthouse of Bigbee County, Mississippi, and stopped at the guard station. "I have an appointment with the county attorney, Mr. Hugh Nash." He took her purse and briefcase and put them through the X-ray machine. She was shown the direction of Nash's office, she entered, and the woman at the desk asked her to sit down.

When she was called back, Nash stood up and shook her hand. "Well, counselor, it seems we have a dilemma, don't we?"

Arian shook her head. "It seems pretty cut and dried to me. I'm going to enjoy going to court over this."

Nash smiled. "Well, we'll see, won't we? What is your complaint? As I understand it, the CIA doesn't want any publicity on this."

Arian smiled as well. "The CIA doesn't have anything to do with this. It boils down to this." She took some photos out of her briefcase. "Here is an in-car camera shot of my client. You see the time-and-date stamp in the corner? Here is a dash-cam shot of my client being handcuffed. It was taken from one of your squad cars, and you see there's not a mark on him. Here is a security-camera shot of my client as he was released from the police station. Now, how are you going to explain the broken jaw, the eyes swollen shut, and the lacerations and bruises he received while in handcuffs? The CIA doesn't need to get involved in this, but you bring them in if you think you can. This is not about what he was arrested for. It's about what happened to him while he was handcuffed in your custody."

Nash protested, "It has everything to do with what he was arrested for."

She said coolly, "I believe all charges were dropped against him, correct?"

Nash looked at her and back at the photos, his expression worried. "What is your client asking for in damages—not that we are agreeing to pay anything?"

Arian didn't bat an eye. "Eight million ... the officers in the video beating him, as well as the sheriff, fired and prosecuted."

He laughed. "That's not going to happen—that's ridiculous."

Arian stood up. "Fine. I'll see you in court. Good day, Mr. Nash." She turned to walk out

"Wait a minute. What is your bottom-line price to settle this out of court?"

Arian looked up as if in thought. "Three million and the aforementioned officers fired, take it or leave it. Let me know soon, as the offer expires at five p.m. your time. Bye now."

* * *

Arian was sitting on the bed in her room at the Holiday Inn Express when her cell rang. Nash was on the other end. "Five hundred thousand dollars, and the sheriff stays. He's the county supervisor's brother." Arian hung up without saying anything.

Nash called back an hour later. "One million, and the sheriff stays. That's my final offer."

Arian was silent for a few seconds. "My final offer is three million, and the sheriff goes. If you are going to continue to make ridiculous suggestions, remember that my offer expires in an hour and fifteen minutes. If this goes to court and the citizens of this county find out you could have settled for far less than the court is going to give, the county supervisor will be out of a job—as well as the county attorney. Time is running. By the way, we're going to ask for a change of venue."

He almost yelled, "On what grounds?"

"Hell, if you include the sheriff and all those officers, they're related to everyone in the county, including the county supervisor." She hung up.

At 4:45, Nash called back sounding contrite. "Will you take two million, and the sheriff and officers will be terminated?"

She was silent for a minute. "And prosecuted. I'll be there in the morning and we can finalize everything."

She was watching TV when the room phone rang. She answered it, but no one was on the other end, so she hung up. It rang again. Again, no one was on the other end. It rang once more, and this time she let it ring. When it went to voice mail, it quit ringing but rang again a minute later. Next came a knock on the door, but when she looked out the peephole, no one was there.

Arian called JT and told him what was happening. "I can't call the police. What do I do?"

"Unplug the phone, and don't answer the door. I'll have someone there in an hour, maybe less. If anything happens, get me on the phone. I'll call you when they're at your door."

She nodded, not that he could see it. "Thanks, JT. I'm scared."

"It'll be all right. They're more mouth than actions."

She looked out the window. "If that were true, I wouldn't be down here." Arian sat there and thought a minute. She called Nash's number from her cell phone record, but he didn't answer. She left him a voice mail stating that they were back to her original demand.

Thirty minutes later, her phone rang. "What's the problem? I thought we had a deal."

"The problem, you son of a bitch, is people calling my room and knocking on the door constantly." There was another knock on her door, and she froze. She switched ears with her phone. "Now they are knocking on my door again. I withdraw my offer. Eight million, and you and the county supervisor resign along with the whole sheriff's department." She hung up.

Twenty-five minutes later, there was another knock on the door, but she didn't move. Then she heard Nash's voice. "Ms. Moss? This is Nash. I can guarantee your safety. Open the door, please."

She walked over and looked out the peephole. It was Nash and two deputies. She opened the door. "You can come in, but any officer connected with this county can't."

Nash walked in, and she shut the door and bolted it behind him. "Ms. Moss, I promise you I didn't know that this was going on, but I'll promise you this: they will be in handcuffs before midnight, please believe me. The officers outside are my son and nephew. They are not in any of the videos, because they weren't there."

Arian's phone rang; it was JT. "Scottie is outside your door with those two policemen."

"Thanks, JT." She hung up and opened the door. The officers were standing between the door and Scottie, so she said to Nash, "I have my own body guard. Please leave."

Nash walked out and down to the elevator with the two deputies.

Scottie looked at her. "Are you all right?" She nodded. "I'll be right outside your door—get some sleep."

She grabbed his sleeve. "No, I want you in here. Take that bed." Scottie removed his coat, and Arian saw the Ruger in his holster. He stretched out on the other bed and watched TV until he nodded off.

The next morning when they went to the courthouse, Scottie said, "I don't think anything will happen in there, and

I'm not giving up my gun, so I'll wait for you down here. Here's my number. Call me if you need me."

She smiled. "Thanks."

She walked into Nash's office with a mean look on her face and found two men standing with Nash. She said, "The people of this county have got to be the dumbest sons of bitches walking the face of the earth."

Nash looked scared. "Please sit down, Ms. Moss. This is County Supervisor Crumb, and this is the man that's going to take the sheriff's job, Bob Harper. He's a former state trooper from Jackson. We regret the harassment you experienced. The man that harassed you is in custody, and it will be a long time before he sees the light of day. Do you want us to bring him over so you can see him?"

She shook her head.

Nash continued. "We are willing to offer your client three million dollars. The sheriff and all the officers in the video will be dismissed. The deputy that did the damage to your client will be prosecuted and jailed. Will that suit you?"

She contemplated the offer for a minute. "Yes, that will be acceptable."

Nash handed her the agreement. She read it over and signed both copies. She put down her pen. "Is that all, gentlemen?"

As all three men nodded, Nash's phone rang and he answered it. "Okay, thanks ... Well, we don't have to worry about firing the sheriff. He just blew his brains out with his service revolver."

Arian stood up. "What a shame. Good day, gentlemen." She picked up her copy, turned, and walked out.

Scottie met her in the lobby, and she told him, "I need to get my rental car back to Tupelo."

He said, "Give me the keys. I'll see that it gets back. We have a helicopter waiting to take you back to Atlanta." She smiled in appreciation.

CHAPTER 14

Ten days later Jessie and Linda, Paul, and Wendy Merton landed at the resort.

JT stood up when Jessie introduced them and apologized for having to talk through his wired jaw. The Mertons were shown to their rooms, and after they had changed clothes, they came out on the shaded patio for lunch. As they were eating, eighteen-year-old Wendy's jaw dropped. When they all turned to where she was looking, they saw a man and woman playing paddleball, naked, on the beach.

Linda said to her daughter, "This is a nude beach. Does that bother you?"

Wendy looked at her mother briefly and then back to the beach. "No, but I'm not going out there naked."

Linda nodded. "Of course. You don't have to."

Jessie told Wendy, "It's a clothing-optional or open beach. You can wear a swimsuit. With my Baptist upbringing, I have trouble going out there naked."

Wendy asked, "You've been out there naked before?"

Jessie nodded. "Once, we went out one morning when the beach was deserted. When we got ready to get out, I found there were three dozen people on the beach, but I had no choice. JT goes out and swims naked every day."

JT shook his head. "First of all, there were only about fifteen people out there. Second, it's her fault that she draws a crowd when she's naked." Jessie hit his shoulder.

The Mertons and Jessie changed into swimsuits to go to the beach. As they walked out, Paul looked at JT. "Are you not going with us?"

JT shook his head. "I might walk out later. You see this piece of my ear that's missing? I lost it to skin cancer. I'm not a sun worshipper." Jessie realized she'd found out something else about JT she hadn't known. She hadn't even noticed the ear.

On the beach they set up beach chairs and laid out towels. Paul and Wendy went in the water. Jessie sat down beside Linda. "Tell me about this social experiment you are going to do."

Linda smiled. "It's not really an experiment. I have tried to raise my children with open minds yet maintaining certain values. I don't really know how I've done, but her reaction will show me. If she's a total prude and doesn't even look at naked people, I will have failed in instilling an open mind. If she strips down and runs down the beach shouting and drawing attention to herself, then I have failed in teaching her certain values. It'll be interesting to see what she does."

Jessie asked, "But you didn't want to know that about your son?"

"I just didn't want him to see his sister naked, or his mother."

"What about the reverse? What about your daughter seeing your son naked, as well as her father?"

Linda grimaced slightly. "I guess it is a double standard, but my daughter doesn't have the raging hormones my son does."

Jessie laughed out loud but stopped when she saw Paul walking back with his swimsuit in his hand. Wendy did a double-take of her father but went back to swimming. Paul sat down in a beach chair on the other side of Linda. He looked at them and asked, "Do you mind?"

The two women exchanged glances, and then Linda said, "No, you're just going with the flow."

Paul looked at his wife's swimsuit. "You're not going with the flow?"

She said hesitantly, "I don't guess there's any way to ease into it, is there?"

Jessie nodded. "Yeah, go topless until you get used to it, and then if you're comfortable with that, take off the rest."

Linda stood up and took her top off. Her breasts were those of a forty-year-old woman who had had two kids.

Jessie raised her voice as they walked away. "Remember, there are parts of the human body that were never meant to be sunburned."

Linda and Paul smiled as they walked off toward the water. Jessie saw them stop and talk to Wendy.

JT walked up behind Jessie and stuck a beach umbrella in the sand. He was wearing shorts, a T-shirt, and a big Panama hat. He sat down under the umbrella, and she moved her chair over in the shade beside him. They sat there for an hour, talking and holding hands.

After a while, JT said, "I might invite my brothers and their families down for a vacation. What do you think?"

Jessie laughed out loud and then looked over at JT. "Who does this villa belong to?"

He smiled at her the best he could.

She shook her head slowly. "I might have known it would be yours."

JT and Jessie looked up and saw all three of the Mertons walking back. Wendy had taken her top off too. JT stood up. "Well, I'm going back to the shade of the patio."

"Don't tell me you are embarrassed to see Linda and her daughter naked."

JT glanced at them and back to Jessie. "It's never bothered me to see people with their children naked. It does bother me to see people that I know and their children naked."

"Her daughter's not a child—she's eighteen," Jesse pointed out.

JT smiled at her. "Yes, she is. It must be my Baptist upbringing." He smiled again and walked off.

When the three got there, Linda sat down in JT's seat and said to Jessie, "I hope we haven't run your husband off."

Jessie shook her head. "No, he's just had enough heat. Some of the antibiotics make him sensitive to heat in general and the sun in particular."

When JT came back out later, Jessie, Linda, and her daughter were putting their tops on. Paul already had his suit on.

* * *

The next day Jessie, Wendy, and Paul took chairs down to the beach. Linda came out and sat down by JT. He asked her, "Are you not going to the beach today?"

"I will later," she said with a smile. "Right now, I thought this would be a good time for us to have a talk."

JT looked back at her. "Ain't I supposed to be lying on a couch or something?"

Linda smiled as she gazed out over the ocean. "Only if that would make you feel better."

He shook his head. "I'm most relaxed right here."

"JT, do you think your wife is afraid of you?"

"No," he said without hesitation. "Quite the opposite— I'm afraid of her. Seriously, I don't think my wife is afraid of anything or anybody."

Linda paused a long time and then asked, "Do you love your wife?"

"To the point it hurts sometimes. I would do anything for her."

"Even give up your work?"

"She would never ask me to do that. If I give it up, it will because I decide to."

Linda took a few notes. "Why do you feel the need to live ... on the edge, so to speak? I mean where you cheat death with what you do."

JT took in a deep breath and mumbled through immobile lips, "The army had me go through a whole battery of test by psychiatrists. Not just me, but anybody who had been a prisoner of war and still liked to live on the edge. Many people get PTSD or some other mental problem, but for some reason I didn't, and that baffled them."

"You didn't answer my question. Why do you feel the need to live on the edge?"

JT thought a few seconds. "I couldn't explain to the army psych's, and I don't know if I can explain it to you. You really have to go through those situations to understand it. When you are in a situation where you know you may die and you come out alive, you get a high like drugs, a sense of euphoria. Because you survived, you want to repeat it. The polite term is called looking for the jazz, and the actual term is looking for shit."

"Now that you're in love, doesn't it scare you that you may not make it back someday?"

JT was silent for a long time, but Linda said nothing and simply waited for him to respond. Finally, he said, "When I went into these situations before, I convinced myself I was going to die in that particular action. Without the fear of dying, I got my men in and out with few casualties. Now that I love her, I can't get that edge anymore. I know I should stop. I even told the company I was quitting, but there were a couple of situations where they needed me, and I went. When I got hurt, I was more afraid of Jessie leaving me than I was of being hurt. Does that make sense?"

She wrote another note and then said, "It doesn't have to make sense to me, only to you. Can you get along without that high from ... looking for shit?"

He nodded. "Since I have a new purpose in life, I think I can adjust. It's going to take time, though."

She glanced sharply at him. "You know she loves you very much, even when she seems ... distant sometimes."

"I know, and I don't have any doubt about her loving me or me loving her. I will tolerate anything, but it hurts when I think she is distancing herself. I'm afraid she's going to get mad enough to leave me."

"I don't think you ever have to worry about that. She just needs time ... like you. I was fascinated about how ya'll came to be married, and I think they should make that into a movie."

He smiled. "Maybe they will."

She stood up. "Well, it was nice talking to you. You are a fascinating man, I'll give you that." She took her notepad in the villa and came out in her swimsuit. As she walked out on the beach, she took her top off. JT saw all three Mertons completely naked later on.

The next day, Paul asked if they would like to go into Puerto Vallarta and do some shopping. Linda shook her head. "Why don't you take Wendy? It's ten o'clock now, and if you come back for lunch, I'll go back with you this afternoon. I have some business with Jessie and JT."

Jessie and JT sat by each other, and Linda pulled up a chair in front of them. "Well, where do you think this relationship is, and where do you see it going?" She raised her eyebrows.

Jessie cleared her throat. "I love him so terribly much, and I can't comprehend losing him. I know I treat him bad and withdraw, but I don't mean to, and I don't realize it at first when I do. After I realize it, I get mad ... at myself mostly. I won't ask him to quit—he'll have to decide that on his own. I'll never leave him, and I hope to God I don't push him away. I need his love and understanding, and I think he does understand. It boils down to ... I hate to see him hurt, whether it just happened or if it happened a long time ago. When he's not doing his work, he is loving and caring and treats me like a queen. I just want that, all the time."

Linda looked at JT with the same questioning eyebrows but said nothing. He returned her gaze and said, "I love her something terrible. I know I can't continue doing what I did, but I can't just walk away. There's a lot of people who depend on me for their livelihood. I've already trained someone to take my place. I just keep being pulled back in occasionally. It's happening less and less and will eventually quit. We just need to go slow. I need her to have faith in me that I'll always come back, and I'll get to the point where I won't go at all." He looked away and back at Linda to let her know he was finished.

Linda put her pen down. "Well, it's obvious that you two love each other. It's understandable that Jessie feels the way she does, and it's understandable that JT feels the way he does. You two want the same thing, but it's going to take time to get there, so don't give up. JT, you know she can't help feel she could lose you. Only you can change that, but it must be your decision. Support and understand her when she goes through the episodes and withdraws. Jessie, when you start feeling angry and withdrawn, let JT know; he'll understand. I would like to talk to you both in another month or so." They nodded and kissed, and Jessie blotted the tears in her eyes.

* * *

After three months of sporadic visits from Jessie, JT finally got his jaw unwired. He had lost eighteen pounds drinking only milkshakes and protein shakes. He flew into Memphis, and Jessie met him at the airport. They drove back to the house and had lunch.

As they ate, their eyes lingered. "You look like you have something on your mind, Jessie." Her eyes reflected the weak smile that flashed across her lips so quickly JT wasn't sure he saw it at all.

"Yeah, I'm glad Dr. Merton says I'm not as crazy as I think I am. I love you so much that the fear of losing you makes me undergo a form of depression. I seem to withdraw and don't realize that. Then I become agitated to the point I say things that I wished I hadn't said. I mean, I know I talk to you in some ways that are mean and sound like I'm spoiling for a fight. I think I can overcome this, but I need your help and, most importantly, your understanding." She looked at him, clearly waiting for a response.

He nodded. "I'll be glad to help, because I don't see living without you. I thought to myself, if you divorce me, I was going to buy the house across the street so I could be near you." This time he was sure of her smile. "I'll try my best to stay out of harm's way. I told Scottie and Margaret that I want to withdraw from any action other than planning. If I can't do that, then I'll quit the company altogether. One other thing—when I see you slipping away, I'm going to gently whisper to you and bring you back. Okay?"

She kissed him.

CHAPTER 15

One day the following month, Jessie came home and sat down beside JT. He turned off the TV and looked at her. She obviously had something on her mind. "I got a call from a Dr. Wellesley in Nashville. He says he has something that he thinks will appeal to me and wants me to come and meet with him in Nashville."

JT nodded in understanding. "Are you going?"

"It's got my curiosity up. Strange thing though, he asked me to bring you with me."

"Me, why me?"

"He just said that what they want me to consider should be a family decision. What do you think?"

JT shrugged. "It does make one think. I'll go with you if it's something you want to consider."

"I don't have any idea what it might be. He is chief of staff at Vanderbilt Hospital, so maybe a job or a position. I graduated from Vanderbilt with my law degree, you know."

He smiled. "No, I didn't. You're full of surprises. Where did you go to medical school?"

She laughed. "I have never surprised you like you have me. I went to UT Knoxville for my pre-med and UT Memphis for my doctorate."

Two days later, they loaded up JT's Range Rover and headed toward Nashville. They could have taken his Cessna, but the weather was threatening. They arrived at the famous

Maxwell House Hotel four and a half hours later. They checked in, but instead of the room reserved for them, JT upgraded them to a suite.

Jessie's phone rang. "Hello? Yes, we just checked in. Fine, we'll see you at six." She turned and looked at JT. "Well, we are meeting Dr. Wellesley downstairs in the dining room at six. That gives us a couple of hours to waste. Got anything in mind to kill the time?"

He smiled, kissed her, and led her into the bedroom. They made love longer than they meant to so they had to hurry to shower and dress to get to the dining room on time. As they walked in, a distinguished-looking man in a three-piece suit walked up. He had graying hair and a goatee to match. With him were another man, short and slightly pudgy, and a nice-looking woman who stood over six feet tall. "Dr. Logan, I'm Sean Wellesley. This is Mr. Douglass Crater and Mrs. Martha Brown. Follow me, please."

They were seated in a private dining room, Sean gave his recommendations as what to order, and they chitchatted for a while. Finally, JT said to Sean. "Can I ask you a question, Dr. Wellesley?"

"Of course, Mr. Logan, but please call me Sean."

JT looked at the other two and then back at Sean. "Okay, and you can call me JT, but why are we here?"

Sean raised his eyes and smiled at Douglass and Martha. "The man doesn't waste time. I like that. What we asked you here for, Dr. Logan, is to ask, if you would be interested in running for public office."

Jessie sat there with an expression of shock on her face. "First, call me Jessie, and I don't ... why me? I have never had a desire for politics."

"That's why we think you should consider running. You are an accomplished surgeon, a lawyer, and you are being recruited for public office. That will make a difference when you seek votes, a sort of non-political, if you will."

Jessie sat back and was speechless for a moment but then said, "What do you think, JT?"

"What office do you have in mind, and what party affiliation are we talking about?"

Sean replied, "The Democratic Party of course. We have a Republican-controlled government in this state, and we desperately need to change that. As for the answer to the next question, we are thinking of several offices in the state government, but we are also looking down the road to national office. You need to get your feet wet statewide first."

Jessie put her hand on her chest. "Wow, this is going to require some deep consideration."

Sean laughed. "Of course. I'm sorry to spring this on you, but I was afraid you wouldn't have come if I had told you the reason over the phone. Listen, Jessie, this will be a long-term campaign, and you may not win the first time. The important thing is to start getting your name circulated in the public. We need to get away from the look of a professional politician. You are a surgeon, a lawyer, married and never divorced, and you have a war-hero husband. We haven't looked into either of your backgrounds deeply, but from what we do see, we see a win-win situation here."

Sean glanced over at JT. "What are your thoughts on your wife running for office? Would you support her in her efforts?"

JT didn't say anything for a minute. "First, my wife knows I would support her in anything she decided to do, but I think she has too much baggage to get elected."

Sean frowned at him. "What baggage does she have?"

"Me," JT said, glancing at Jessie. "Do you remember, a year or so back, that a man was tried for war crimes, specifically for killing men, children, and women in Iraq?"

"I remember it was seen as an attempt to discredit a war hero, and it backfired on the congressman who started that whole thing," Douglass said, chiming in. "We can certainly spin that into a plus."

"Why?" JT asked. "I'm not running for office."

"Well, so it would reflect in a positive way on your wife and not negatively. They couldn't use that against her."

JT looked at the three of them. "You know that was a Democratic congressman that did that, don't you? I don't know what Jessie will do, but if this goes forward, then be prepared to answer anything concerning me, and I've been accused of almost everything thought convicted of nothing."

Sean appeared to be deep in thought. "We haven't fully vetted Jessie, but I haven't seen anything yet that would change my mind. Anything else, JT?'

"How is it going to look with your candidate running for the Democratic Party married to a staunch Republican?" JT said as his gaze drifted to Jessie and back to Sean.

Sean appeared concerned for the first time, but Martha said confidently, "I think we can turn that into a plus also. It shows she is willing to listen and cross party lines, something that is lacking in any candidate that I know of. Do you have any desires for politics, Mr. Logan?"

JT shook his head. "No, I dislike politicians more than I do lawyers."

Sean looked taken aback until he saw Jessie smile. He laughed. "Of course that's not true, but I like your sense of humor."

JT face was somber. "I wasn't joking—I was dead serious. I don't like politicians and most specifically Democrats."

Martha gave JT a surprised look. "What have you got against Democrats?"

JT pressed his lips together. "We see differently on many subjects, such as the second amendment and gun control."

Martha sat up. "You don't believe in gun control?"

JT pulled his jacket open, exposing his .40-caliber Kahr. "Does it look like I believe in gun control? We're getting off the reason we're here. If my wife wants to run for office I will support her, both emotionally and financially, but I think I am too much baggage for her to get elected. The higher you go in politics, the more adverse effect it will have on her. You vet her, and you won't find anything but good there. You vet me, and you will find all kinds of stuff with every stone you overturn. Just remember, accused of almost everything but convicted of nothing. I have said my piece, so I'll leave you to talk to my wife. Good night." JT got up and left the dining room.

Sean cleared his throat and said, "Well, that's something I didn't expect. We may have to rethink strategy here. Jessie, I still think you would make a great candidate, so let us fully vet you, which will include checking your husband, and we will be in touch with you. Your room has been paid for."

Jessie smiled. "Thank you, and I am flattered that you thought of me. I will think on it, and you do your due diligence. We'll talk later, and my husband won't let you pay for the room, but thank you anyway. Good night."

* * *

On the way back to Memphis the next day, both were quiet. Finally Jessie said, "Had any more thoughts on this?"

JT shook his head. "I don't have to have any more thoughts. You know how private a person I am. The thought of people checking into my background and making claims that can't be defended makes me uncomfortable, but this is not about me. It's about you, and you have to decide what you're going to do."

She was silent for a minute. "What do you mean, claims that can't be defended?"

"Well, I'm a contract agent for the CIA. When I do extractions, I purposely try to involve the CIA in some way so I will be covered by the national security blanket. I don't have to tell anyone anything about it because it might compromise national security. That won't stop people from making the claims, though, and an unanswered claim makes you look guilty. Not only have I quit doing something I loved doing, but if you're elected, the CIA won't use me anymore. But like I said, this is about you, not me."

She sat back and absorbed all that JT had said. "I want us both to be happy, but I don't know if I want to give up being a surgeon or lawyer. I will have to give this a lot of thought ... and prayer."

JT glanced over at her. "Think about what you want to do first, and then think about me second."

Jessie went back to Nashville by herself several times to meet with the members of the Democratic committee. She made so many trips, JT bought a condo in Nashville. She'd been gone for a few days on one such trip when JT's phone rang. "Hello?"

Dean was on the other end. "JT, I could use your help on something if you're up to it."

JT narrowed his eyes. "Does it involve the possibility of getting shot, beaten, or my jaw broken?"

Dean laughed. "Nothing like that. I need a babysitter for a couple of weeks."

"Okay, Dean, you have my attention. What do you want me to do?"

"We'll discuss it over a steak at O'Charley's—one o'clock then?"

"A steak that I'm paying for, I suppose."

Dean laughed. "Hell, yeah. You're the one making the big money. I work for the government—I don't make shit."

JT laughed. "Okay, I'll see you there."

JT walked into O'Charley's at quarter past one. "Sorry I'm late. There's more traffic than I thought there would be."

Dean smiled. "No problem. I'll get right to the point. I have a big Saudi businessman that wants to ... experience America, Las Vegas in particular. I need someone to watch him and make sure he doesn't do anything that will embarrass his government or jeopardize his influence with the government. If he does that, he'll be of no use to us."

JT nodded. "What role will I play? Do I shadow him, herd him, or what?"

Dean chuckled to himself. "I need you to be his best friend for ten days to two weeks. Fly him around in your jet, bankroll his gambling, and pay for his whores. If he drinks, pay for his liquor, and if he needs a hit, pay for his drugs. I can give you a contact in Vegas that you can get the drugs from with no danger. I have a feeling he'll leave the drug scene alone, but who knows what will happen when he gets turned loose. Send us your bill for the plane, cars, gambling money, and so forth, plus whatever you're going to charge for this. The biggest danger to you is being seen gambling big in a casino or entering a whorehouse. It might affect your relationship with your wife and, more importantly, her political career."

JT looked at Dean. "You heard about that, huh?"

"Hell, we knew they were looking at her before they asked her. Has she decided if she wants to do it or not?"

JT shook his head. "She's still exploring the 'what if's.' I hope she doesn't, but it has to be her decision."

Dean nodded. "Yeah, we hope she doesn't either, because we would hate to lose you."

JT looked at Dean, knowing he was saying that if Jessie were in public office, they would have no more use for him. He just nodded. "When will this take place?"

"If you can swing it, we need to start in ten days. I need you to pay for everything, and we'll reimburse you. I can't have any trace from our government to him. It will be just a big businessman from the Middle East being wined and dined by a big businessman in the US." Dean asked him, "You speak Arabic, right?"

JT nodded. He looked out the window and then back at Dean. "Let me think it over and check my schedule as well as my wife's schedule. I'll call you tomorrow and let you know." Dean nodded, and they chitchatted over their food.

Jessie returned from Nashville, and JT kissed her as she walked in. "Well, what's the latest?"

"Well, we would have to move to Nashville, so I'm glad we have the condo. I'll be up there a lot."

JT nodded. "That goes without saying. If this ever gets any bigger, we would have to move to the DC area." He looked at her, waiting for a response.

"I'm more on the fence than I was when they first asked. I want to do it, but then again, I don't." She gave him a weak smile. "What are you thinking? I can see it in your eyes."

"I figured you could. Dean needs my help for a couple of weeks."

"No! JT, you said you wouldn't do that anymore."

"Calm down, and let me tell you about it. It's not dangerous."

She took on a mean look. "Yes, it is, or the CIA wouldn't have you doing it—they would be doing it themselves. Isn't that why they use contract agents?"

"Listen to me for a few minutes, okay?"

"No, do you really expect me to?"

He narrowed his eyes. "I expect you to give me the same courtesy as I gave you about running for office. Now, will you listen? If not, I'll explain it all to you when I get back, so what's it going to be?"

"I'm sorry, but I've never been beaten, shot, or had a broken jaw for you to worry about. Do you understand what I'm trying to say?"

"Yes, I do. Here's the scoop. A businessman from the Middle East is coming over. They want to make sure he's treated right and doesn't do anything to get himself in trouble with his own government. If he gets drunk or in a traffic accident, he won't be any good to them. I'm just babysitting. He doesn't have any enemies, with the possible exception of some rednecks that don't like Middle Easterners. I will be gone ten days to two weeks. I'll be in touch, and you can call me at any time."

She looked at him. "Why can't a regular agent do it?"

"Because there can't be any connection between the US government and this man. It's just going to be a businessman from the US entertaining a businessman from the Middle East. I'm going to be paying for everything, and they will reimburse me. Besides, you never can tell when I might need the money to finance somebody's political campaign."

"I'm sorry, I just get scared when you do anything like this. Please be careful, and please don't come home hurt. And I can call you anytime, day or night?"

He nodded. "If I'm playing poker or something, I will tell you I'll call you back as soon as possible, okay?"

"Where are you going?"

"We'll start with Vegas and then anywhere he wants to go. I'll have the Lear jet tied up all this time."

She kissed him. "I love you, and I don't mean to be such a thorn in your side ... but if you come home hurt, I'll kill you. Understand?" He smiled and nodded.

The following week, JT flew to New York and waited for Bema Fouad to get off the overseas flight. He spotted him from the picture Dean had given him. He walked up and introduced himself in Arabic.

JT took him to the private airport in a limousine. They got on board the Lear and sat back. Bema gazed around at the plane. "Very nice. Whose plane is this?"

JT didn't bat an eye. "Mine. Where do you want to go?"

Bema looked back at him. "Let's start with Las Vegas."

JT picked up a phone by his seat, and the pilot answered. "Go with the original plan to Vegas," he said, and she acknowledged his request.

After they landed, another limo picked them up and took them to the Paris Casino. They went to their suite, and JT put $200,000 in the room safe and deposited $400,000 with the casino. When JT asked if he would like to gamble a little, Bema raised one eyebrow. JT handed him $10,000 in cash. Bema grinned, and they got up and walked down to the casino. JT played sparingly so it wasn't obvious to Bema or anyone else that he was babysitting.

Bema went through the $10,000 in about three hours. JT discreetly handed him another ten grand. That lasted him four and a half hours. After that, they decided to eat and go back and rest. They ate at the La Creperie, and the smell as they entered was so aromatic it made JT's stomach growl. Bema had a goat cheese crepe, and JT had a ham and cheese crepe.

They went back to the suite, and JT asked him what he would like to do next. Bema looked at him. "You speak Arabic very well. Where did you learn it?"

"The army taught me. I was stationed in the Middle East for several years."

Bema looked at him again, and JT knew he had something on his mind. Bema smiled. "Even though it is against my religion to drink alcohol, I think I would like a little Scotch if possible."

JT went over to the small bar in the suite's sitting room and opened the doors on the wall behind it. Inside was everything imaginable to drink. Bema smiled and went around the bar to fix his own drink. JT poured himself a little Jack and Coke and nursed it through the six drinks that Bema had.

When Bema's eyes got heavy, he decided to get some sleep. JT had given him the master bedroom. JT left his door open so he could hear if Bema got up and so he could see if Bema tried to leave without him.

Jessie called just before he drifted off. They chatted a few minutes, and she seemed satisfied she could call him anytime.

About ten hours later, Bema emerged from his room. It was daylight, and Bema said, "I think I would like to gamble some more."

JT nodded, took another ten grand out of the safe, and handed it to him. They went back down to the casino, where Bema held his own for about five hours and came back with about $2,800. Bema wanted to see Las Vegas, so JT got a limo and they drove around. They stopped at a traffic light, and a woman knocked on the window. Bema lowered it, and she gave him a booklet. JT had stuck his hand under his jacket and rested it on his gun. Bema looked through page after page of beautiful naked women, and JT could tell Bema was interested.

JT told the driver where to go, and they drove for an hour until they reached a place called the Bunny Ranch. Inside were twelve beautiful women in various stages of undress. Bema shook hands with each one as they introduced themselves and then turned back and scanned the line of beauties. He pointed at the whitest blond JT had ever seen. She took Bema back, and the madam walked up to JT and said, "What about you?"

JT smiled. "No, thank you. I'm just showing my friend around."

The girl that went back with Bema came out and spoke to the madam, who walked back over to him. "Your friend said you were paying for everything. Is that true?" JT nodded. "Well, how long does he want to stay?"

JT handed her a credit card. "We'll know that when he comes out, won't we?" The madam smiled, looked at the girl, and nodded.

As JT waited, several of the other girls came over and tried to get him to take the dive. He laughed. "Are any of you married?" They all shook their heads. "Well, say you found someone that you loved and wanted to spend the rest of your life with ... how would you feel if someone tried to talk them into cheating on you?"

One girl looked at him seriously. "I had that happen once, and if I ever see that bitch again, I'll kill her with my bare hands."

JT smiled. "Well, I'm showing my friend around Vegas. I have a wife who is waiting on me to come back, and she trusts me not to do anything stupid. The greatest pleasure you could give me wouldn't be worth the pain of losing her, understand?"

One came over and said to JT, "That's the sweetest thing I have ever heard. We won't ask you again, but can we talk while your friend is busy?"

JT nodded. "Sure, talk about anything you want." They asked him what business he was in and made other small talk. Two hours and fifteen minutes later, Bema came out.

The madam walked over with a credit card slip. "The regular party cost $4,000, but your friend had a special request that cost another thousand."

JT smiled, signed the credit card receipt, and stuck his copy and his credit card in his pocket. As they walked to the door, Bema turned to look back at the girls. "Maybe I will be back tomorrow. Good day, my love."

The girl he had been with blew him a kiss, and they left and went back to the casino. Bema decided he wanted to shoot craps. That was something that JT was not well experienced at. When Bema stepped up to the table, the pit boss raised his voice. "New shooter coming out, new shooter." JT stood by Bema and watched. He seemed to be doing pretty well. He soon had more than two hundred chips of various denominations.

Someone tapped JT on the back. "Excuse me, sir. If you're not going to gamble, can I ask you to step back and let someone else up?"

JT looked over his shoulder at the guy. "I'm bankrolling my friend. If I leave, I'm taking him with me and what looks to be about thirty thousand of your money to another casino. What'll it be?"

The man quickly said, "You're fine, sir. Good luck to your friend."

Everything was going okay until a loudmouth in a Chicago Bears Jersey stepped up and started mouthing off.

Bema kept winning, and the loudmouth kept losing. He finally glared down the table at Bema. "These goddamned Arabs have all the money in the world from screwing us with oil. Now they come over to take our gambling money by cheating." He started down the table, and men stepped back and let him pass until he got to JT. He looked at JT menacingly. "You want to move, or do you want me to move you?"

JT kept his tone even. "My friend, you've had too much to drink. It's just a friendly game."

The man scowled at JT. "Back when I played for the Bears, I went through a bunch of guys that thought they were as tough as you. Now move."

JT said, "Is there nothing I can do to change your mind? We don't want any trouble."

The Bear stepped up and looked at JT eye to eye. "No. Now am I going to have to—" JT head-butted the man, and as he staggered back JT kicked the inside of his knee. Everybody heard it break, and the man went down screaming.

Suddenly two security guards walked up to JT. "Will you come with us, sir?" JT shook his head, knowing they wouldn't touch him. Bema went on gambling as the paramedics employed by the casino tended to the man's broken nose and leg. Thirty-five minutes later JT saw four sheriff deputies coming his way. He said quietly to Bema in Arabic, "If I am arrested, go back to the room and wait until I join you. It may take an hour or two."

Bema nodded and started gathering his chips. The four deputies walked up to JT, and one of them said, "Sir, put your hands behind your back. You're under arrest." JT complied, and they handcuffed him and led him out. They stopped outside and searched him. The officer frisking him said, "Gun," and the other three each drew his sidearm. The first officer pulled JT's gun out, ejected the magazine, and laid them both on the hood of his car.

He turned JT around. "Do you know it's against the law to have a gun in a casino?"

JT looked at him. "So arrest me."

The officer grabbed him by the arm and walked him over to his car. "That's exactly what I'm going to do."

JT had an uncomfortable ride to the station in as nice a police car as he had ever been in. It didn't seem to have the urine smell most of them did. They took him in, undid one cuff, cuffed it to a ring in the wall, and then searched him again. "Do you have any ID on you at all, sir?"

JT reached inside his belt and pulled out the ID card Dean had given him. He handed it to the booking officer and said to him, "I want to see a supervisor, please."

The officer looked at the card with JT's picture, the CIA logo, and agent ID number on it and said, "I'll be right back."

He returned almost immediately, and then fifteen minutes later, a captain came over to JT and told the booking officer, "Take the cuffs off." The man did, and the captain motioned to JT and said, "Follow me, please."

They went into a small office, and the captain turned and faced him. "We checked you out, and we're sorry for the inconvenience." He handed JT his ID, weapon, and magazine. "Is there any way we can discourage you from carrying that while in the casino?"

JT smiled. "If trouble breaks out in a casino, I'll be the best friend you ever had, and you'll be glad I was there. Excuse me, I need to get back."

As he walked out past the front desk, he heard a man telling the desk sergeant, "I'm from the Paris Casino, and I need to bail Mr. JT Logan out. How soon can I do that?"

JT walked over. "I'm JT Logan. Can you give me a ride back to the casino?"

"Certainly, sir. Let me say, sir, that the management has reviewed the tapes, and the manager who did this has been given severe a reprimand. We are truly sorry for the inconvenience."

JT nodded. "Just get me back as quick as you can." The man dropped JT off at the front door. He made his way through the sound of slot machines to the suite to see if Bema was there; he wasn't. Suddenly, there was a knock at the door, JT opened it, and a manager was there with a bottle of champagne and a fruit basket.

"Sir, the management—"

"Locate Mr. Fouad for me, quickly."

"Sir, I was just told—"

"Do you have a radio?" The manager produced it instead of answering. "Call surveillance and locate him—and hurry up about it."

The manager keyed his radio and told them they needed to locate Mr. Logan's party. JT grabbed the manager by the arm and started downstairs. "Come with me. You have a radio, and I need to know when and where you locate him."

They got to the casino, and JT started across the floor through the maze of people. "Keep up with me and watch for him." He went back to the craps table Bema had been playing at, but he wasn't there. He started toward the high-stakes poker room, looked around, and saw Bema in the high-stakes blackjack room. JT stopped, and the manager ran into the back of him. JT told the manager, "There he is, no thanks to you and your crack team of surveillance experts."

The manager called on the radio and informed them that Mr. Logan's party had been found. Walking fast to keep up with JT, he said, "Sir, if there's anything I can do—"

"Yeah, get the hell away from me."

The manager left.

JT walked up behind Bema. "Are you winning, my friend?"

Bema replied, "I was just passing the time until you returned. I'm down $3,000 here, but I am up $85,000 at the craps table. I would like to return to ..." He hesitated, glancing around to see who was near.

JT didn't let him finish. "I know where you want to go. Come on."

They walked toward the front, and another manager came up to them. "Mr. Logan, we are extremely sorry for the inconvenience—"

"Yeah, well, let's see how fast you can get me a limo." As he walked out the door, the Bear was being brought in, in a wheelchair. He had his leg in a cast and a bandage over his nose, and both eyes were black. JT stopped, as did the Bear, and JT narrowed his eyes. "Get the hell out of my way, or I'll kick you out the door." The man pushing him pulled the wheelchair backward and off to the side.

When JT and Bema walked out the door, a limo with the Paris logo on the door was waiting for them. They got in, and the driver asked, "Where to, sir?"

"The Bunny Ranch."

"I'm sorry, sir, but I'm not allowed—"

"Why don't you call the management and ask if you can." The driver pulled his cell phone out and talked on it in a low voice as he drove. The driver looked in the mirror at JT, nodded, and kept driving. After a ride through the hot Nevada sun, they pulled up to the Bunny Ranch, and Bema seemed excited as a kid. Most of the same girls were there, but some were in the back with clients. The young girl Bema had been with the day before came running up and kissed him. They walked to the back, the madam came up, and JT handed her the credit card. She smiled, took it, and walked off.

Two hours later, Bema walked out smiling with his arm around the girl. He sat down in a lounge chair, and the girl sat in Bema's lap. They kissed and cooed at each other. JT sat off to the side, watched, and thought it was nauseating. He couldn't fathom touching a woman that no telling how many others had been with in the last twenty-four hours.

The madam came out and said, "There's the regular party that cost $2,500, and there was a new kink that cost an additional two thousand." JT signed it, and she gave him his copy.

Bema finally got up and walked out toward JT, and they went to the limo. On the way back, Bema asked JT, "You do not wish to engage in a party with one of those beautiful girls?"

JT shook his head. "My job is to see that you have a good time, and I can't do that if I am with a girl." Bema nodded in approval.

They went back to the casino and ate, and then Bema played more blackjack at $15,000 a hand for about two hours. He didn't ask JT for money, so JT assumed he was doing well. The next six days were pretty much the same thing, with a visit to the Bunny Ranch every day. The seventh day Bema came out of his room in a hurry, saying, "My office called, and I must leave immediately. Take me to the airport. There is a plane waiting for me."

JT nodded, and they went out and got in the limo that was always waiting for them. As they pulled up at the airport and waited for the driver to get Bema's luggage out of the trunk, Bema turned to JT. "Will you do me a favor?"

"Sure."

"Will you give this money to Sassy? Tell her that I love her and I'll try and return for her as soon as I can." He handed JT a wad of bills and got out. JT got out as well, shook Bema's hand, and then got back in the limo, and it pulled away.

JT lowered the window between himself and the driver. "The Bunny Ranch, please. I have a delivery to make, and I won't be long." The driver nodded, and when they pulled up, JT went in. The madam met him at the door.

JT looked at her. "Can I have a moment with Sassy? I have something for her from Mr. Fouad."

The madam said, "She's in a party right now. Care to wait for about ten minutes?"

JT nodded and sat at the bar. The plush lounge chairs looked comfortable, but he saw several girls spread out on them, and the skin contact with the chair was greater than with the barstools. After ten minutes, Sassy came out on the arm of a man wearing a huge cowboy hat. She kissed him goodbye, and they both said, "I love you." The man promised her he would be back to take her away from all this.

Sassy saw JT and walked over. "Where's my sugar daddy?"

JT stood up. "He had an emergency and had to return to ... his office. He asked me to give you this." He handed her the bundle of money. JT didn't count it but figured there to be in excess of $50,000 in it.

She looked at it and beamed. "He's so wonderful. Is he coming back?"

JT started to say, "Not if he comes to his senses," but decided not to. "He said he would be back for you as soon as he could."

She smiled. "He said he was going to take me to his country and I will live like a queen. He said women in his country don't take it up the ass." She looked seductively at him. "This money will cover anything you need ... want to come on back?"

JT shook his head as he smiled. "No, but thanks for the offer, but let me ask you something. If he takes you back to his country and puts you up like a queen, isn't it going to be a little crowded with that cowboy you just told that you loved?"

She dropped her smile. "Fuck you. Get out."

JT smiled and lifted his chin in acknowledgement to the madam. He left and on the drive back to the casino called his pilot and told her to prepare the plane, file a flight plan to Memphis, and call him as soon as she was ready. He went back, packed, and left for the airport. The pilot called to tell him she would be ready by the time he got there. On the way, he called Jessie. They had talked intermittently though the week, though often when she could talk, he was asleep, and when he could talk, she was in surgery or court.

"Hey, I'm on the way to Memphis. Are you busy tonight?"

She sounded distant. "No, it's Sunday. I'm just going over some briefs. Do I need to pick you up?"

JT wondered why she would even ask. "No, I'll get there. You sound like you need to study briefs, so I'll see you when I get there. I love you, bye."

She hung up without saying anything, so he knew something was wrong. He didn't know if she was depressed or what. He got on the plane and called Dean. "Hey, your client is on the way home. He got an important recall from his office."

Dean laughed. "What kind of expenses did you have?"

"He had about $6,000 in room expense. He went through approximately $440,000 of gambling money. He won a hundred grand or so but didn't offer to give it back. He did donate over $50,000 to a whore. The only other expense was about $22,000 with one particular whore."

Dean whistled. "Twenty-two thousand dollars for a week's worth of pussy? What did she look like, and do I need to come out there?"

JT laughed "She wasn't that bad, but she apparently let him in the backdoor, which he told her women in his country do not do. She was the whitest blond I've ever seen. She had no color and apparently didn't get in the sun much. I've noticed that many Middle Easterners go for blond white women, whether they are marrying them or paying for them. Speaking of marrying, Bema fell in love with this whore that serviced him all week and has made an oath to come back and get her and take her away from all this."

"Oh shit, I'll have to get someone working on that. That dumb bastard. What else?"

"Well, there's about $100,000 in plane expenses and my fee of $400,000. Other than that, it was a cheap week for you."

Dean was silent for a minute. "Less than a mil for your expenses. Man, you're getting old. That's the cheapest we ever had for you."

"Yeah, well the expense is measured by the danger involved. I was only arrested once and only got in one fight."

"What were you arrested for, and who did you fight?"

JT told him about the events. Dean told him that was worth it and promised to have the money in his account in a day or two.

JT got to Memphis, got his car out of the hanger, and drove home. He walked in, and Jessie got up and kissed him briefly. He looked at her and said, "Sit down and talk to me. Are you having an episode of depression, or do you have something you need to talk about?"

She looked at him for a few seconds. "Sean called and said they had someone checking on you. They said they saw you go to a whorehouse every day you were in Vegas. Is that true?"

"Yes, I went in the whorehouse with the guy I was watching. I sat in the lobby area while he was busy, but I didn't have a whore, and I didn't drink much. I did gamble some, but that was to look inconspicuous. Jessie, I didn't cheat on you, and I'm hurt and surprised that you would think I did. I love you. How can I convince you of that?"

"I told myself that I wasn't going to believe that until I talked to you, and I told myself to reserve judgment until you told me about it. My mind did wander, I guess. I'm sorry."

JT said, "I'm unhappy with your Democrats. They shouldn't have told you all that. I was going to give you details when I got back because I have nothing to hide."

She smiled and kissed him. "Did you get in any fights or get arrested? If you didn't do either one, then I'm perfectly happy with you." She smiled and looked at him expectantly.

"Uh oh," he murmured.

She narrowed her eyes. "What 'uh oh'?"

"Well, this Chicago Bear has-been was drunk and went after my guy. I broke his nose and his leg. I was arrested, but they let me go, and when they viewed the tapes, they apologized with champagne and a fruit basket ... oh and a free limo the rest of the week. I didn't get hurt, and I have no arrest record. Now, go ahead and give me hell—I deserve it."

She smiled and kissed him again. "I can accept that. You're always honest with me, and I appreciate that. On another, yet similar, story, I'm going to meet with Sean and tell him I don't want to go into politics, especially after they scared the hell out of me with their stories of you spending every day at the cathouse. Is that okay with you?"

A wave of relief washed over JT. "I'm good with whatever you want to do. I've always said it was your choice."

CHAPTER 16

JT had to go back to Paris for some long-range planning. He assured Jessie that there were no jobs pending, and he wouldn't be in any danger; it was just planning. He asked her, "You want to come with me?"

She smiled. "I would love to, but it will have to wait for another time. My schedule is fairly busy for the next month. I spread it out so I wouldn't be working day, night, and weekends."

"In that case," he said, "I'll get down to business and get back here. We have a ten-day meeting planned, but I'll see if we can get it done in less than a week."

"Thank you for that." She leaned over and kissed him.

She took him to the airport, and he flew commercial from Memphis to New York and then another commercial to Paris. He got off the plane and got on a bus that took him out to some buildings beyond the runways. When he got off the bus, Scottie was there waiting to drive him the hour back to Paris.

JT asked Scottie, "Well, how's business?"

Scottie looked over at him with a smile. "We don't have any extractions planned, but we have picked up quite a few companies that want key personnel insured against kidnapping. That's worth about 50 million a year now, enough to get us through the lean times. The building is completely rented out, and that's about $3 mil a year in your pocket. Let me tell you what I'm doing nowadays. When we have down time, some of the guys don't know how to manage money, and they run out. I loan them money against their take on the next job." He glanced at JT for his approval.

JT nodded his head slowly. "That sounds like a good idea if they don't get too deep. Maybe that will keep them from trying to make money selling us out."

"That's certainly true, but I have a good feel about the group we have. Everyone is happy, willing, and patient ... except Dutch. His little girl died yesterday." He looked at JT again.

JT was gazing out the window. "Damn. Make sure his bills are paid and he has enough to live on. Take it out of my account."

Scottie shook his head. "Everybody's kicking in. They would want the same thing if they were ever in that circumstance."

They arrived at the Trans Global building and pulled into the parking area for all the top businessmen in the building. Scottie smiled again without looking over. "As I said, we pull in about three million a year in rent, and we're full. I did build an apartment for Margaret in the office next to hers. She doesn't get out much, and she monitors a lot of deals for us, twenty-four hours a day. I put in drop-down partitions in case anybody ever wanted to take over the building or her office. She monitors the security-camera feed to the building, so she can button down before anything got to her floor."

JT smiled. "Damn, when you take over a position, you really take it over, don't you?"

Scottie dropped his smile, but JT lightly punched him in the shoulder. "I'm proud of you. I told you I thought you would do a better job than I could." When they got to the office, JT hugged Margaret, who was a short, redheaded woman about five foot six. They went to the conference room, and JT sat in on financial, planning, and logistic meetings for several days. They discussed upcoming jobs, personnel changes, and the need to buy and stash ammo and weapons in several places around the world.

On the fifth day of his stay, JT, Scottie, and Margaret got on the TGV train in the first class carriage and rode at 200 mph for two hours. They got off in a little village near the French Alps, where Dutch was waiting for them. JT walked over and hugged him, and Dutch held onto JT and cried. Margaret and Scottie also hugged him, and then they went to the funeral for Dutch's daughter. They got back on the train that afternoon and returned to Paris.

The next day JT went to Margaret's office early and visited with her. She was showing him around her new apartment and the office when one of the security monitors above her desk caught JT's attention. Margaret asked him a question, but he didn't answer, so she turned to look at him. He was staring at a monitor; he pointed at the screen. "That looks like Estefania."

Margaret frowned. "You haven't seen her in what, ten years?"

JT continued staring at the screen. "You remember I was going to marry Estefania Anguilla from Peru about fifteen years ago, but she dumped me and disappeared. I looked all over South, Central, and North America for her but couldn't find her."

Margaret nodded. "I remember, but that's not her. That girl couldn't be over fifteen years old herself." She quickly looked at JT as the same time as he turned his gaze to her.

He turned back to the screen. "Call down and ask the guard what and who she's here to see."

Margaret got on the phone and talked in French to the guard. She held her hand over the phone and turned to JT. "She's asking for you."

JT said, "Tell him to tell her I'll be right down." Margaret spoke in the phone and hung up. Before he walked out, JT said, "Call Scottie and tell him something weird is happening." He knew Scottie would go down and watch from the second-floor railing that overlooked the lobby.

JT walked up to the young girl sitting on a couch. She looked up at him and stood up. He just stared a few minutes and finally came back to earth. He said in Spanish, "Are you Estefania Anguilla's daughter?"

She replied in French, "I am, and my name is Gabriel Anguilla. I was told that you are my father."

JT felt the strength leave his body; he had to sit down because his legs were weak. "I didn't know. I loved your mother, and ... she left me, but I never knew there was a child. I searched all over the American continent for her."

She smiled, leaned over, and hugged him with tears in her eyes.

He said, "You are the exact image of your mother. How ... where is she?"

Gabriel looked down and then back up. "She died a few weeks ago, but she wouldn't tell me who my father was. She said it was for my own protection, but my grandfather finally told me. He said after she ended your relationship, he moved my mother and me to Cherbourg to live with his half-sister."

JT looked up at the ceiling. "No wonder I couldn't find her. I was looking all over Peru and the American continent for her, and she was right here in France under my nose." He stood up. "Let's go out back. There's a garden there, and we can talk."

* * *

As JT and Gabriel made their way to the garden, Scottie called Margaret and told her what they were doing. He kept the two in sight.

Margaret was quiet a minute. "There's something not right about this. Keep an eye on them. I'm going to call in the guys for backup."

Scottie paused and then said, "Just bring in my A team. I don't want to attract a lot of attention. Have the others within striking distance on standby. Check the security feeds, especially on the outside of the building, and see if anything looks out of place."

"Okay, but what am I looking for, Scottie?"

"I don't know just yet."

JT and Gabriel walked into the garden and followed the trail up a hill. They got to a spot where the trail forked and took the right fork, which led to a bench. Scottie went back in because he could no longer see them.

* * *

"What happened to your mother?"

Gabriel wept. "She was working in a hospital and got a staph infection and died from it. She was thirty-six ... but I guess you knew that."

JT suddenly felt something wasn't right. He nodded at Gabriel in understanding but scanned the area to see if anything was out of place. When he looked up through the trees, he saw a man was coming down the path from further up the hill. He was moving cautiously, so JT stood up and pushed Gabriel behind him as they stepped behind a tree. The man, who was carrying a gun, didn't see them when he got to the bench. He backed up toward them while looking through the trees. JT reached around, grabbed the man's chin from behind, and gave it a quick jerk to the left. He heard the neck snap, and the man crumpled to the ground.

Gabriel appeared ready to scream, but JT put his hand over her mouth. "Please do as I say—we are in great danger." He took her down the path and stopped at a retaining wall about seven feet high. "I need you to do something for me. I'm going to lift you up and put you up here. Lie down and stay there. Don't show yourself or make yourself known in any way until either I or a man named Scottie comes for you, okay? Will you do as I ask?"

She nodded. "Who are these people, and who are they after?"

He bent over, picked her up, and laid her on the top of the wall before answering. "Me, they're after me. Put your head down and stay here." She nodded and did as he said.

JT went back and turned the man over. In his hand the man had a silencer-equipped nine-millimeter, which JT took. He also had an earpiece on and a phone in his pocket; JT took those as well. He dragged the man's body back up the trail and rolled him under some bushes to conceal him. He heard a voice in the earpiece speaking in German. "Move out in intervals, and don't expose yourself until I give the word."

JT pulled out his phone, put it on vibrate, and called Margaret. "Something's going on. I just offed one bad guy. I have their communications, and they are moving out at intervals, but I don't know from where."

Margaret came back. "I'll tell Scottie and ... JT, I see a big cargo truck below the garden. Two men just got out. Now there's two more getting out."

JT moved through the garden and came out above the truck. He saw the men climb up a trash discharge chute from an office on the third floor that was being renovated. He watched the first three men climb in and then shot the fourth man in the back with the silencer. He fell back, slid down the chute, and landed in the dumpster in a cloud of sawdust. One of the other men came back and looked through the hole in the wall, no doubt to see where the fourth man had gone, but almost immediately went back in.

JT climbed over the rock wall that surrounded the garden, stepped from there to the top of the truck, and climbed down a ladder welded to the back. He looked in the side mirror; the driver was asleep. He knew the truck was set up with men and electronics because the AC unit was running and there were several antennas. When he walked around the corner, one of the truck's doors opened, and a man came out holding a gun under his coat. Before the man could react, JT shot him in the forehead. He grabbed the man, pulled him around to the far side of the truck, and rolled him under it.

JT took the gun, which was also fitted with a silencer, from the body and went back around; the door was still open. Numerous cameras on the truck pointed at the building. He stayed under them so they couldn't see him, got in the truck, saw another door, and eased it open. Four men sat with their backs to him at a long console mounted on the wall, looking at TV monitors. He shot the first two men in the back of the head before they could turn around. The other two reached for guns on the shelf above the computers, but JT shot them before they could do anything. He then moved toward the front of the truck to another door. It was locked, so he knocked. The door lock clicked. He shoved the door open and was facing a startled man in a plush office chair. The man glanced at the gun lying on his desk about twelve inches from his hand; JT said in German, "You might as well try it, because I'm going to kill you anyway."

The man reached for the gun, but a bullet from JT's silencer hit him in the forehead before he could reach it. He slumped over on the desk with blood running onto his keyboard and then onto the carpet. JT then opened a small sliding door that separated this section from the cab of the truck. The driver was still asleep, and JT put a bullet in the back of his head. The man's body then went limp.

JT went back to the exterior door of the truck and peered out. He could see no one, so he called Scottie and told him what had happened. "Get to the office and watch out for Margaret."

JT dropped one gun in the truck, put the other gun under his jacket, jumped out of the truck, and shut the door. He then went to an entrance of the building where a guard was sending everyone through the metal detectors. The guard recognized him and opened a side door to let JT bypass the queue.

The bad guy's radio squawked. "Okay, boss, we got one more floor to go. Is he in there?" After a few seconds of silence, the voice said, "Boss, are you there? Bernard, anybody, come in."

JT called Margaret. "Margaret, lock down, go to the safe room."

"I am, the doors are down, and I'm in the room. I see three men coming up the east stairs."

"We're on the way up." JT called Scottie. "Where are you?"

"Going up the east stairwell. I've got two more floors to go."

By now JT was in the elevator. "Watch for a bad guy times three. Margaret's in lockdown. She's safe." When JT got to the top floor, the elevator door wouldn't open. He went back down a floor and headed for the west stairwell. As he opened the door to the executive floor, he heard the *zip* of a silencer. He walked to the hallway, and a bad guy raced toward him, looking back. Then the bad guy turned and saw JT standing there with a gun. A bullet hit him in the forehead, and he dropped. JT saw Scottie running toward him. JT called Margaret. "We're outside—you can open up."

Margaret replied, "I know. I'm checking the security cam before I open up."

JT looked at Scottie, and they both smiled.

Gunter called to Scottie, "I hear the sirens screaming. What do we do?"

Scottie turned to JT. "I don't mind telling them we killed them, but what are we going to do about why we're carrying guns with silencers?"

JT glanced from his gun to Scottie. "I got mine from one of the bad guys. Where'd you get yours?"

Scottie reached down and picked up another gun off a dead bad guy. "I'll be damned—that's where I got mine too." Scottie grabbed his phone and called everybody on his team, telling them to secure their own weapons and take one off the bad guys for the cops' benefit.

JT ran back to the elevator and went to the first floor. The guard came up to him. "The police have us locked in. No one gets in or out."

JT got back in the elevator and went to the third floor. He got off, ran down to where the trash chute was, jumped on it, and slid down it as if he was surfing. When he got to the bottom, he jumped onto the wall of the garden and ran to where he had left Gabriel. "Gabriel! Are you up there?"

She raised her head, and he could see that her eyes were red and swollen from crying. JT picked her up and sat her down on the ground. She said, "What was that? Why were they trying to kill you?"

JT looked at her. "We're going to go back and get you some rest and food, and you and I will sit down, and I'll tell you everything. Okay?" She nodded, and he walked her down the path away from the building. He hailed a cab, took her back to his apartment, and asked her if she had any clothes.

"They're in a locker at the train station."

At his request, she gave him the key, and then JT called Charles. "Are you locked down?"

"No, boss, I'm on the outside watching the show. What's up?"

"Come to my apartment. I need you to do something for me."

"I'm on the way."

About forty-five minutes later, Charles knocked on the door, and JT opened it. "Come in, Charles. I need you to go to the train station and go to this locker and get everything that is in there and bring it back here."

"Which train station?"

"Well, hell, how many train stations does Paris have?"

Charles looked at him with a frown. "Six."

JT glanced at Gabriel. "The train station from Cherbourg." He gave Charles the key, and he left.

Gabriel walked up behind him and hugged him around the waist. He turned around, put his arm around her shoulders, and walked her over to the couch. They sat down, and she leaned on him and sobbed.

Eventually she looked up at him. "You're not going to send me back home are you? I have no one now. My *grand mere* died, and my *abuelo* is too sick to come over here."

JT hugged her. "How about you come to the United States and live with me?" She smiled and squeezed him. He pulled his phone out and texted Scottie, "Let me know when it's okay to come back."

Gabriel got up, sat in his lap, and put her arms around his neck. She seemed to want to be where she could touch him so he wouldn't disappear again. He sighed. "Let me tell you why your mom threw me out and wouldn't tell you about me or tell me about you." He went into a lengthy story about how he'd had people after him when he was with her mom. "Someone tried to stab me one night when we were out, and I ... killed him in anger because he had put your mom in danger, and your mom saw it. I went through several years like that, and your mother was afraid she would be killed, I would be killed and ... I guess the straw that broke the camel's back was when she found out she was pregnant with you. I guess she decided to end it once and for all. She disappeared, and I spent the next year looking for her."

She looked up at him. "You didn't abandon her or me, did you?"

"No, no, no. I loved your mom. I was willing to change my life, and I have. In all these years, I have never had anybody come after me ... until now. I used to think I was lucky, but not anymore." He told her of living in the United States and marrying Jessie. "Will you come to America and live with me? Have you ever been to America?"

She smiled. "I was born there."

He frowned. "Born there, where?"

"In Iquitos, Peru."

"That's not America."

"It's South America, but it's America." She gave him a big smile.

He laughed. "I guess it is. This is going to be hard on me, because you're smarter than I am."

Charles got back with her suitcase, and JT gave him the pistol with the silencer to dispose of. They stayed in the apartment for three days before Scottie called him and told him it was okay to come back to the office. Dutch pulled up to pick him up, and JT and Gabriel got in the car.

Dutch looked puzzled, so JT said, "Dutch, I want you to meet my daughter, Gabriel. Gabriel, this is Uncle Dutch." They all three smiled. As they drove through Paris, JT looked in the side mirror. "A green Mercedes is following us."

Dutch chuckled. "I thought Gunter was better than that. You spotted him right after I did."

When they got to the Trans Global Building, JT took Gabriel up to Margaret's office.

"Margaret, I want you to meet my daughter, Gabriel."

Margaret stood up and hugged her. "I knew your mother many years ago. You are as beautiful as she is."

Gabriel's expression grew sad, and JT quietly told Margaret that Estefania was dead. Then he said, "Can I leave her with you, while I meet with Scottie and the crew?"

Margaret nodded, hugged the child again, and took her to her apartment.

JT went in and sat down at the table with Scottie and Dutch. Scottie looked at him and said, "The bad guys were Basque separatists. They were paid to kill you, and they had this planned pretty well. I found out that a crime kingpin in Spain paid them. Of the ten we killed," he said, looking at JT, "you killed seven of them. Anyway, I got in touch with the crime kingpin in Spain named Reno. It appears you cost him a bundle by ruining his kidnapping-for-hire business. I told him that ten were dead and the remaining four got away, but we know who they are. We have them on footage, and I told him if they kill themselves, we would spare their families. Otherwise ..." He frowned. "I haven't figured out how that young girl works into this. I first thought she was designed to get you out of the building, but if she hadn't, we would have never known they were coming. Who is she?"

JT smiled and looked out over the Paris skyline. "She just happened to be here when they hit. She's a daughter I didn't know I had. There is no connection between the two other than just dumb luck."

Scottie looked at JT and down at the table. "I made a deal with Reno. He will leave you alone in return for your quitting Trans Global. I told him you would go to the US and live there, and you and your family will be all right. If anything happens to you, we'll come after his family. You'll still be the CEO of GTI, but you need to stay low for a couple of years. I'll put the word out that we bought you out and you retired."

JT felt a great weight lift from him. He knew it was time to leave Trans Global though and Scottie wanted him to stay, but he also knew Scottie knew he wanted out. JT nodded.

Scottie said to him, "You will still receive five mill a year plus the rent on this place."

JT had regrets but knew this was what he had to do to stay married to Jessie. He knew she would eventually get as scared as Estefania had, and he knew he had to do it to stay alive and keep his daughter safe.

He stood up. "That'll be fine. Thanks, men. I'll miss you and the work, but this is the best thing that has ever happened to me. I have a wife I love and a daughter I want to get to know." He walked around, shook each man's hand, and hugged him.

Scottie had wet eyes as he turned to Dutch. "Get him and his daughter on the first available flight to the States." Dutch smiled and nodded. Scottie hesitated. "You will be available for consulting work, won't you?"

JT nodded. "Oh, yeah."

The next day, JT and Gabriel went to the airport and waited to board their flight. When his phone rang, he got up and walked a few steps away. "Hello, Jessie. I'm about to get on a flight to Atlanta. I'll be in Memphis about eight tonight, and I have a few surprises for you."

He heard nothing but silence. "JT, I've had a strange feeling all this week. What did you do?"

"I didn't go on a job, if that's what you are thinking. I'll tell you one surprise, but you'll have to wait until I get there for the other. I retired from any activity with the company. They don't even want to talk to me for a couple of years."

"Really, JT? You're not kidding me, are you?"

"No, honey, I'm not. One other thing—when I come out of the security area at the airport, you had better have a mattress strapped to your back."

He heard her chuckle. "It's a deal, but you better be the first man through the gate." He laughed.

JT and Gabriel got on the plane and talked for nearly all the nine-and-a-half-hour flight to Atlanta. Soon after they got on the Memphis flight, Gabriel fell asleep. When they walked out of the secure area in Memphis, Jessie was standing there, and she frowned as she looked at Gabriel.

JT walked up and kissed her. "Jessie, I want you to meet my daughter Gabriel Anguilla. She was born in Iquitos, Peru ..." He looked at Gabriel. "How many years ago?"

Gabriel smiled as if she were embarrassed. "Fifteen."

JT quickly said, "Two things I want to say before you hit me. I didn't know I had a daughter until she walked into the Trans Global building the other day. The second thing is you know everything about me now. I have no more surprises for you."

Jessie smiled and kissed him and then turned to hug and kiss Gabriel. They walked to the parking garage, got in JT's Range Rover, and drove home.

* * *

JT and Jessie legally changed Gabriel's name to Logan.

Jessie continued as a surgeon and a lawyer. JT separated from the Trans Global Insurance Company except for advisory work. He kept in touch with Margaret and Scottie but settled down to a different life.

The End

Printed in the United States
By Bookmasters